George Matthews Arnold

**Robert Pocock**

The Gravesend Historian, Naturalist, Antiquarian and Printer

George Matthews Arnold

**Robert Pocock**
*The Gravesend Historian, Naturalist, Antiquarian and Printer*

ISBN/EAN: 9783337025557

Printed in Europe, USA, Canada, Australia, Japan

Cover: Foto ©Raphael Reischuk / pixelio.de

More available books at **www.hansebooks.com**

# ROBERT POCOCK,

THE

## GRAVESEND HISTORIAN, NATURALIST,

## ANTIQUARIAN, BOTANIST, AND

## PRINTER.

BY

### GEORGE M. ARNOLD,

AUTHOR OF

" REMARKS ABOUT GRAVESEND IN OLDEN DAYS," ETC.
MEMBER OF THE COUNCIL OF THE KENT ARCHÆOLOGICAL SOCIETY.

"Why, he is dead and gone these eighteen years! There was a wooden tombstone in the churchyard that used to tell all about him, but that's rotten and gone too! "—*Washington Irving.*

London :

## SAMPSON LOW, MARSTON, SEARLE, & RIVINGTON,

CROWN BUILDINGS, 188, FLEET STREET.

1883.

# Dedication.

TO MY FELLOW-TOWNSMEN OF GRAVESEND

I DEDICATE THIS LITTLE EFFORT

OF GATHERING ALL I COULD GLEAN

TOUCHING THE CAREER OF ONE OF THEMSELVES,

## ROBERT POCOCK,

IN THE HOPE THAT,

AMIDST SOME OCCASIONS FOR SORROW IN THE RECITAL,

THEY MAY FIND MANY FOR COMMENDATION,

AND SOME EVEN FOR JUST PRIDE.

# PREFACE.

It is fifty-two years to-day since Robert Pocock found an obscure grave away from his native town, and it seems just that some tribute should be paid to his memory.

He was eminently a student of nature, and not only an acquirer of useful information but its indefatigable disseminator.

The toilsome search for a fossil, the active pursuit of any new butterfly, the unwearied scanning of the heavens, the discovery of a rare plant,—these were his recreations.

Ever accessible at his humble shop—one day to a waterman freighted with some outlandish fish, on another to a countryman laden with a curious bird or some unusual plant—it was his delight to supply their names and classification ; but student of nature as he was, he knew that well-nigh every parish in his ancient county—Kent—is decorated with a hundred memories of historical interest, and hence his antiquarian pursuits kept pace with his study of natural history.

If he had evinced less of these qualities and had been more of the shopkeeper, he might have accumulated money in lieu of dying houseless and a wanderer. But his higher instincts ever led him to seek knowledge, and to publish it even in its most elementary form, so much so that his place of honour is among the very pioneers of elementary literature, in the production of the " Easy Reading Books for the Young," which supplanted the old Horn Books of less lettered generations, while his Navy List and his " Companions " (the origin of the modern Guide Book), are proofs that there was existing in Pocock not only the apt and ready detection of a public want, but the energy and skill to supply it, so far as his limited means enabled.

Let me add, that at the age of twenty-six he first introduced to his native town that mighty engine of literature the printing press, and I think I have advanced enough to justify this attempt to honour Pocock's memory.

True it is, that the retrospect of his trials, his museum broken up and dispersed, himself ejected without money or furniture from his shop, his last days of discouragement and death at his son's house at Dartford, present reflections sufficiently depressing; and yet, as he says in an epitaph which he drew up for himself, " he produced a History of Gravesend and Milton, with other works, which will perpetuate his memory." To secure him some of this posthumous honour is the object of my present effort.

And therein I have endeavoured to give only such of his published matter as could not properly be dispensed with, and as much of his unpublished writings as I fairly could. Nevertheless I have collected all I could reach that seemed to bear upon his life and character, so as to make the biography as complete as possible ; yet, probably this would have appeared to higher advantage if it had been set forth by greater literary experience than the arduous duties of a laborious profession have allowed me to acquire.

Another motive I must avow in addition to a sense of justice to Pocock's memory ; like him I am a townsman of Gravesend, and love my native town and feel interested in its credit and repute.

This is not the place to descant upon the merits of the authors it has produced since Pocock's day, but I am unwilling silently to pass by the memory of Mr. Robert P. Cruden (twice Mayor of Gravesend), whose researches into the history and incidents of this locality and of the Port of London are so creditable an emulation of his early predecessor, William Bourne ; nor of Mr. Coombe (the immediate precursor of the present popular town clerk), who wrote upon the evidences of Christianity ; and descending to native authors yet living, still less would I wish to omit a passing tribute to my brothers, Edwin Arnold, C.S.I. (who has written various historical and poetical works, and largely contributed to Oriental literature), and Arthur Arnold, M.P. for Salford (the author of works of political and social economy and travel, as well as in the lighter paths of fiction), while the Rev. W. D. Johnstone, the Rector of Milton, has published more than one treatise upon the doctrines of the Church of England, and Mr. W. F. Harvey, M.A., of the Inner Temple, has lucidly illustrated the civil law in the domain of contracts. But without enlarging the list, if we would wish to discover local traces of the true mantle of Pocock, the love of letters and pursuit of knowledge amidst the apparently discordant calls of trade and the harassing claims of the family, it would not be necessary to travel far from the scene of his labours; indeed, within scarce a stone's throw of his house the reader could this day enter the modest shop of Mr. G. Newman, from whose published poems the following pleasing lines are taken at hazard, and who conducts his daily industry with an energy which might well have interdicted all hope of any successful cultivation of the muse :—

### Lyric.

*Written on the anniversary of the day on which the author's (Mr. Newman's) brother left his native land.*

'Twas once my happiness to own
   A brother, kind and dear to me ;
Though years have now successive flown
   Since 'neath our old home's shelt'ring tree,
In boyhood, joyous, wild, and free,
   Like as the tendrils of the vine
Twine round each other, so did we
   Our joys and sorrows intertwine.

His joys were mine, my pleasure his,
    Our own each other's every care,
And all our hopes of future bliss
    In love were intermingled there;
Unknown to us each plot and snare,
    Which would in after-years be laid,
To give to each of grief our share,
    And turn life's sunshine into shade.

.     .     .     .

He heard, and o'er him soon the spell
    An overpowering influence bore;
To friends and home he bade farewell,
    Perchance to meet again no more.
He started for the far-off shore;
    My pangs at parting, who can tell!
E'en now doth mem'ry o'er and o'er
    Sound in my ears, farewell! farewell!

Years now have fled, and through the gloom
    Of "days gone by" will Fancy rove,
Back to our childhood's happy home,
    E'en till again a brother's love
Seems round my heart like tendrils wove;
    But soon the bubble bursts, and I
Have but the hope that yet in love
    Our souls shall meet beyond the sky.

Years now have fled, and deeper still
    Grows the dark veil through which mine eye
Would pierce to see or good or ill
    Surrounding now his destiny:
But no! not e'en a glimpse for me
    Of good or ill, or weal or woe;
Impenetrable mystery
    Forbids me all I long to know.

Must it be so? and must his fate
    Be lost beneath oblivion's gloom;
If yet alive—unknown his state;
    If dead—alike unknown his tomb?

Oh, if the grave's capacious womb
Has long closed o'er him, still to me
'Twere sweet to know immortal bloom
Succeeded dull mortality.

Again, let us turn our eyes to the neighbouring nursery-grounds. Who is yon son of toil, working spade in hand at his laborious vocation, but the author (Mr. C. J. Clarke) of published poems, from which the following extract is culled?—

### POETRY AND LOVE.

'Tis poetry and love alone
Can cheer and sweeten life,
Amidst its wearying routine
Of care, and toil, and strife.

For poetry refines the sense,
And elevates the soul;
While love's endearing influence
Sheds fragrance o'er the whole.

These twin-born sisters from above
Our purest pleasures give;
Deprived of poetry and love,
I would not wish to live.

They shed a beam in darkest night,
A pure and heavenly ray
Of sunshine bursting into light,
To guide us on our way.

Then, ye who grovel here below,
And raise no thought above,
Despise not what ye cannot know,
Sweet poetry and love.

The reader, I trust, will kindly excuse the length of these extracts, not only on account of their own merits, but because they would have been welcome to Pocock, —their literary feeling would have cheered him—their native origin pleased him, while their authors' "self-help" would have encouraged him; and that these and their other stanzas would have been right welcome at his press who can doubt it ?

GEORGE M. ARNOLD.

MILTON HALL, GRAVESEND,
  26th October, 1882.

# CONTENTS.

*Robert Pocock*

*Signature to will 19 Oct- 1797*

# CHAPTER I.

I care not, Fortune, what you me deny ;
    You cannot rob me of free Nature's grace,
You cannot shut the windows of the sky,
    Through which Aurora shows her brightening face ;
You cannot bar my constant feet to trace
    The woods and lawns, by living stream, at eve :
Let health my nerves and finer fibres brace,
    And I their toys to the great children leave ;
Of fancy, reason, virtue, nought can me bereave.

JAMES THOMSON.

THE interesting biographies, written by Mr. Smiles, of
Thomas Edward the Scotch naturalist, and of Robert
Dick the Scotch geologist and botanist, illustrate how
a career of laborious industry (that sweat of the brow
by which most men's daily bread must be earned) may
run side by side with remarkable self-culture, and be
accompanied by the truest of enjoyment which flows
from the love and study of Nature—an enjoyment
perhaps intensified by the very difficulties thus excep-
tionally encountered.

We have only to transport the scene from the
north to the south of the Tweed to see in Robert
Pocock, author, naturalist, botanist, antiquarian, and
printer, an English example of the love of Nature and of
a thirst for the acquisition and distribution of knowledge,

B

outstripping the confinement and trammels of commercial pursuits and narrow means, and vindicating for
itself a real and honoured, and (in the best sense) a
successful place in the drama of life.

His efforts are all the more worthy of record in that
they were " cribb'd, cabin'd, and confined " by the " res
angusta domi ;" till at length, driven by dire necessity
from his native town, he lived to see his museum and
books dispersed, and finally died broken-hearted, " all
unwept, unhonoured, and unsung," with no memorial
however humble to mark his resting-place,—some fifty-
two years ago.

Robert Pocock's father was a freeman of Gravesend,
where we find that he was duly sworn on the 26th March,
1745, " to be a true liege man, and true faith and truth to
bear, to our Sovereign Lord King George the Second,"
before Henry Thames, Esq., the then mayor of the town
and parishes of Gravesend and Milton ; at which time
he further deposed that " to the best of his skill, wit,
cunning, and power, he should maintain and uphold all
the liberties, franchises, good customs, orders, and
usages of these towns and corporation thereof," and
thereupon was admitted a freeman of such corporation.

It is doubtful whether John Pocock was a native, or
had come from Sussex to this town of his adoption ; but
it appears from his will of 1766, that he was then a settled
shop-keeper, occupying his own house in the High
Street, part of which had formerly been known as a separate tenement, under the sign of the " Hat and Feather."
There he presumably flourished as a grocer, and though
the date of his marriage is unknown, it is clear that on
the 21st February, 1760 (just 122 years ago), Robert
Pocock himself (his father's second son) first saw the

light.   His father died, and was buried at Gravesend some twelve years later, on the 4th May, 1772, followed by his widow, Martha Pocock, on the 30th January, 1776.   When at the age of sixteen years he became an orphan, he drew up, and he has left behind him, a semi-humorous epitaph intended for his father's tomb, which is subjoined :—

AN EPITAPH.

The Merry Soul
of
JOHN POCOCK
departed
From Earth to Heaven,
May 4th, 1772.
During 52 years
It animated his body
with
An agreeable deportment ;
to which add
Sobriety, Industry, Honesty,
and
Civility to his Customers,
For those Virtues
Preserved his reputation.
He satisfied his Creditors
by paying them
Twenty Shillings to the Pound,
and
Died comfortably,
Leaving an Overplus for his Family.

*Mem.*—He lies buried within six feet of the door (now stopped up) near the vestry-room window in Gravesend Church.

There is little doubt that such education as Robert received was obtained at the free school of the town— situate in King Street, previously known as St. Thomas'

Street, in honour of St. Thomas of Canterbury, and afterwards as School Street, and probably under James
Giles, sen., who died on the 9th December, 1780, aged
61 (and who was one of the witnesses to his father's will),
or else under his son, such store of erudition as a boy of
fourteen years of age can accumulate was acquired.
This is confirmed by the kind notice which Pocock makes
of them both in his "History of Gravesend," where he
writes under the head of "Literary Persons: "—

"Mr. James Giles, although not to be reckoned a
literary person, yet was such a character as no parochial historian should pass unnoticed. Mr. Giles, in
the early part of his life, was bred to the business of
shoe-making, which he quitted, and, untutored, engaged himself to the study of arithmetic; this brought
him to be somewhat acquainted with the more abstruse
branches of the mathematics, and upon the Rev. Mr.
Locker's leaving the free school in Milton, Mr. Giles
was appointed to succeed him.

"Mr. James Giles, son of the above, succeeded his
father, and from his classical abilities many bright lads
have been sent forth from the free school. Mr. Giles
was also the constructor of the curious sun-dial at
Milton Church, and of an orrery; and besides being
an electrician was the author of an elaborate work
called 'English Governing; or, Parsing Recommended
to School-masters and Private Teachers of Grammar
as the most easy method of attaining a thorough
knowledge of that science: Nothing of this sort had
ever appeared in Print.'"

Pocock does not mention it, but he was himself the
publisher of this useful work. Thus he was an early
pioneer of the "Society for the Diffusion of Useful
Knowledge" of later times.

At an early age, and concurrently with his free school education, it is believed that Pocock held the post of an errand boy in his father's shop, but whether or not he became actually apprenticed to the grocery trade does not appear; probably not, for his intellectual habits and craving for literary pursuits, and his love of Nature, seem to have made the pursuit of that trade repugnant to him. At all events, it is clear that he attached himself by preference to the trade of printing, and in some way acquired the needful knowledge of that business so as to establish himself in it. It was probably about 1779 that he married his first wife, Ann Stillard, the spinster daughter of Edward Stillard, who held a situation in the old East India House, in Leadenhall Street, London.

His marriage, and the birth of three children successively in 1780, 1782, and 1786, no doubt stimulated his industry for the necessary maintenance of his growing family, and we have good proof of his energy since, when scarce twenty-six years of age, he established a printing-press, and collected a library for the use and benefit of his native town.

Meanwhile, that hi s practical knowledge of printing was more than usually compl ete appears from his having, in after-life, cast his s on's type for printing. The follow-ing entry under his own hand, in his "Local Chrono-logy," is simple and devoid of all rhetorical flourish.

" 1786. The first printing-press and circulating library established in Gravesend by Robert Pocock writer of this Chronology and compiler of the ' History of Gravesend.' "

At this period he seems to have possessed all the emotions of youth, both in his antipathies and friend-ships, and to have been much given to the composi-

tion of epitaphs. These tendencies are well illustrated
in the case of his friend, Mr. Sawyer, who united in
his own person the practice of medicine with the
mastership of the Gravesend Workhouse, of whom he
wrote, upon the occasion of his death, as follows :—

To the Memory of
MR. EDWARD BUSH SAWYER,
Doctor in Medicine,
Master of Gravesend and Milton Workhouse,
Brother of the Ancient and Honourable Society of Free Masons,
Member of the Lap-eared Club,
Visitor of the Bugnapping Board,
A youth of the Ringers and Post Master General,
who,
by his Frugality and Industry,
maintained his Family genteelly,
which raised him to
a Pitch of Envy never before known to those
who like the Dog in Manger
would neither get a living themselves
nor permit (if in their power) others to do it.
After giving their Words for his Support,
like Snakes they basely turned against him,
and joined consent to give him Warning to quit
his Profession ;
which so knawed on his Vitals,
that it brought on his Death,
November, 1787.

Pocock makes the following note of the funeral ceremony :—

"Mr. Edward Bush Sawyer, master of Gravesend
and Milton Workhouse, was buried on Sunday, in
Gravesend churchyard, when the procession began as
follows :—

"1st, the tyler of a mason lodge with a drawn sword—
2 links—an excellent band of music—2 links—about
12 couple of free masons with all their insignia of

office—2 links—the 'Lap-eared' Club, about 20 couple—
2 links—the minister, clerk, and undertaker—2 links—
the body, with six pall-bearers and five couple of
mourners, closed the rear. Many hundreds of people
attended the funeral—the music played very solemnly
going to the interment; after which the bells rung a
dumb peal."

Pocock was fond of the dissemination of learning,
and impressed with the absence of elementary works, he
at an early period turned his attention to the more easy
instruction of children in the rudiments of spelling
and reading. Perhaps one of the most useful of his
efforts, was the publication of the children's books,
"Reading made Easy," which he published under the
titles of " The Child's First Book ; or, Reading made
Easy," and " The Child's Second Book ; being a further
Improvement in Learning." These publications speedily
superseded the ancient horn books, of one of which
(discovered on pulling down an old house at Newbury)
a recent correspondent of " Notes and Queries " gave
the following account :—

" It consists of a page of letter-press which measures
$2\frac{7}{8} \times 2\frac{1}{8}$ inches, mounted on a piece of oak of slightly
larger size, the lower end of which is shaped as a handle.
It is covered with a sheet of transparent horn, which
is kept in its place by means of narrow strips of
thin brass, fastened with small nails. The letter-
press, which is surrounded by an ornamental border,
consists of the alphabet, preceded by a +, first in small
letters and then in Roman capitals. Next are, on one
side of the middle line, the vowels alone, followed by
the vowels with the consonants, *b, c, d ;* on the other
side the same reversed. Following, is, first, ' In the
name of the Father,' &c., and lastly, the Lord's Prayer.

At the same time and place there was found one of George I.'s lead Bombay pieces."

Mr. A. J. Dunkin, the antiquary and printer of Dartford, states that these reading-books for the young, by Pocock, preceded the well-known publication by Rusher, of Banbury, fully two years, and that the original woodcuts were in his possession in 1842. They are now deposited in the library of the Guildhall of the City of London, by Mr. Fooks, Q.C., in behalf of Mr. Dunkin's sister, where they have a honoured home.

If Mr. Dunkin is correct in this claim, it would follow that Pocock had established his printing-press in consequence of the encouragement which he had derived from the publication of these elementary works. The title of Rusher's Book is "Rusher's Reading made most Easy; consisting of a variety of useful lessons on a rational plan, proceeding from the alphabet to words of two letters only, and from these to words of three, four, and five letters, &c. &c., so disposed as to draw on learners with the greatest ease and pleasure both to themselves and teachers;" and on examining the date of its production, it affords evidence that Pocock must have published prior to September, 1786.

That Pocock thus led up to the provision of a great new and recognized want is apparent from the circumstance that the above copy of Rusher, now in the British Museum, is a print of the 220th edition.

By the kindness of Miss Dunkin inspection has been made of the engraved blocks above mentioned, and they are found to consist of illustrations of the nursery verses apropos of the death of " Cock Robin," " The House that Jack built," &c., &c., suitable to the apprehensions of the juvenile minds for whom the book was designed.

The period dating from our author's first marriage, and of his probable greatest domestic felicity, was drawing to a close, since, in the month of March, 1791, he lost the wife of his early manhood, whom he followed to the grave on the 20th of that month.

It was not probably until the end of the following year that he remarried, when he was united to a lady whose social position was in advance of his own, and by whose family the alliance was consequently deemed unsatisfactory. She was a daughter of John Hinde, Esq., solicitor and coroner for Kent, living at Sittingbourne in that county; and whilst of his first marriage there was issue two daughters and one son, of this, his second marriage, there were ultimately four sons and three daughters.

Side by side, however, with his efforts in behalf of elementary education, he had devotedly utilized his spare hours in compiling a Chronology (1790) of local events connected with his dear native town, with a list of its successive mayors from A.D. 1632. The list is not, however, very complete, as he plaintively states in the preface to this Chronology " that he only laments that it is not in his power, at present, to render the Chronology more complete and copious, having been denied access to the records of the town, whereby much information might have been gained. Thus cut off from the grand magazine of intelligence, he now only offers his gleanings from others, in miniature, as a prelude to a future work (whenever he shall be favoured with the names of 300 subscribers) to be called ' The History of Gravesend and Milton,' and wherein his utmost endeavours shall be used to make such a local publication useful, entertaining, and instructing."

Pocock seems to have added fresh pages to his Chronology as occasion required down to 1796— George Arnold, Esq., appearing as the mayor of that year—but he still retained the old frontispiece, with its date of 1790.

The next work, of which we have any account, is the unpublished MS. of what would have been an apparently useful publication, entitled,—

The
FARMER, GRAZIER, AND BAILIFF'S ASSISTANT
for the year 1795.
To be continued annually.
Containing

A new methodical arrangement of keeping the affairs of a Farm, by setting down in a clear and concise manner the employment of the servants, and where employed; the number of live stock; moneys paid and received, to whom or upon what account; with the various occurrences that happen upon the Farm every day in the year.

A Farmer's Chronology.
Useful things necessary to be known by Farmers.
Laws relative to corn.
The gross duty on hops from 1711 to 1793.

Tables showing the gross weight of hops reduced into neat weight, what price the hundred at any price the pound, and what duty is to be paid for any quantity.

Recipes in Farming,

Together with pages ruled for the insertion of all the names of fields on the Farm, serving as an annual account to show what each was sown with, the number of bushels sown, when cut, what produce, what sold for, and to whom.

Gravesend : Printed and Sold by R. Pocock.

No printed copy of this work has been discovered, and it remains another of the efforts of a great and useful activity, always limited and frequently strangled by the want of material means. The conception and design were, so far as his personal labour was involved, unflinchingly executed, but the means of publication, the expenses of printing and paper, remained insoluble obstacles.

Adverting to the refusal of the corporation to afford him access to its archives for the purposes of his History; it seems clear that he possessed a friend in the then mayor, or had acquired other partisans in that body, since in his "History of Gravesend and Milton," printed by himself and published in 1797, he gave *in extenso,* at page 183, the town charter of the 7th Charles I. (A.D. 1632).

This public invasion, however, of the privileges of the close incorporation (as then understood), was most distasteful to the majority of its members, and it was resolved by way of punishment that Pocock should lose their corporate support in regard to the public printing. This he felt very acutely, and the timely establishment of a second printing-press in the town enabled the infliction to be carried out with all the greater promptitude and exactitude. The following is the title-page of his "History of Gravesend," upon 256 pages, small quarto :—

THE HISTORY
of the
INCORPORATED TOWN AND PARISHES
of
GRAVESEND AND MILTON,
In the County of Kent.
Selected with accuracy from Topographical Writers.
And enriched from Manuscripts hitherto unnoticed,
Recording
Every event that has occurred in the aforesaid Town and Parishes
from the
Norman Conquest to the present Time.
Learn the Laws by which you are Governed.
Gravesend : Printed by R. Pocock.
1797.

It is hoped that it may not prove too wearisome to give the preface to this volume, which was one endeared to Pocock by many ties, though it would have been superseded by the fuller and complete work which he afterwards decided upon, and in copiousness and character would have been surpassed by his later projected " History of Dartford and Wilmington,"—projects, each of which was arrested in publication by the want of means.

The preface is as follows :—

" To know the history of our native place should be the first desire of every person possessed, in the smallest degree, of literary knowledge : under this idea, the compiler of the following work thought of collecting together (for his private amusement) all the materials he possibly could proper to give such information. In this he succeeded beyond his utmost expectations, by having access to the libraries of two gentlemen in the neighbourhood of Gravesend, to whom he returns his sincere thanks, and likewise to the Rev. Mr. Denne of Wilmington, for the list of ministers, and to Mr. Tracy of Brompton, for the kind communication of his intelligence.

" Being thus in possession of manuscripts hitherto unknown, and of a sufficient number of quotations from the laborious and topographical writers upon the County of Kent, by the persuasions of a few friends he puts the same in print; flattering himself that the ' History of the Town and Parishes of Gravesend and Milton ' will be instructive, entertaining, and useful, not only to the resident inhabitants of the town and of its environs, but likewise to every person occasionally visiting the place.

" This being the first compilation of ' The History of Gravesend' that ever appeared in print, and the compiler of the same not having that leisure time requisite for its critical inspection, by other business interfering, it is hoped that the candid reader will excuse any errors that he sees in the performance of it."

It is clear that even in 1790 he had virtually compiled his History, which only saw the light in 1797. It is nevertheless more than doubtful if his finances would have, even at this later date, enabled him to have launched the volume if it had not been facilitated by the fortunate incident that he happened to be present at a sale of the stock of a paper-mill, and was thus enabled to purchase at quite a presumably nominal price a quantity of unsized paper, cut into sheets too small for profitable or general use in the trade. By this acquisition he came to be able to utilize the accumulations, both antiquarian, natural, and local, which his untiring energy and industry had secured.

In those of the fragmentary diaries of Pocock which have been collected, traits of his general character will sufficiently appear, and in the most natural way ; but candour does not allow us to say that his domestic relations, arising out of his second marriage, always exhibited the completest harmony. It was with him as with many who similarly give their days to public rather than private objects, they to a proportionate extent withdraw time and energies which would otherwise have been more completely focussed upon the domestic hearth. In how many cases of literary men do we not naturally find the same causes productive of the like results. And if on the part of his conjugal helpmate there existed the conviction that naturalists were ever more welcome than relatives, that his humble abóde was rather a resort for all who had information to impart or inquiries to make, than was consistent with the economy of time and of money, and more profitable pursuit of business, it would have been more natural than strange or reprehensible.

About the year 1800, Pocock appears to have made a few manuscript notices in a little waste-book some of which are subjoined, the very first of which seems to disclose the existence of these occasional domestic differences.

His grandson, Dr. Jones (to whom an obligation is due for much kind information), remembers that he was very exact and methodical in his habits, but inclined to be strict with his family. His custom was to rise early, and to take, whenever he could, long walks and excursions with any naturalist whose company he could secure, tendencies doubtless obnoxious, more or less, to his wife, and little conducive to commercial success.

The following is one of the above-mentioned entries supposed to be inscribed over Mr. Pocock's door:—

Want of unanimity.
Here lives a young Pair
Who lost the Flitch of Bacon
Within the year.

This was in 1800, and without wishing to adjudicate between husband and wife the respective blame too closely, the following letter from Mrs. Pocock to her Lord, temporarily absent in London, is certainly more matter-of-fact than redundant in terms of exuberant wifely endearment :—

"Monday, May 3rd.

"*Mr. Pocock,*—If you can get a case of mathematical instruments very complete at two guineas and send me down to-morrow, a gentleman who has bought several things will be obliged to you. Our set has not enough instruments in it. You will be able to get one at Martin's, I think; if not, don't go to pay ready money for one but rather lose the sale.

"Yours, &c.,<br>"F. Pocock.

"Shedrach is much pleased with your leather breeches, as he is very fashionable in *pantaloons.* I have altered them. I have had another pair altered for every-day, and Luscombe is making a coat of your two blue ones. Mrs. Muirs and I have done one shirt to-day, and another I will make in a week or two. He must have a hat in a month or two, and then he will do again.

"Mr. Pocock,
at Mr. Gent's, Hairdresser,
Watling Street,
Near St. Paul's, London."

Another entry is as follows :—

"Retort.

"A foppish young fellow upon coming to the White Hart, Gravesend, ordered a bill of fare to be brought, but nothing contained there would please him, when after keeping the landlord a long time he said, 'Go directly, sir, and dress me an elephant.' 'Sir,' said the landlord, 'I have nothing so large; but I will roast a young monkey just come in.'"

### " A Trick upon Vice.

"About the year 1790, I printed a small book of moral songs, the sale of which I knew would depend much on the title. I therefore entitled it 'The Frisky Songster.' It was called for with rapidity, and the edition soon sold, but the purchasers were disappointed (although pleased) when they found the contents and title did not agree."

### " Angel.

" A good woman is an angel; but where are angels to be met with ?—not on earth I believe."

The following in 1801 :—

### "A Female English Historian.

" On Friday, October 2nd, 1801, I visited Westminster Abbey, desiring (with the promise of a gratuity) the conductor to proceed *slowly* in his descriptions of the monuments.

" The pleasure I received from viewing the venerable remains was much enhanced by a female, whom curiosity had likewise brought to visit the Abbey. This lady no sooner heard the name of the Deceased mentioned than she immediately followed it with the most curious anecdotes of the family, and entertaining parts of English narration, and this in such a sprightly, familiar, and condescending manner as to gain the ears and affection of the company present. Her retentive memory and knowledge in English history exceeded the powers of any person I have ever met with ; nor did her talents end here, sculpture and statuary she could criticize; nor must I forget that upon coming to the tomb of Queen Elizabeth she said,—

" ' Here is that vixen Queen Bess, for Lavater says a sharp chin is the sure guide for it.'

" She then made remarks on the similarity of the family faces of Mary Queen of Scots and Queen Elizabeth with such judicious comments upon the whole exhibition that I was determined (although a stranger) before I quitted this Phœnix of English history to learn her name, which upon soliciting, assigning as a cause the entertainment I had received and hoping for a further acquaintance, she politely gave that of Mrs. Morhall, No. 18, Castle Street, Holborn."

"GENERAL MONK.

" The conductor of Westminster Abbey, upon show-ing General Monk's effigy, said a French lady the day before was tall enough to kiss his chin. Upon this saying Mrs. Morhall stepped up and made a belief to kiss his cheek, when the conductor said,—

" ' Madame, you had better kiss me.'

" ' If I do so,' said the lady, ' I should have kissed two inanimate beings.' "

"DEBTOR AND CREDITOR.

" Sanders and Lemon were partners and carters at Gravesend (1801), generally employed by Mr. Gillbee, a coal-merchant there, who owed them 6*l.* for labour (Lemon had not behaved very honestly to his employer) ; and when they went to ask for their money, Mr. Gillbee began beating poor Lemon most violently for some distance, Sanders following, when Gillbee turned round to Sanders and said,—

C

"'Well, Sanders, what have you got to say?'

"'I say, sir, if this is the way you pay debts, you owe me nothing! you owe me nothing!'"

## "MAJOR WADMAN.

"The Major of the Northfleet Volunteers being dead, Captains Allen and Wadman were the next in seniority for the choice of the corps, who being assembled, Captain Allen addressed them thus:—

"'Gentlemen, I am sorry to acquaint you with the death of your Major; you must choose another, and I shall be proud of your votes to succeed him.'

"Then Captain Wadman spoke,—

"'Gentlemen, you know your Major is after being dead, and Captain Allen or myself must succeed him. Away, you dogs, to my house and consider of it; there is plenty of roast beef and strong beer.'

"'Oh! Wadman for ever! Wadman for ever!' they cried; and so Wadman was elected."

## "VERY TRUE.

"In the English language the use of the expression 'Very true' is a tautology, and you may as well pronounce the inelegant repetition of 'True, true.'"

## "MAJOR WADMAN.

"West the bricklayer having set off to walk to London, met the Major riding home to his country seat.

"'Good morning to you, Mr. West, and where are you after going to?'

"'I am going,' says West, 'to London, sir, to employ a lawyer against you for my money.'

"'And do you mean, man, to walk all the way?'

"'I must, sir, for I can get no carriage.'

"'By my soul, man,' says the Major, 'you shall do no such thing. Here, take my horse, and I will walk home.'

"He did so. Soon after West put the sheriff's officer into his house, when he sent for West and said,—

"'I don't blame you, Mr. West, for I think you have done right! Now you will get your money. We have always been friends, and I know of no person I would so soon send to as yourself to be bail for me in case I was arrested!!!'"

To resume. It does not appear that the demand for the "History of Gravesend" was sufficient to have made it remunerative, although in an advertisement of the time it is stated that nearly all the copies had been sold; for speaking of himself, Pocock says at a later period "he would have added another volume to the 'History of Gravesend,' but not finding that encouragement among his townsmen he could have wished for, he dropped it."

In the year 1800, having increasingly turned his attention to antiquarian subjects connected with his native county, he published his interesting account of the Tufton family, Earls of Thanet, whose pedigree he traced from an early period. The book itself he dedicated or inscribed to his friend, R. Gough, Esq. It is a small octavo of 156 pages, and bore the following title-page:—

MEMORIALS
OF THE FAMILY OF TUFTON, EARLS OF THANET,
deduced
from various sources of authentic information.

c 2

"From lives of many a good example may be drawn."
Gravesend :
Printed by R. Pocock,
and sold by Messrs. Robinson, Paternoster Row, London,
and all other Booksellers.
1800.

This work is replete with interesting detail, to which, however, its main scope and object are never allowed to become subordinate; but what should have particularly induced this selection of the topic of the Thanet family is hard to say, as more prominent Kentish subjects could have been suggested. It may have arisen from the local connexion of Tilbury Fort with Gravesend, for he remarks that "Col. Tufton, on whom the earldom of Thanet descended on the decease of Thomas, Nov. 19, 1694, was in the reign of James II. chosen governor of Tilbury Fort, and probably the first who received that honour after the old Blockhouse Platform, built by Henry VIII., with other like fortresses on the coast (out of the vast plunder of the religious houses, by way of amusing the people after their loss), had been enclosed with works, and reduced to the regular fortification we now find it."

The following is extracted from our author's "Introduction" to the Tufton family, Earls of Thanet :—

" Before the reign of Queen Elizabeth, it was thought a rarity in the course of a century if one historian appeared to record and transmit to posterity the glorious actions of our forefathers, or to set forth the topographical beauties of this respectable and delightful island. Under the patronage of Her Majesty several literary luminaries arose during her golden age. Mr. Lambarde, the father of local historians, honoured Kent by making it the subject of the first county history ; and in his time a general collection of the antiquities of the kingdom was comprised into a thin quarto in Latin by his contemporary Camden. Not long after these authors, all that was then thought worthy of notice among the monuments of Britain was given by Weaver, in a folio ; and it was not, I believe, till the beginning of the eighteenth century that any town or even city was judged capable of affording sufficient materials for a distinct publication ; but whether from the accumulation of recorded and interesting events respecting places and families, which are not now, as formerly (before the invention of printing), soon hurried into oblivion, or from the growing taste for a know-ledge of men and manners in past ages, or probably from both these causes, aided by an increasing popula-tion, which renders what was once a narrow theatre of action now complex and diversified ; whether from all or either of these causes, it is certain that a single town, parish, the smallest village or meanest family may afford documents worth relating for the benefit of future generations," &c.

\*    \*    \*    \*    \*    \*    \*    \*

" No apology is needed for offering in this separate form memoirs of the family of Tufton ; but it may be necessary to premise on behalf of the execution of the present work, that the occupations of a man who has not the happiness to enjoy affluence and a peaceful re-treat naturally stand in the way of study and research.

" The writer nevertheless hopes that his labours will not be found wholly uninteresting or useless.

" He has availed himself of all sources of information that were accessible to him, and has endeavoured to illustrate with as much accuracy as he could the career of this family.

"He has particularly aimed at impartiality (steering clear of the extremes of political phrensy), and has concluded at a period most consistent with the respect due to living characters."

A person perusing the above work might recognize in one of the epitaphs the idea which Pocock adopted in that which he wrote to his mother's memory.

It is the monumental inscription of Thomas, Earl of Thanet, who died in 1729, eighty-five years old, and who lies buried with his ancestors at Rainham Church, adjoining Chatham, in Kent, and after stating his birth, &c., it records his marriage with Catherine, daughter of the Duke of Newcastle, and proceeds (speaking of the deceased) thus,—

"Who believed that no woman on earth would have made him so happy as she did."

This is a tribute to the Countess all the stronger as she died in April, 1712, some seventeen years before her husband, and by consequence at least that distance of time remote from his kind and faithful record of the conjugal happiness which she had brought him.

Pocock, in penning his mother's epitaph, writes as follows :—

The
Prudent Conduct,
Constant Care, Frugality,
and
Good Housekeeping
of
MARTHA POCOCK
enabled

Her Husband John to prosper;
For she knew
That no man can thrive or be happy
unless
His Wife likes.
On January 30th, 1776,
At 56 years old,
She died
A Pious Churchwoman,
and
Lies buried in the same Grave
With her Husband.

The social and domestic virtues thus depicted for her by her son derive confirmation from her husband's will; for not only did the latter appoint her his sole executrix, but refers to her in the expressive terms of " my loving wife Martha."

In the year 1802 our author compiled and published " The Memoirs of the Families of Sir E. Knatchbull, Bart., and of Filmer Honeywood, Esq.," a small octavo; and at the end he added a note, promising an enlarged account of these Kentish families, with fine engravings, provided a sufficient number of subscribers could be obtained. This was never the case, and the supplemental book never saw the light.

It will be seen that Pocock throughout his career exhibited constant proofs not only of literary industry, but of order; indeed without these qualities he would never have compiled the materials for his collections, and secured the publication of such of his published works as saw the light. He carried this exactitude into the affairs of his private life, as is illustrated by his having in the year 1797 (the year of the publication of his " History of Gravesend "), on the 19th of October, carefully written out his will on three pages of MS.; and after mentioning that his wife Frances was sufficiently provided for, and releasing all marital ·control over her little property, gave whatever he might leave to three trustees, for his children equally, a disposition which sadly survived all that it was designed to confer; expiring itself indeed of inanition, it remains to this day in the lawyer's pigeon-hole, a never-to-be-fulfilled testament !

It was in 1802 or the previous year that he exerted himself to establish a library and reading-room. His methodical statement of the literary supplies with which the subscribers were to be refreshed will not be without interest; it was accompanied by the following proposals :—

" The entrance to the library and reading-room shall be by a private door and passage adjoining to the Globe public-house, and not through his (Pocock's) shop, viz. the circulating library.

" The room shall be fitted up in a commodious manner, and open for the admission of the subscribers from nine in the morning to nine at night; well lighted with candles, and a fire kept during the winter.

" The subscribers shall be furnished with

" The Canterbury Paper twice a week,

" The Maidstone Paper once a week,

" The Times Paper daily,

" Lloyd's List twice a week,

" The Public Ledger daily, or some other, provided the subscription will allow it;

" And monthly with

" The European Magazine,

" The Gentleman's Magazine,
" The Critical Review,
" The Monthly Review,
" And Steel's List ;
" And yearly with
" The Annual Register, and such other books and pamphlets as the subscription will allow of. Exclusive of these, the library shall be furnished with all the historical and valuable books (novels excepted) now in Mr. Pocock's possession."

The yearly cost of these periodicals and coals and candles he estimated at 48*l.* 1*s.*; and doubtless the enterprise had a happy rise, and, as is often the fate of such local undertakings, was followed by a gradual decay.

In after-days, writing of his efforts at this period and in previous years, he says, not without some tinge of bitterness,—

" Prior to 1786, Gravesend could not boast of any institution of this sort, but in that year the writer established the first printing-office and first bookseller's shop in that town ; but literature was at such a low ebb, that upon the words 'Circulating Library' being placed over his window, many of the inhabitants came in to know their meaning. Since that period they are a little improved, but they have a further opportunity of enriching themselves by more often visiting Pocock's library, which will also enrich the librarian, who has done his endeavours to render his native townsmen prosperous, and to cultivate their ideas, for which purpose he also established a scientific society ; but some of the members, thinking they would be ruined by the trifling expense per week, fell to and sold off the property among themselves, to their eternal shame and disgrace."

This society was presumably the Natural History Society of the County of Kent, of which he was both founder and chairman.

We must remember, however, in justice to the uninformed townsmen, that the era of " Mudie " had not then arisen; and it is interesting to note that only four years before the establishment of Pocock's printing press, these unsophisticated people had been seriously imposed upon in listening with much interest, on the Sunday before his commitment, Sept. 3, 1782, to a *pseudo*-Rev. John Lloyd, really a highwayman, who, with forged letters of ordination, had preached an edifying discourse at Gravesend parish church, taking his text from the Epistle of St. Paul to the Philippians, "For I have learnt, in whatsoever state I am, therewith to be content."

The MS. sermon was found in his pocket when apprehended, and in it occurs the following amongst many similar passages :—

"The remembrance of a well-spent life, and of the many benefits and kindnesses done by us to others, is one of the most pleasing things in this world."

Indeed the experience of the inhabitants had not been happy in ecclesiastical affairs. The church-wardens fell under the censure of the great Bishop Fisher in 1522 (a prelate of whom Dean Hook rightly says, that to his transcendent virtue and noble qualities justice has never been done); while in 1710 we find the Mayor busily taking the information of Arthur Gibbon, of Milton next Gravesend in the county of Kent aforesaid, glazier, upon oath, that, " being at the

Faulcon ale-house, situate in Milton next Gravesend, Arnold Syddall Clerk, curate of Gravesend, was there in, company with this deponent and others, and that he then and there heard the said Arnold Syddall declare and say that the Pretender, the Prince of Wales, was King James's true-begotten son, and born of the Queen's own body;" while again, eleven years later, Bishop Atterbury suspended the then curate for allowing the Dutch soldiers (who sat covered during their sermon) the use of the parish church for their service. So highly ran the politico-religious animosities of the day.

Indeed, even at an earlier period the inhabitants of Gravesend were unfortunate in regard to their ecclesiastical buildings; and the churchwardens were exposed to constant proceedings in the spiritual courts, for their old church of St. Mary became more ruinous as it grew to be more and more remote from the receding population, which, in view of the supreme importance of the river traffic, had been for the last three centuries steadily leaving the interior for the river-side. Within six years of the rebuilding and reconsecration of the old church by Bishop Fisher, we find the churchwardens cited to the Consistory Courts in consequence of its neglect and disrepair, and this continued repeatedly until Henry VIII., "in terra Supremum Caput Ecclesiæ Anglicanæ," by his licence of 1544, authorized the abandonment of St. Mary's, and the substitution of St. George's Chapel as the parish church.

Owing to the dearth of material, we cannot, until we shall have further advanced in the century, command much unpublished information respecting our printer; but continuing for the present to confine ourselves to his publications, he issued in 1802 :—

"THE GRAVESEND WATER COMPANION;
describing all the Towns, Churches, Villages, Parishes, and
Gentlemen's Seats as seen from the River Thames between London
Bridge and Gravesend Town, with observations on whatever is
curious or worth remarking in that distance, calculated chiefly for
the amusement and entertainment of those who frequent the
Gravesend Passage Boats, Margate Hoys, and for all Captains,
Passengers, and Mariners.
'Oft we pass'd them unobserv'd,
But now observ'd we do admire.'
Gravesend:
Printed by R. Pocock.
Sold by Messrs. Robinson, Paternoster Row,
and all other Booksellers.
1802."

This little volume, the precursor of the now familiar
"Murray" and of our modern guide-books, is not perhaps
very felicitously entitled "Water Companion;" but a
perusal of its pages discloses a very useful and superior
publication of the kind, octavo in size, and of thirty-five
pages. It is pleasantly descriptive of the places of
interest on both sides of the River Thames in an
upward journey from Gravesend to Billingsgate, with
an abundance of matter showing careful and extensive
topographical research.

Simultaneously was published by the author a
continuation of his descriptive account of the places on
the banks of the Thames as far down as Margate,
under the title of

"THE MARGATE WATER COMPANION;
describing the River Thames from Margate to Gravesend, being a
supplement to the Gravesend Water Companion; both to be had
stitched together of any Bookseller in the Kingdom.
Price One Shilling."

The following extract will show the easy and pleasant style of the author. Opening his work with Gravesend Reach, he proceeds :—" In this reach lies the town of Gravesend, noted for fish, asparagus, watermen, and a well-frequented and cheap ferry (to that metropolis which has no equal), by means of the boats which depart each flood upon the ringing of a bell. Opposite to this town on the Essex shore lies Tilbury Fort, a regular fortification, having a great many guns and a very few old soldiers within it, who have for their comfort continual agues to vex them, unwholesome air to breathe, and very bad water to quench their thirst. Leaving them to their piteous situation, we pass the west end of Gravesend, where the road or tunnel under the Thames is intended to be made, and if completed will be the greatest wonder on (or under) the earth," &c.

The author might well speak of the cheapness of the ferry to London, since it appears from his " Sea Captain's Assistant," hereafter to be mentioned, that the fare then was but one shilling for the whole twenty-four miles or thereabouts. No doubt this river route was both pleasant and popular, and as in very disturbed social periods the road to London over Shooter's Hill was often infested by footpads and highwaymen, it is not difficult to imagine the busy scene normally displayed at the Gravesend Bridge (the local name for the pier or embarking-place), which has been amusingly written of by many, and amongst them by Mr. Straycock, a pilot, who often visited the town, and who writing of " Gravesend at low water" says,—

"The ebb is done; list how yon bell's loud charms
The ears of anxious passengers alarms.
Now busy boatmen run from side to side,—
'Sir, Madam, Miss, do you go up this tide?'
'Here, Serjeant, Master, let us put you off;
We're the first boat (at this the others laugh);
We start directly, Sir, we never wait;
In three hours hence you'll be at Billingsgate.'"

In the same connexion occurs on a fly-leaf of a
MS. in the Bodleian Library, entitled "The Pricke of
Conscience," the following curious reference to what
must have been a well-known and most popular mode
of travelling to London from Kent:—

"The Grave Counsell of Gravesend Barge
Gevethe John Daye a privylege large
To put this in prynt for his gaynes,
Because in the Legend of lyes he takethe paynes,
Commandinge other upon payn of slavery
That none prynt this but John Daye the prynter of Foxe his
Knavery."

This was probably the same John Daye as the
printer of that name of Foxe's Martyrs, and of the
seven satires upon the doctrine of the Real Presence in
the reign of Henry VIII. (for which at the time he
got into great trouble), such as his dialogue between
John Bon and Master Parson.

In the same year (1802) as the above guide-books,
Pocock wrote and published his

### SEA CAPTAIN'S ASSISTANT;

Or, *Fresh* Intelligence for *Salt*-water Sailors; giving an account of
Merchandise exported from or imported into Great Britain; with
the names and residences of the principal Brokers, Consuls, and
Agents; the Monies and Ministers in Foreign Ports.

Also,
The Flags of different Nations arranged in a new form; the
Public Maritime Offices in London; a list of the Trinity-house
Pilots, with the Pilots of Deal and Dover; a Naval Chronology,
&c., &c., &c.
Gravesend :
Printed by R. Pocock,
And sold by the Booksellers in Paternoster Row.

The following preface which he drew up will best
exhibit his aims and the objects of the publication :—
" The public are presented with a pamphlet on a new
plan, and although small, yet the compiler presumes he
has introduced such information as will prove useful
to maritime gentlemen, to whom he begs in particular
to pay his highest respects, and at the same time to
solicit their patronage.

" From the merchant and broker he hopes to receive
such matter and correction as will enable him at some
future period to bring forth another edition more
deserving of their favours.

" Therefore communications and corrections will be
thankfully received (post-paid), addressed to the
Editor of the ' Sea Captain's Assistant ' at Mr. Bird's,
Bookbinder, Ave Maria Lane, London, or sent to the

" Public's humble servant,
" R. Pocock,
" Book and Chart Seller,
" Gravesend.
" Dec. 1, 1802."

The title-page and preface sufficiently shadow forth
the contents of this little publication. It appears from
its pages that no less than seventeen coaches then
passed upwards daily from Gravesend to London,

and fifteen in the other direction.  The manual is an
octavo of forty-eight pages, replete with evidences
of careful preparation, and it must have proved
at the period of its publication an extremely welcome
means of reference in the hands of the maritime trading
community, especially such of it as was connected
with the port of London.

Mr. A. J. Dunkin, indeed, in his "Nundinæ Can-
tianæ," 1842, claims that our author projected the
Navy List, and published it several years alone, and
afterwards in conjunction with Steel.

The publication of that name we have seen, was comprised in the works provided by him for the subscribers
to his library (p. 25).

## CHAPTER II.

Stranger of heaven ! I bid thee hail !
Shred from the pall of glory riven,
That flashest in celestial gale,
Broad pennon of the King of heaven !
Where hast thou roam'd these thousand years ?
Why sought these polar paths again,
From wilderness of glowing spheres,
To fling thy vesture o'er the wain ?
And when thou scal'st the Milky Way,
And vanishest from human view,
A thousand worlds shall hail thy ray,
Through wilds of yon empyreal blue.

JAMES HOGG.

As we shall now be proceeding to Pocock's Diary for
1811, in which he records the appearance of the great
comet of that year, it suitably enables us to direct
more especial attention to our printer's love of nature,
and his ardent pursuit of natural history. This he
evinced in 1809, in his

### NATURAL HISTORY OF KENT,

Arranged in a systematical Order.
To which is added
An Alphabetical Index
of
All the Parishes in that County ;

D

Also
The Specific Names
of every
Animate and Inanimate Production of Nature
found in and about
Great Britain.
By R. Pocock, Author of the Tufton Family,
History of Gravesend, Margate Water Companion, &c.
Gravesend : Printed by R. Pocock.
1809.

He wrote a preface to this work as follows :—

" The foundation work of this Natural History of Kent is adopted from Dr. Turton's octavo edition of Linne.   His method, and systematic order, is followed (because better cannot be found), but the merit and usefulness of that publication is not lessened, as no article is stolen or copied therefrom (which is too often practised), but overlooked or new information is added, whereby this may rank 1st as a continuation of that excellent universal collection, 2nd as an extra volume to Mr. Hasted's octavo edition of " Kent," and 3rd as an original work.

" It is not presumed or expected a volume of this nature can be perfect (for much is yet left to be known and done) ; yet the candour of the public is claimed for all deficiencies, especially when it is considered that the labour of this *first* systematically arranged natural history of a county is greater than superintending twenty future editions.

" Much difficulty occurred at the beginning.   It was once thought the best way to give the produce of each parish under its head, but repetitions of articles would have extended the work to an enormous size, to avoid which an alphabetical index of all the parishes in Kent is added, with the pages wherein they are mentioned : this will prove of great advantage to a parochial historian.

"GENERAL DISTINCTIONS.

" The scarcity or plenty of things is remarked by the following words in italic type :—

"*Most common* means what is found in *every parish,* and *daily seen,* as horses, hogs, sparrows, &c.

"*Common* means what is found in several *parishes,* but not daily seen, as moles, hawks, &c.

"*Not uncommon* means what is found in *some parishes,* but *not so often seen,* as otters, badgers, &c.

"*Uncommon* means what is found in few parishes, and but *seldom seen,* as martens, cats, horned owls, soap-wort.

"*Most uncommon* means what is rarely met with in the county, or visit the shores, as whales, seals, eagles.

"*Not heard of* means has not come to the author's knowledge.

"*Var.* means a variety."

He dedicated this labour to the President and Council of the Royal Society in the following words:—

"Gentlemen,—The British nation is greatly indebted to our Sovereign Gracious Family by the incorporation of the Royal Society, which has so often and laudably issued forth rewards for improvement of scientific knowledge, whereby many useful inventions have been brought to perfection and carried into effect, which otherwise would have lain dormant and been lost in oblivion. The encouragement held forth by your

Royal Society first stimulated me to begin a Natural History of Kent, which work I have now the honour to lay before the public, with hopes that it will deserve their approbation.

"I remain, gentlemen,

"Your most humble servant,

"ROBERT POCOCK."

But alas! he was never able to publish these his labours, and they fell sterile, like so many other of his efforts, for want of encouragement and pecuniary support.

It is satisfactory to be able at length to pass to some of the author's Diaries, which have been to a fragmentary extent saved; for it is ever easier and truer work, certainly pleasanter, to judge of a man and to form an estimate of him from his own words, than to depend upon the researches and speculations of others, however disinterested and impartial. Indeed he who writes a Journal often involuntarily portrays his own character.

### CHRONICLE OF 1811.

"*September 1st*, 1811, *Sunday.*—Visited Essex, and bought a loaf at Leigh, and then to Old or Holy Haven in Canvey Island, Essex, where there is only one public-house; but did not enter it, or take any refreshment, because I had heard from *several* that the landlord's name was not Mr. 'Civility.'

"*September 2nd, Monday.*—Read the Gent.'s Mag. for last month, the value of which has lately been increased by the correspondence of Messrs. Lettsom, Foster, Richardson, Hall, and others.

"The Gent.'s Mag. I rank as one of the first British periodicals.

" I take delight in perusing this magazine, because it contains variety; yet I think the editors confine themselves too much to the antique, especially in the counties about the metropolis. The plates of churches carry with them a sameness. Ormskirk Church, I have been told, has at one end a spire and at the other a tower: such as have a similarity about them ought not to be introduced.

" Dr. Richardson must accept my thanks for the goodness of his communication of the Fiorin, and must also forgive the harsh treatment of Mr. S. The public surely would have liked Mr. Urban to have given a plate of this grass.

" Dr. Lettsom, by publishing Mr. Neald's letters, has done more good to society than any individual since the days of Mr. Howard; but I cannot help remarking, that whilst the philanthropist is exerting himself to relieve forlorn, dejected, petty debtors, to the comfort of their families, on the other hand there are in the country a set of pettifogging attorneys continually trying to establish Courts of Requests (Courts of Conscience, *alias* without conscience) managed by a set of commissioners, mostly tradesmen under the influence of those attorneys who distress the poor debtor frequently by imprisonment, illegally proclaimed.

" Mr. Hall (it is to be hoped) will favour us again with his communications.

" *September 3rd.*—The eclipse of last night passed over without my knowing it; but it would not have been so if I had consulted Moore's Almanack, which I have frequently disregarded on account of the prognostications contained therein. Surely those might be omitted, and more useful matter substituted.

"*Wednesday, 4th.*—Saw the moon rise; supposed my neighbour's house on fire.

"*Thursday, 5th.*—Visited Lord Darnley's gardens at Cobham. At nine at night, coming home from Cobham, observed in the north-east a circular haze which I supposed to be a comet. Thought of my friend Mr. Overton of Plumstead, and the great telescope at Slough. Caught this day at noon a brimstone butterfly.

"*Friday, 6th.*—I mentioned this morning to my wife that I had certainly seen a comet last night. Heard in the course of the day that a comet had been announced in the newspaper. Saw the paper, where a gentleman at Kelso had discovered it in August. I found this evening the comet take another appearance; it now had a tail in the direction of about an angle of forty-five or fifty upwards, tending north-east. Ran about the town to borrow a celestial map or globe, but without success. Found the inhabitants not attached to the sciences, and more of astrologers than astronomers.

"*Sunday, 8th.*—Foggy morning, but the finest day and starlight evening I ever beheld. The Milky Way most conspicuous, and the comet brighter, with longer rays. First saw it through a common spy-glass, when it appeared like a hazy star of the first magnitude. The field of the glass took in a star out of its rays below it, and a star in the rays above it, rather to the right hand. Observed, whilst looking, a falling star or meteor descend into its tail. The water on the oars appeared very luminous—a prognostication of a southerly wind.

"Visited Lord Eardley's gardens at Erith, where

the village was like a fair, owing to the Gravesend boats not being able to get farther. Observed there an ancient low house with two doors, the spandril ornamented with leopards' heads and a coat of arms, well worth a plate in Mr. Urban's magazine. Walked into Lord Eardley's, and saw the gardens: the pleasure-grounds are charmingly rural, and a great variety of scarce trees and shrubs. Accidentally met with two of the household female servants, who escorted us to the top of the high tower that overlooks the trees, and from which we had a fine prospect of the river and adjacent country. Could do no less than thank our guides for the view, and politely endeavoured to salute one, which seemingly was not taken amiss; but in performing the ceremony I was so awkward that my hat fell off. Surely, I thought, this, like many other things, wants practice. A good general should be cool, wait for opportunities, and not be too rash. Descended the tower, and took leave of our kind, sociable strangers.

"*September*, 1811.—Had a gossip with Mr. H., a river pilot, by some called Mr. 'Milk and Water.' Why this name should be attached to a worthy man, I know not; perhaps it is that milk and water is often thought incapable of doing harm, whilst it may do good, an instance of which occurred last week. A little boy Mr. H. observed, in company with a soldier at Gravesend, inquiring the road to Chatham and seemingly dejected, sitting on the steps of a trades-man's door; whereupon Mr. H. called the boy in, and challenged him with running away from his parents. This the child did not deny, and to the honour of Mr. Bryant, linen-draper of Gravesend (who took the child in for that night, he being destitute of money) it was restored to the parents, implement-makers in Shoe Lane, the next day. So much for the kind conduct of Mr. H. Too much cannot be said in praise of milk and water !

"Went to the sale of my old acquaintance, Mr. Adams, a bricklayer, who lately died worth some thousands. He left, I hear, two of them to a person no way related, although he had several poor relations. No accounting for the unfairness of wills !

"How much good would a few thousands have done to a few industrious tradesmen tottering on balances of 50*l*. ! I did not find a book of science, or English topography, or cyclopædia, &c., in his sale, which contained a library of 230 chosen volumes, which fetched a price about equal to 1200 volumes of novels lately disposed of at Mr. Lance's library.

"The young sparrows pick and spoil my black cluster grapes, but not my white sweet-water. Counted my bunches, and found I had 404.

" Found this year, as I have before noticed, that the tenderest, sweetest, and best grapes are those covered with leaves. A gentleman some time since asked the reason of withered bunches. I think it arises from the lateral branch being shortened. Worth trying the experiment next year on different laterals. This day my sister died.

"*Wednesday, September 11th.*—Fine sunshine morning and day. A small air from the north. Observed the moon plainly at nine in the morning, whilst the sun was very bright. Guessed it would be with the sun in four days' time, so that the sun, moon, and comet will be nearly on a meridian line.

" In the course of this day the young lady called from the Orkneys who sent me the drawing of the wonderful sea snake which came on shore at Stronsa. What would Pontophidan have given for such ! Greatly disappointed and vexed that I was not at home to receive her, as she is a bonny girl—not a bony girl, but a bonnie girl. What can I do for such a kind female, who exposed herself to inclemency and danger to visit a distant island to gratify my request ? Why, send her some books to pass her hours in the dreary winter. I have so done, and through fraud they never reached her hands. Then send her some grapes, for out of 404 bunches surely a few may be spared, and grapes at the Orkneys are nearly as rare as sea snakes.

" *Thursday, September 12th.*—Had a large green grasshopper brought me. Saw the newspaper with an account of the comet by Capel Loft, who supposed it to be fast approaching to Ursa Minor ; but I am not of that opinion, as it tends more to the tail of Ursa Major. At four p.m. set off for London, not in a balloon, but in a swift bird, the *Petrel,* which flew with me to that stinking place called Billingsgate, which I could not quit so soon as I wished. Heard a boat had gone through bridge, and carried away mast. Had a glimpse of the comet. Just before I arrived a mad dog bit a man (September 10th) and an old woman. The father of the boy sent to Birling directly for that never-failing remedy.

" *Friday, September 13th.*—Peeped into the auction mart—not fond of the last-named place. Met with the City Solicitor, and had some discourse on a boundary-stone of the City, which I had discovered. Went to Margaret Street to see a friend just arrived from East

Indies.   Sorry to hear that the petty officers in that
service are generally dissatisfied, it being a losing
concern.   Went into a public-house, where a letter was
read, received from Slough, describing Dr. Herschell's
telescope, which has a diameter of forty-seven inches, a
platform for six to stand at its top to take a peep—at
the bottom a mirror, which was stated to weigh 250lb.,
and traverses on a platform of forty feet.   I informed
the company that a baker (a neighbour of mine, Mr.
Mathews) could make as good as the composition for
such mirrors, and this was some years since made
public in the Nautical Almanack, a publication more
useful but not so much known as Moore's.   A better
account of Moore and Dr. Herschell's telescope is requested in the Gent.'s Mag.   At near midnight I re-
treated to Merlin's Cave, where I passed the night.

"*Saturday, September* 14*th.*—Visited Mr. L., of Titch-
field Street.   Gave him some sand from Ascension
Island, and a piece of Sydnea Australis, and heard a new
edition of twenty vols. of Buffon was in the press.   Saw
the comet in the evening.   Heard the tail took a direction to the north-west in the morning.   Embarked at
twelve at night from the Dundee Arms in clean,
commodious boat called the *Glory.*   Soon after a
very thick fog came on.   Anchored four times, and once
got on ground.   Time tedious, but much passed
away in conversation with a young female traveller
from Scotland.   Found she had read nearly every
play and poet.   Landed at seven o'clock a.m. at
Woolwich.

"*Sunday, September* 15*th.*—Found Woolwich greatly
increased since my last visit.   Walked towards Crayford, but missed the road.   Passing by Captain Ed-

meades's, of the East India service, in Bampton Lane,
found the vervain mallow in bloom. Had only found
it once before in Kent. Plucked some seeds, as it is
well worth a place in private garden. Observed at
the same place in bloom, by the side of the ditch, the
scarlet pimpernel in a great state of luxuriance.
Bampton Lane is solitary, and not such a desirable
spot for a residence as I should choose. Refreshed
myself at Crayford, where I found that madder was
lately cultivated, but now totally rooted up, it being
a losing concern, as it took three years to bring it to
perfection, and much trouble in getting up the roots,
which run four or five feet in length. Crayford
famous for calico-printing, carp, trout, and good
singers. Saw a large green grasshopper. Strong
wind east. Faintly saw the comet. Starlight to eight.
Arrived at Gravesend at ten, greatly fatigued.

" *Monday Night, September* 16*th.*—Heard that on
Saturday last a man put in the cage on a charge of
stealing two odd shoes from Mr. Newman, proprietor
of coaches, had cut his throat. However, by timely
assistance, and the skill of Mr. Beaumont, surgeon, it
was sewn up, and the man is likely to recover.

" Miss B. from Orkney called. Gave her some
grapes, being the greatest present to take to Orkney.
Mr. C., my young antiquarian and scientific friend,
informed me that during my absence he had been
engaged in trying the utility of a new screw and machine
for the purpose of navigating vessels. I told him the
proprietor of the machine, Mr. S. of the Strand, should
have called on my neighbour, who knows more about
screws than half the screw and machine makers in the
kingdom. Two French prisoners taken to a madhouse.

"*Tuesday, September* 17*th.*—Fine Sunday morning.
Company of the 42nd Regiment arrived from Scotland,
following the regiment which passed through this
town within a few weeks. Had a present made me
of a copper "Nero."

"*Wednesday, September* 18*th.*—The watchman pro-
claims 'past two o'clock and a fine starlight night.'
Got out of bed on hearing this, and peeped at the
comet, which was more conspicuous than before. Now
seen in the north-east, its tail apparently more
upright, and in an oblique direction at the square of
the Great Bear. With much persuasion prevailed on
my wife to have a peep also (for the first time !), which
she did, with indifference declaring she never cared
for the Great Bear nor Little Bear, and that I had
better come to bed than be looking at such creatures,
and that the stars would do me no good. The finest
morning I ever beheld ! Wind at E. Brisk, yet
pleasant. At sunset a general gloomy reddish haze,
which I thought portended rain, and many meteors ;
however, it turned out starlight. Near nine a meteor
from the Great Bear passed over the tail of the comet
just above its head. Looked at the comet with a
common glass, and found the rays proceeded from the
circumference, making a vacuum.

"*Wednesday, September* 25*th.*—Four fine horses
shipped by Mr. Woodgate for America. One was
valued at 1200*l.*, as certified in the cocquet at the
Custom-house.

"Many Jews and crimps about the town ; a sure sign
of an Indian fleet arrived. Among the crimps are
many well-dressed women. As the business of crimp-
ing is unknown in the interior of the kingdom, let

me inform you that crimps are a useful set of people, acting as a medium between the captain and sailor. The established fee for procuring a seaman is two guineas.

" *Thursday, September 26th.*—Went to the sale of Mr. L., lately ruined by having gunpowder on board his vessel. There are penalties for having it in a ship when at certain parts of the river. The police officers are well skilled in Acts of Parliament wherein *qui tam* abounds. The martins flew very low this day in the rain. Several cut down by boys with whips. Many conjectures are given about those birds. I know of no place where so many abound as Sheppey.

"The Church of Minster in Sheppey is remarkable for having a horse-head on the top of the spire in lieu of a weather-cock, from which we have an improbable traditional story; but many persons resort in summer to this village, and upon visiting the church seldom leave it without hearing something of this tale, which we shall entertain our reader with in poetry.

"MINSTER.

" Of monuments that here they show
Within the church, we draw but two;
One an ambassador of Spain's,
The other Lord Sharland's dust contains;
Of whom a story strange they tell,
And seemingly believe it well.
" The Lord of Sharland on a day,
Happening to take a ride this way,
About a corpse observed a crowd,
Against their priest complaining loud,
That he would not the service say
Till somebody his fees should pay.
On this his lordship too did rave,
And threw the priest into the grave.
' Make haste and fill it up,' said he;

‘ We'll bury both without a fee.’
But when he cooler grew, and thought
To what a scrape himself had brought,
Away he gallop'd to the bay,
Where at that time a frigate lay
With Queen Elizabeth on board ;
When (strange to tell) this hair-brain'd lord
On horseback swam to the ship's side,
There told his tale, and pardon cried.
The grant with many thanks he takes,
And swimming still, to land he makes ;
But on his riding up the beach,
He an old woman meets (a witch).
‘ This horse which now your life does save,’
Says she, ‘ will bring you to the grave.’
‘ You'll prove a liar,’ says my lord,
‘ You ugly hag !’ then with his sword,
Acting a most ungrateful part,
The generous beast stabb'd to the heart.
  “ It happen'd after many a day
That with some friends he stroll'd that way,
And this strange story, as they walk,
Became the subject of their talk ;
When on the bank by the sea-side,
‘ Yonder the carcase lies !’ he cried,
As not far off he led them to't,
And kick'd the skull up with his foot,
When a sharp bone pierced thro' his shoe,
And wounded grievously his toe,
Which mortified ; so he was kill'd,
And the hag's prophecy fulfill'd.
See there his cross-legg'd figure laid,
And near his feet the horse's head.
  “ The tomb is of too old a fashion
To tally well with this narration ;
But of the tale we would not doubt,
Nor put our cicerone out.
'Tis a good moral point at least,
That gratitude's due to a beast.

"*Saturday, September* 28*th.*—Read part of Du Lolde's 'Embassy to China.' Found the mode of drinking tea the same as at present, except the spout was closed to infuse the tea better, and a little salt to give it a flavour. The death-watch heard at ten.

"*Sunday, September* 29*th.*—At ten the Earl of Darnley arrives in the town as hereditary High Steward, and according to custom breakfasted with the Mayor, Geo. Rich., Esq., and corporation, in their Town Hall, on hot roast beef, moistened with plenty of arrack-punch, and then walked to church, where a discourse was delivered by Dr. Watson, Rector of Gravesend.

"A fleet from China passed by. Evening star and moon light, with low clouds. Comet seen making nearly a triangle with the two last stars in the Bear's tail. The tail of the comet faint, probably arising from the glare of the moon. Whilst observing it about eight, a faint reddish Aurora Borealis shot from the north-west. Those phenomena were frequent before the American War, and are yet often seen by our fishermen to the north of Scotland, making a hissing, snapping noise.

"*Monday, September* 30*th.*—The Corporation of Gravesend walk in procession to church to hear divine service, and on their return choose Mr. Dennett as Mayor for the year ensuing.—Mem. Most corporations now are petty tyrannical governments ruled by the caprice of their town clerks. They should be an object of government constitution. They should either have a heavy tax imposed on them or be dissolved.

"The rays of the comet appear faint, it being bright moonlight. Whilst looking at this time and moonlight, a meteor shot forth in the westward, passing along horizontally a great space, and entered or went behind a cloud, making its appearance again in a clear space, and once more entered a hazy cloud that reached to the horizon. This was a singular phenomenon. I guess about next Friday the comet will eclipse, or be very near the last star in the Great Bear's tail. The town full of hissing serpents (fireworks), following a lawless rabble called ' Mock Mayor,' who go from door to door collecting alms for drink and riot, and imitating his Worship the Mayor, his mace-bearer, and the rest of this singular body, who demand 20*l.* for the privilege of a man becoming free of the town, but deny this freeman the privilege of voting for any one, either mayor, jurat, or common councilman! "

" *Tuesday Morning, October 1st.*—A person from Dover called and told me that David Anderson, a pilot of Deal, had met with his death in a tragical manner. He was coming up in a south whaler, which ran foul of an East Indiaman, and received such a shock that it was expected she was sinking, whereupon all the men of the whaler, except two, jumped on board the Indiaman ; but Mr. A., in jumping, either missed his hold or jumped short, and fell between the ships, which at that instant suddenly came in contact twice, and squeezed him fatally. The whaler, with two men on board, drove on Margate Sands, losing one of the two men. What has become of the ship is unknown, as she is not now seen on Margate Sands.

" Had this morning a violent pain at the bottom of my heel, which affects the back part of my leg. Never had such a pain before ; surely it must be the gout for

the first time. If so, it certainly arose from my standing out on the damp ground last night to view the
comet and fireworks. Had this day brought me a
sphinx moth, convolvuli, &c., which flew on board a
vessel *ten leagues* off the coast of Scotland. Had also
a lump-fish sent me.

"Pain in my heel increases, making me lame. First
used spectacles, and found great benefit therefrom.
Took up Greig's 'Astrography.' Not well pleased with
this work, and opened the book with much prejudice,
because I remember a work of authority beginning
with abstruse characters instead of the most simple
elements. Perused some of the pages of this 'Astrography' with pleasure. Every leaf I turned over
diminished my prejudice. I find the book full of well-
selected information on a new plan, as the title expresses ; therefore I earnestly recommend it to both
young and old as a useful manual of astronomy,
mythology, and history. More knowledge can be
derived from this close-printed pocket edition (which
costs only five shillings) than from ten quarto volumes
of the more ancient men printed on royal paper with
royal margins. Went to Dr. Thornton, No. 1, Hinde
Street, Manchester Square, to see his paintings.

"*Thursday, October 3rd.*—Read an American newspaper. Philadelphia Museum State-house—a mammoth there, twenty-five cents for a peep.—Mem. The
bones of a mammoth can be seen at the British
Museum for nothing.

"*Friday, October 4th.*—Swallows and martins fly
about house high. Sun out at two o'clock. Read the
Gent.'s Mag. for last month, and understood it very
well (except the epistle by a young clergyman), I

E

made my wife laugh (a very singular thing) at the
humour there related in a paragraph styled the 'Times.'
I hope this humorous writer will continue Mr. Urban's
constant correspondent.

"*Saturday, October 5th.*—This evening at eight
my neighbour, the mechanical turner, &c., ran in
and wished me to see the comet that instant, as it
was in more splendour than ever; its tail lengthened
to the square of the Little Bear; the stars about it
unusually bright for a few moments: and its tail
embraced two stars of fourth or fifth magnitude, whilst
a star of about third magnitude was below it. Several
meteors or shooting stars seen in less than ten minutes.
They were noticed as if flying with the wind. Observed a circular haze the size of the moon round
Lyra, which continued five minutes. This appearance
was so singular that I was on the eve of calling out
'Another comet.'

"*October 11th.*—"A Painted Lady Cardinal" flew
from my grape-vine. Read a small pamphlet on comets
by Mr. Rivers, wherein he gives an erroneous list of
comets, omitting that which appeared in October and
November, 1807, and likewise one which I remember
seeing about forty-three years ago, nearly of a similar
appearance to the present.

"*Wednesday, October 16th.*—A flight of birds (star-
lings) flew over the town to the westward. This I
have observed several years. Read this day a pamphlet on comets printed at Stamford, which gives a
much better account than that of Mr. Rivers. My
friend Mr. Crafter called, and says it is not the hottest
day of the year, as on one day it was ten degrees hotter.
Read a letter from my son, wherein he appears to be

afraid of asking a young lady to alter her name. I write 'Courage, my lad; the lady will say, Don't, sir; pray do.'

"*Thursday, October 17th.*—Insulted by a grinning dog or biped puppy. Mr. Bedingfield's Clerk called with a message from the party.

"*Sunday, October 20th.*—Soon after eleven alarmed by the watchman with a smell of fire. Got up, searched the house, and found the smell arose from some asafœtida or other drug injected through the keyhole—suspected to be put there by one C. (assistant to Mr. B.) and others.

"*Monday, October 21st.*—Morning at eight. Wind E. Sent a letter to Mr. B., of which the following is a copy:—

"Sir,—Surgeons and apothecaries are expected to have more gravity and good sense than the generality of men, and when otherwise they are a disgrace to their profession.

"You keep dogs, and have a grinning one that goes about the streets in the evening (with others) to the annoyance of the neighbourhood. This is to caution you to keep him within, or likely enough he will some night return with a good horse-whipping by the hand of

"Yours, &c.,
"Robert Pocock.

"P.S.—When you have read this, show it to the puppy."

"*Tuesday, October 22nd.*—Death's-head moth found at Gravesend.

"*Thursday, October 24th.*—Gravesend Fair. Small

rain. Some men taken up in the fair for gambling. Gathered my last grapes.

"*Monday, October 28th.*—A bat flying about the market inthe forenoon ; rain in the afternoon. Mr. Foreman, of the Ferry House, Tilbury, called, and said he had started this day a post-coach to Chelmsford daily. Sets out at seven in the morning, returns at three, and arrives at Tilbury Fort at eight in the evening. Heard that Mr. Rashleigh, jun., performed divine service as curate of Gravesend yesterday for the first time.

"*Wednesday, October 30th.*—Evening at eight. Moonlight night. Comet very faintly discerned, owing to lustre of the moon.—Mem. The lustre of the moon does not seem to affect the brightness of Lyra. A pilot-fish taken alive at Gravesend, size of a mackerel. Three spines on its back near the tail.

"*Sunday, November 10th.*—Conger-eel came on shore at new tavern, about five feet long, and supposed to weigh 18 lb.

"*Tuesday, November 12th.*—Read the Maidstone paper that at the Wrotham meeting for making a new road to Tonbridge were present Earl Camden, Earl Darnley, Sir William Geary, Sir Henry Twysden, and about twenty other gentlemen, among whom were George Rich, Esq., and Laurence Ruck, Esq.

"*Wednesday, November 13th.*—Wrote this day a letter to the committee on the proposed new road to Wrotham from Gravesend. Tide ebbed and flowed twice at Gravesend.

"*Thursday, November 14th.*—Two black women, Tobitha Isaacs and Maria De George, about going to Santa Cruz. Said they would send me some shells.

Perplexed by bills being printed for the parish by Caddell for the militia." [The rival press.]

" *Friday, November 15th.*—Spent the evening at ' the George.'

" *Sunday, November 17th.*—Walked to Northfleet with Mr. Crafter into the cliffs, where we saw a martin flying about. One of the men said two martins had been flying about in the morning, and also yesterday. Bought a virgin flint for sixpence. Saw in bloom wild endive (dandelion).

" *Monday, November 18th.*—Mr. Lancaster, a fisherman, brought me a left-handed whelk, and a piece of rock from Lewis Island, which appears as crystallized hornblende.

" *Tuesday, November 19th.*—It appears that the comet passed its perihelion about September 12th, 1811, when its perihelion distance was about 95,000,000 miles, and made its nearest approach to the earth about the middle of October, being then 10,800,000 miles distant. The space in the heavens occupied by its train extended 12°, so that the length of its tail was not less than 33,000,000 miles. The inclination of its orbit was about 73°.

" *Wednesday, November 20th.*—Heard that a stone had been placed yesterday on the sea wall at the extremity of the parish of Milton, having on one side the words ' Port of London, 1811,' and on the east side ' Port of Leigh.'

" *Thursday, November 21st.*—43rd Regiment came into town from Billericay. Went with Mr. Clarke from Exeter to see a machine invented to move forward boats and vessels in canals (by Mr. Sheldrake, of the Strand, London). Found the machine composed of a vertical wheel worked in with oblique iron screw, and turned by another massive iron wheel, to which was a horizontal lever pulling back and forward in the boat. On the whole it is a clumsy contrivance, and certainly will not answer the intended purpose. It was fixed with heavy apparatus of six or seven hundredweight to the stern of a boat about fifteen tons.

"*Friday, November 22nd.*—Mr. Richardson, the surgeon, called and said that his pointer dog died last Saturday mad, and that about six weeks since the dog had bit him through his coat in his arm, and had drawn blood in two places. The dog bit him, irritated by Mr. Richardson's correcting him whilst hunting. I persuaded him to lose no time in getting the 'Birling' remedy as an antidote. He seemed to say he would go on Monday; but I said, 'Why delay an hour when life is at stake?' Before this happened I had told the doctor I had heard his dog had been bitten by a mad dog, and to be careful of him. This was about the middle of September, subsequent to the dog's biting the brewer's servant.

"*Saturday, November 23rd.*—Laid a wager on spelling Brightlingsea, a town in Essex. I found this was the right way by the index to Morant's 'History of Essex,' but found that there were eight ways of spelling it. Remember Mr. Ball of Lockhill, who possessed a capital museum. Mr. Moore, the fisherman, brought me some shells from a vessel's bottom. Told me Mr. Roxburgh had got a small dog-fish with two heads.

"*Tuesday, November 26th.*—Mr. Crafter brought a red gurnard called a piper, taken at Long Reach in the river near Gravesend.

"*Saturday, November 30th.*—Sold to Mr. Salmon of Meopham thirty-three bushels and a half of coal ashes

at threepence per bushel as manure, used by him to
sprinkle over sainfoin and clover. Within a few years
fish have been used as manure. Sprats last year sold
for eightpence per bushel, and herrings this year for
about the same. They have been found to answer
well.

"*Sunday, December 1st.*—Met with Mr. George
Bruce, a man lately come from New Zealand, and most
curiously tattooed. Says the Zealanders are not can-
nibals; that the island produces flax, potatoes in
abundance, with mackerel and various fish. Called on
Mr. Roebrook with Mr. Crafter, who took a drawing
of the double-headed dog-fish caught off Cape Wrath.
It was eight inches long, and parted about the pectoral
fins into two heads, and the other parts were completely joined in a vertical manner, the same as if two
perfect fish had been placed together. It was one of
five found *alive* within the body of a shark about four
feet long.

"*Monday, December 2nd.*—This evening Mr. George
Bruce, naturalized New Zealander, and husband to the
late Princess Aetochoe, youngest daughter of Tippa-
hee, King of New Zealand (the title which a pamphlet
of his gives, printed by T. Plummer, Seething Lane,
Tower Street), called on me, and promises, whenever
he should be able to get to New Zealand, to send
some coral, emeralds, and shells, with skins of birds
and other curiosities. He has been at Gravesend about
a month, waiting for a ship going to the South Seas (Mr.
Bennet, or Mellish, owner), and has, whilst at Gravesend,
worked for Mr. Ditchburn, the rope-maker. He showed
me a letter from the Earl of Liverpool (by his secretary),
wherein his lordship declines interfering in his interest.

He therefore appears in his native country as a neglected alien. His pamphlet says he has had a ' liberal ' education ; but here it is wrong, as the word should have been ' common ;' for upon my asking him to read the title of a Botany Bay newspaper, he did it with difficulty. He has a fine pair of lips, good eyes, and if he had not been so much tattooed he would have been a very likely man. He is about five feet eight inches high, thinly made, and has lost two fingers. Mr. Crafter called with the drawing of the eighteenpence piece.

" *Wednesday, December 4th.*—Read the *Medical Journal* published this month, and pleased with the abstract of Mr. Lambert's ' Notes on Botany ' from the MSS. of Peter Collinson. Afternoon fine, with large white rocky clouds on azure sky ; starlight evening Between six and seven viewed comet, now to the southward of bright star in Aquila, at one-third distance of either two stars in it. It appears very faint, its tail not longer than the three stars of Aquila.

" *Thursday, December 5th.*—Out of temper, had tea, instead of a dinner off a very fine hare sent by Mr. R. H. yesterday. .

" *Friday, December 6th.*—My wife affronted me. Went to Greenhithe. Heard that the Poet of Greenhithe was the Rev. Mr. Bradley. This gentleman has produced some excellent pieces of poetry.

" *Saturday, December 7th.*—In the *dolldrums* all day. The New Zealander called for his pamphlet.

" *Sunday, December 8th.*—Taken at night with a violent shiver attended with fever, certainly owing to standing still in the damp.

" *Wednesday, December 11th.*—Paid a poor cess of one

shilling in the pound, said to be collected for the expense of a new goal at Maidstone, which I do not think was wanted, there being plenty of ground behind the present erection to have built an extra one. Many words passed which were quick and loud this evening between my wife and self. Not all true. I wished she was dumb.

"*Thursday, December* 12*th.*—Double stocks in bloom. Heard Captain Elphinstone sent (the other day) his servant on board man-of-war for wearing his shirts.

"*Friday, December* 13*th.*—Met with Mr. Millen, just come up in the *Drake* from Flushing.

"*Saturday, December* 14*th.*—Heard Mr. Cope's house was on fire from a pipe being thrown into the window.

"*Sunday, December* 15*th.*—Miss Phipps called and drank tea. She is not handsome, but agreeable. Heard some of our watermen had been up to London about Mr. Forseka the crimp being taken up on a charge of murder eighteen years ago, and that he was dismissed.

"*Tuesday, December* 17*th.*—Heard the Tower guns fired yesterday for news of Batavia being taken. Heard that Forseka the crimp was admitted to bail on charge of murder.

"*Wednesday, December* 18*th.*—Mr. Walker of Paternoster Row called in evening.

"*Thursday, December* 19*th.*—Buckingham Militia marched into town. Mr. Hinde and his son Robert Hinde called, when I sold them my house and premises. At the same time I paid Mr. Hinde every farthing I owed him, and at the same time he advanced 200*l.* on a note. Mr. Rowe, myself, and tenants gave possession, our rents to him to commence from Christmas Day coming."

This is a significant paragraph, and probably affords the key to the family discord disclosed in the previous pages.

It indicates that Pocock parted with his little patrimonial house and shop by sale to his father-in-law, and yet remained a debtor in 200*l.* to him!

"*Thursday, December 26th.*—Met with Mr. Cuthbertson, fifth mate of *Asia*, bound to East Indies, who promised to bring me home shells; and met with a medical man, who has sailed to South Seas. Has been on the Isle of Desolation, where a black man has resided several years. Helped by Mr. Bennet of Greenwich, who orders his captain to repair his house when wanted, and when the ships are absent he goes " a sealing," and sends Mr. B. the skins. The Desolation man's wife keeps a public-house in London.

"*Monday, December 30th.*—Walked to Chatham and back. Observed many gulls flying over the land. Met at Chatham, behind Gad's Hill, with Mr. H. (a brewer), son of the Kentish historian, who informed me his father lives at a town called Corsham in Wiltshire, ninety-six miles from London. Got change at the Chatham bank for a cheque I received from my brother. For the clerk's civility (Mr. Vining) bought a ticket in Dr. Thornton's lottery of him, price two guineas, No. 2965, and so did my friend Mr. C. Twelve field-mice killed by the snow (*sylvaticus*). A good print of them in the Rev. Mr. Mindey's ' Memoirs of British Quadrupeds.' "

# CHAPTER III.

Nature inanimate displays sweet sounds ;
But animated nature sweeter still,
To soothe and satisfy the human ear.
Ten thousand warblers cheer the day, and one
The livelong night ; nor these alone whose notes
Nice-finger'd art must emulate in vain,
But cawing rooks, and kites that swim sublime
In still-repeated circles, screaming loud,
The jay, the pie, and even the boding owl
That hails the rising moon, have charms for me.

WILLIAM COWPER.

THUS close the fragments of Pocock's Diary which
have been collected for the year 1811, and they are here
followed by similar collections for the year 1812 ; but
in reproducing these entries, which are given to the
public for the first time, it has been necessary to
eliminate many of the meteorological facts, and other
matters of inferior importance or of purely private
concern.

" *Thursday, January 2nd,* 1812.—Morning delightful, with sunshine. Ground wet. Report of guns
about half-past twelve—likely Woolwich. Read in a

magazine that an explosion took place at Waltham
Abbey on December 3rd, at eleven o'clock.  Referred
to that day, and what I supposed was the "proof" at
Woolwich certainly arose at Waltham Abbey, where
eight lives were lost.

"*Sunday, January 5th.*—Gulls flying over the land.
Saw the gaoler's boy trying to drive three hogs into
the cage, because Gravesend is not worth a pound.
Not long ago two hogs were there impounded, and
shortly after an old woman was put into the same
place !  The Mayor of the place is a linendraper,
and very religious.  Tried to translate ' Dulce Domum.'
Only did two verses, and they were not to my liking,
so I gave it up.

"*Monday, January 6th.*—Morning at nine.  Wind
W.S.W.  A breeze.  Sun out at noon.  Paid Mrs. T.
what I owed her, with thanks.  Recollected 'a friend
in need is a friend indeed.'

"*Friday, January 10th.*—A man fell from the
*Cuffnell's* (East Indiaman) yard, and killed on the
spot.  Mr. Williams called to-day.  Said he was seventy-
three years old.  Much broken in health since I saw
him last.  Bid him farewell (I dare say for the last
time).

"*Monday, January 13th.*—Went to London, thinking to do much business, but met with an accident at the Talbot Inn, Borough, that nearly deprived
me of my right eye and almost of life.  Confined at the
Inn ill a week, and came home on Monday with a
black eye, owing to the false step.  Continued ill
at intervals, no particular circumstance happened,
unless a small watch-box, made out of a cart at the
canal, caught fire on a Sunday night, but being wheeled

into the canal was extinguished. My little boy tells
me he saw a hawk flying among the sea-gulls. Last
year about this time I observed the same bird taking
delight with them.

" *Tuesday, February* 11*th.*—Went to Chatham (being
the first time of getting out since my accident),
and it proved the finest day possible—sunshine, mild
and pleasant. Heard proof at Gad's Hill twice from
Woolwich. Observed snowdrops in bloom. Heard
that Dr. Katterfelto's daughter lived at Whitby.
Another daughter married a Mr. Carter, a naturalist
at Scarborough.—Mem. I remember visiting Dr.
Katterfelto when his huff was about his black cat.

" *February* 13*th.*—A detachment of the Stirling regiment of militia passed through, supposed to be going to
quell rioters. On this day an East Indiaman of 700
tons was launched from Mr. Pitcher's yard, Northfleet,
said to be a gift from the East India Company to a
son of Mr. Pitcher's.

" *February* 14*th.*—Wet, boisterous weather to-day.
The Gravesend boats put back, a very unusual thing,
as they are excellent boats to stand the weather.

" *Saturday, February* 15*th.*—Heard that a day or two
ago the dock-master of the canal had broken the stone
put down by Mr. Gilbee to ascertain the port of London as regards the duty on coals.

" *Thursday, February* 20*th.*—Went into my garden
and cut my grape-vine, which should be done before
March, as then it begins to bleed.

" *Friday, February* 21*st.*—This is my birthday : now
fifty-two years old.—Mem. My father died at fifty-
two, and my mother at fifty-six years.

" *Sunday, February* 23*rd.*—Mrs. Creed brought to

bed of twins. In Gravesend also Mrs. Loft of twins, Mrs. Elliot, Mrs. Yates, and Mrs. Barnard.

" *Thursday, February* 27*th.*—Damp day. Church Lecturer chosen. Ship launched at Northfleet (— guns) named the *Gloucester.* I think she got damaged, as it was a bad launch.

" *Friday, February* 28*th.*—A detachment of the 83rd Regiment from Essex marched in, on their way to Chichester and Portugal.

" *February* 29*th.*—Had a dragonet-fish brought me by Mr. Crafter, called the fox-fish. Dr. Tyson called them the yellow gurnard.

" *Sunday, March* 1*st.*—Jessup's wife buried in Milton churchyard. This woman, six feet high, was so strong that she had often carried a sack of flour.

" *Tuesday, March* 3*rd.*—This afternoon the foundation stone of a new chapel was laid in the late garden of the New Inn. A hymn was sung on the spot, but no money put under the foundation stone. [Wesleyan.]

" *Saturday,* 7*th.*—Very ill with the toothache or swelled face, which has kept me in bed several days. Cured in a few minutes by applying hot toasted Turkey figs held (to my gums) in my mouth. Heard the Sussex Militia was in the town.

" *Sunday,* 15*th.*—Wind N.E. Very cold. Fine morning. Sleet in afternoon. Brought up several sea-gulls. Spotted lungwort in bloom.

" *Friday,* 20*th.*—A strong equinoctial gale. The Rev. Mr. Davies, a teacher at Hall Place Academy, Bexley, chosen lecturer for Gravesend parish. It is said this minister preaches the Gospel, as many Dissenters have left "the meeting" and come to the parish church on account of this preacher. The Rev. Mr.

Phillips, Vicar of Grain, has been lately appointed
curate (under the Rev. Dr. Watson, rector, late keeper
of the academy on Shooter's Hill).

"*Sunday,* 22*nd.*—Walked to Chalk Church to see the
ridiculous figure of a buffoon (with a jug in one hand
and a purse holden by the other arm, seemingly laughing at another figure placed above somewhat like a
Merry Andrew, as he is in the act of looking through
his legs) placed over the entrance of the porch into
the church, within which is seen the remains of the
basin wherein the holy water was placed. In my walk
I saw out for the first time this season a land lizard,
called an eft in Kent. My son tells me he saw a water
eft the day the ship was launched. The flowers in
bloom this day were shepherd's purse (*bursa pastoris*),
barren strawberry, dandelion, sweet white and purple
and dog violets, blue veronica, lesser celandine or pile-
wort, and primrose. Of garden flowers were spotted
lungwort, beautiful blue veronica, blue and yellow
crocus, daffodils, snowdrops, polyanthus, and coltsfoot.
The sharp winds have damaged the leaves of my fly
and bee orchis, but have not affected the spider orchis ;
so that it is a good time to go in search of it. The leaves
lie close to the ground, and are not above an inch
long and half an inch broad. Neither the butterfly,
bird's-nest, latifolia maculata, or canopsea orchises are
yet seen above the ground.

"*Easter Day,* 29*th.*—Wind blew strong. Walked to
Hollow Dean Field, Sutton, and got four or five roots
of the lizard orchis—now four or five inches high.
Saw in my walk three brimstone butterflies, and one
scarce insect like a spider. Great ants out, and cock
chaffinches.

"*Thursday, April 2nd.*—My grape-vines have not begun to shoot, yet by my memorandum-book I find my white grape put forth leaves and the fruit was seen last year on this day. Marched into town the first division of an Irish regiment, the Carlow Militia. Heard three proofs at Woolwich at noon.

"*Friday, April 3rd.*—Another detachment of the Carlow Regiment marched into town. They had come from Hastings in Sussex on their route to Hull. Gurnards plenty; also dried haddocks and cod-fish. Read the *Monthly Magazine,* and observed, as I have done before, that the person who styles himself 'Common Sense' writes the best sense, especially in his severities against that nefarious set of pettifogging scoundrels called lawyers—*alias* vultures—who prey on the substance and vitals of honest men! Had a tarantula spider brought me by Mr. Fox, waterman.

"*Saturday, April 4th.*—Another detachment of the Carlow Regiment marched in. Walked on over hill, and observed in bloom common chickweed, red nettle, white nettle, furze, nailwort, and white violets. Kidney potatoes in our market sixpence per gallon; champions fivepence. The sun went down clear, and Venus, the evening star, seen with others of the first, second, and third magnitudes very clear. Mr. Jackson, the pilot, says he has seen from Gravesend Reach the flash of the Admiral's gun at the Nore, and heard the report about a minute after, frequently (of a still night) when he belonged to the Gravesend boats. It is a distance of about twenty-one or twenty-two miles. The rue-leaved whitlow grass is nearly in bloom; I think it will be this next week.

" *Sunday, April 5th.*—I heard the Rev. Mr. Davies, the chosen lecturer, preached this morning to a *small* congregation, as he was not expected. In the afternoon there was a great congregation ; but when they saw the Rev. Mr. Phillips, the curate, prepare to mount the pulpit, the major part of the people left the church, to the mortification of the latter reverend gentleman ! (Mrs. C. was so affected with the sight as to cause her to faint away.) Another occurrence is related. Some years since, Dr. Watson, the rector, was on a visit to Mr. Champion (my brother-in-law), a professed Dissenter, and at that time Mr. Phillips was ill, and Dr. W. sent his compliments, offering to officiate for him ; but Mr. P. refused his offer, arrogantly thinking that Dr. W. was a Dissenter also, because at Mr. Champion's house. Wonderful change !

" *Monday, April 6th.*—The Carlow Regiment marched out, leaving three of their men in the cage to answer for assaults committed last night ; but it was proved they were provoked by the Gravesend watermen, and so were discharged by the Mayor.

" *Tuesday, April 7th.*—My grape-vines bleed much, which shows they ought to have been pruned before March, as I have observed before. The tortoise-shell butterfly seen in the house.

" *Wednesday, April 8th.*—Wind N.E. Mr. Robert Hinde called about Rowe's purchase.

" *Sunday, April 12th.*—Blackthorn first seen in bloom ; wood anemone also. Eggs of thrush seen ; also blackbird's eggs. Chaffinch's nest not built. Violets, blue, fetch eightpence per quart when picked. Beef steaks

F

and new ropes of one price, viz. one shilling and twopence per pound. Fine clear starlight evening. Venus shone bright.

"*Monday, April* 13*th.*—Wind strong, E. Went with Mrs. P. to West Tilbury. Returned, having got some oxlips, double polyanthus, and flowers from an old woman. In going up Tilbury Hill found a piece of sandy pudding-stone. Woodlark sings. Gulls hovering over the river. Observed water ranunculus in bloom. Bees out, and being fed in elder with honey.

" *Wednesday, April* 15*th.*—Went with G. and C. P. to Thong. Saw first hitchwort in bloom; also tuberose moschatel and wood sorrel. Thought I heard a nightingale. My nectarine has been in bloom these three days.

"*Friday, April* 17*th.*—Mrs. P. went to Dartford. Hail two or three times in the course of the day. Returned in the evening, and said a girl about twelve or thirteen was buried that day at Dartford, who had been burnt to death by her clothes taking fire; and that a lad had been killed that day by a cart going over him.

"*Saturday, April* 18*th.*—Found in bloom blue cresses on the hill (Latin name unknown); also geranium, purple bloom, which falls off.

"*Sunday, April* 19*th.*—Botany Bay ship came down (the *Indefatigable*). Got a root of wall rue from Northfleet Church. Mr. Smith's gardener called, who said that Sir. Joseph Banks within five or six years had altered the name of Orchis Militaris to Latifolia, and the Orchis Mascula to Maculata. I doubt this story, although I look upon this gardener to be one of the most practical, yet his knowledge of the terms may be deficient. Young rooks on the terrace. Dust flies in the roads.

" *Wednesday, April 22nd.*—Had Mr. Young, a journeyman, come to work, but sadly troubled with an asthma. Recommended him to smoke the stramonium (because it is now the popular remedy). Saw a large blowing fly.

" *Thursday, April 23rd.*—The first leaf of my white grape appears.

" *Friday, April 24th.*—Walked in Northfleet Cliffs. Found a gooseberry-tree in full flower. Got it up, and transplanted it in my garden. Dry bleak weather all the month. White periwinkle in bloom. Saw several water-efts in the ponds of Northfleet Cliffs.

" *Saturday, April 25th.*—Met Mr. Masterman, who said he saw two or three swallows (the first) fly to the westward to-day ; that he had seen a cuckoo, and that a nightingale had been caught by Bowie. Cowslip in bloom.

" *Monday, April 27th.*—Three troops of the 7th Regiment Dragoon Guards came into town from Sittingbourne in their way to Romford, and thence to Northampton. Saw two or three swallows at Northfleet. Nightingale heard.

" *Tuesday, April 28th.*—More of the 7th Dragoons came. A ship, the *Minstrel*, Capt. Reed, with 140 women and some boys, convicts, came down, bound to Botany Bay. Sent out to Mr. Lewin, at Sydney, the ' Monthly Magazine ' for March, 1812. Marched through the town, having halted half an hour, the 2nd Regiment of Somerset Militia of 700 men in their way to Nottingham. They came from Chatham, having

F 2

received their route only at eleven this day. The first head of asparagus seen coming out of the ground.

"*Wednesday, April 29th.*—More of the 7th Dragoon Guards came into the town on their way through to Islington. Walked to Shorne. Got a lilac double primrose.

"*Thursday, April 30th.*—Mr. R. Hinde called, and with Mr. Rowe and Bedingfield marked out the ground Mr. Rowe had purchased for 200 guineas. The whole month has been bleak and dry for the most part. Mr. Woodgate cut the first 150 heads of asparagus.

"*Sunday, May 3rd.*—Some soldiers (I believe a regiment) passed through the town early this morning, about five or six o'clock, on their way to Dartford. The cold wind ceased, and the sun set very fine and unusually clear at the horizon, putting on the appearance of a rim of an earthen pot or crown, which disappeared before it had totally set. This setting indicates a fine day to-morrow.

"*Monday, May 4th.*—A very beautiful day, the first all the year. A meeting held this day in the Town Hall, calling the inhabitants together to take their opinion on a renewal of the East India Company's charter, and wishing to have the E.I.C. trade confined to the Port of London, when the Corporation of Gravesend subscribed 50*l.* and the inhabitants more, to the amount, it is said, of 200*l.* In the afternoon walked to Greenhithe. Got some bee orchis in bloom. Saw the sulphur and tortoise-shell butterflies.

"*Tuesday, May 5th.*—First saw house martin. Troop of the 3rd German Legion came across from Essex to-day. Went to Chatham with Mr. Crafter, and saw Mr. Penn's auriculas, who bought some good polyanthus of Mr. Frost at one penny per root. Mr. Jarvis, the bricklayer, gave me some roots. Heard a proof twice this day at Woolwich, about twelve o'clock. Visited Mr. Foreman, the barrack-master, at Chatham. Not so polite as Lord Chesterfield. Gave Mr. Plant a bee orchis.

" *Wednesday, May 6th.*—300 more 3rd German Horse Legion came in. The first thin long brown beetle seen. It jumps, with a sudden jerk, when placed on its back, up to the height of seven or eight inches.

" *Thursday, May 7th.*—About 170 more of the German Horse Legion came in. Walked into Clarke's garden, the nurseryman, and found he had made near twenty shillings from a piece of Botany Bay clover.

" *Friday, May 8th.*—Mr. Crow of Faversham called, and Mr. C. and self walked with him to Shorne. Got there some narcissus on the Warren Hill, and found the Orchis militaris in and about Chalk Hole near Beefsteak House. Saw the swifts first time.

" *Saturday, May 9th.*—Sale of evergreens at Lady Fermanagh's, Crayford.

" *Sunday, May 10th.*—A nest of six eggs taken on Gravesend Hill. They were unknown; larger than a hedge sparrow's, of a clear colour, and somewhat like a robin's. The nest was shallow, and lined with horsehair. Wind strong, W.

" *Monday, May 11th.*—Several cockchafers first observed in the evening. First white caterpillar seen.

" *Tuesday, May 12th.*—Heard Mr. Percival, the Prime Minister of State, was shot last night. This day there was a meeting of delegates at Maidstone from various parishes to oppose the building of a new gaol, &c., for the county of Kent.

" *Wednesday, May 13th.*—Thunder and lightning and

rain during dinner (about one o'clock). Mild and
pleasant just after. Venus, Jupiter, and the moon
seen in a straight line this evening; the moon the
lowest, Jupiter next, and Venus uppermost.

" *Thursday, May* 14*th.*—Rain at Shorne to-day, but
not at Gravesend. Saw Rowe of the Prince of Orange
in the street, and had some words with him. Heard
that yesterday some Irish volunteers from a militia
regiment had raised a riot at Maidstone, because they
had not received their bounty-money, and beat their
officers, with other gentlemen of Maidstone, all of whom
they drove through the River Medway.

" *Friday, May* 15*th.*—Several East Indiamen from
abroad passed by the town, unguarded by officers. Sent
a monkey to Mr. Hall, preserver of birds, City Road.
It was killed by drinking arrack, an East India spirit.

" *Saturday, May* 16*th.*—Large blowing flies seen on
the wall, very lively and loving. Casks of tea floating
about; thrown overboard on purpose, because the
Custom-house officers are so strict.

" *Whit-Monday, May* 18*th.*—Walked with Mr. Champion and Henderson to Gad's Hill. Met with Durling,
the ' simpler,' gathering violets for the chemist : a very
religious man, who would not gather herbs on the
Lord's Day. Old Culpeper and Dr. Talmon were his
guides. Praised Mr. Dickson of Covent Garden Market
for his knowledge, but not for generosity. Found the
Orchis militaris in bloom in Gad's Hill Wood, where
I had not known it before. Toads crawl in the path
in the evening. The moon and Venus in a haze.
A thickness came on, but no rain.

" *Friday, May* 22*nd.*—Walked to Betsom to Mr.
Treadwells'. Heard that a Custom-house boat was

upset and one man drowned, and that a man was put into Gravesend Gaol for uttering a forged or bad note. Found a mushroom (not the eatable), and also a large boletus from an old tree.

" *Saturday, May 23rd.*—The person taken up proved to be the same person that came to try a new sort of gunpowder at the fort here some time back by leave of the Board of Ordnance. He called himself then Lieutenant Parr of the navy, but now answers to another name. It is said papers of a treasonable correspondence have been found on him. He is remanded to the gaol.

" *Sunday, May 24th.*—Walked to see Mr. Best's tulips in bloom. Found and got red rattle in Northfleet brooks. Saw two frogs with black eyes. Returned under shore whilst the French frigate the *Pomone* was dropping up. She was taken by the English in the East Indies.

" *Trinity Monday, May 25th.*—Rainy morning. Went with Mr. Crafter to Deptford, where there was an annual procession to the Trinity House, but did not see them, our business being to buy garden-pots. Walked to Lewisham Nursery (late Mr. Russel's, now Mr. Wilmot's), where Mr. C. bought some auriculas from Mr. Chandler, a foreman: found the other foreman, Mr. Winsor, a pleasant man and a good botanist. No gulls seen in the river : they are gone to breed.

" *Tuesday, May 26th.*—The second summer's day this year. At ten minutes after one, a large halo round the sun. A regiment of Leitrim Militia passed through the town towards Dartford. During the halo my flowers drooped very much, as if they were prostrating themselves to implore a blessing or dreading a storm.

This appearance I have observed before, on the day it thundered and lightened last. Therefore I prognosticate that lightning, thunder, rain, or a storm will ensue this evening. During the halo, the swifts and martins were flying about at an uncommon height.

"I remember about 1774-5 three halos of the sun intersecting each other. This halo continued near an hour, and was behind the clouds, as clouds I observed to pass over it.

"*Thursday, May* 28*th.*—Master Page, the gardener, brought me some twyblabe and butterfly orchis.

"*Friday, May* 29*th.*—Two Bow Street officers came down and took away from Gravesend Gaol Mr. Parr and his companion or servant to London, likely on a charge of high treason. This day being the king's restoration the guns were fired from the Hudson's Bay ships, the crews of which are always annually treated with green peas at this place before they proceed on their voyage. The peas, it is said, cost 5 guineas per quart.

"*Thursday, June* 4*th.*—A fine summer's day. Guns of Tilbury Fort and Gravesend fired in honour of the king's birthday. Walked to Northfleet and got roots of chlora perfoliata and fly orchis.

"*Friday, June* 5*th.*—Our man, Mr. Young, left us. A waterman said he saw the mist rising gradually from the horizon six hours before it came and was felt. Such kind of observations are much neglected.

"*Saturday, June* 6*th.*—Fine summer's day. Very ill in the night with cholera morbus. Hay-making (first) in the New Road to Northfleet.

"*Sunday, June* 7*th.*—Visited Esq. Russel's garden at Swanscombe, who has the greatest variety of flowers I ever saw in any garden; the gardener, Lee (a very civil man), says there are above 1500 ; the cherries received a blight from the wind last Friday.

" *Monday, June 8th.*—Poultney, a gardener, was taken up and put into Gravesend Gaol for robbing Mr. Clarke's garden of myrtles, trees, &c.

" *Tuesday, June 9th.*—A badger baited at the Prince of Orange which was taken at Southfleet : they are not so frequent as some years back.

" *Wednesday, June 10th.*—Cold easterly winds for two or three days past in the evening, which check the vegetation. To-day heard America was going to war.

" *Saturday, June 13th.*—Fine summer's day. Mrs. Smith, a lady, called and bought some fossils and Martin's book on fossils. The general complaint of people within the last two or three days is ear-ache, stiff necks, sore throats, and tooth-ache; surely these must arise from the wind suddenly shifting from east to west. To-day at noon was a beautiful long fleecy or drapery sky, having out of it long faint streamers flying from the east : what does it prognosticate?

" *Sunday, June 14th.*—Fine summer's day. Mr. Wells, jun., called; ditto Mr. Robert Hinde. Many people came down by the tide; among the rest a butterfly catcher, for the blue butterfly found, he said, near Gravesend Hill. Saw the moon out at twelve o'clock to the east of the sun which shone very bright : an uncommon sight. Walked to Singlewell and drank three glasses of grape wine at Mr. Barnard's. Showed him how to prune his vines after Mr. Forsyth's plan.

" *Tuesday, June 16th.*—Fine summer's day. In the afternoon I felt uncommonly rheumatic—there was a peculiar chilliness in the air, which prevented me taking delight in my garden. I said there was snow in the air; yet the day was fine—a gentle breeze came on southerly; yet I felt relaxed, came over feverish, and dreaded going out of doors. Drank two glasses of rum and went to bed. It certainly did me much good, counteracting the cold and unusual cold sensation within me.

"*Wednesday, June* 17*th.*—Awoke perfectly free from cold or fever, and found myself comfortable. Fine morning. It had rained in the night. The rum I drank last night was my physician. The rain in the air certainly caused the uneasy sensation I felt in the afternoon.

"*Friday, June* 19*th.*—Walked to Randall Heath—once the residence of Cobham, Lord Cobham and Randall. A windy day (westwardly). Found there a nest of young bullfinches, six in the nest; also green birds and blackbirds. Struck down two large dragon-flies. Found the moss saxifrage in bloom on White Hill. Met a Custom-house officer, who said a seizure had been made at Gravesend from a ship from Havre de Grace of two sacks of French lace worth 20,000*l.*, besides many French watches.

"*Saturday, June* 20*th.*—Nihil. In dolldrums. Luscombe had sent me a green moth with angular wings. Swinny called and said mole crickets were taken at Bexley.

"*Tuesday, June* 23*rd.*—Short storm of hail in the forenoon, also a few flakes of snow in the afternoon. Attended at the 'Compass,' when orders were given to print the club articles.

"*Wednesday, June* 24*th.*—Showery at intervals. Wind at all points of the compass. The air cold and rheumatic, and a peculiar heaviness in the air, which affected my limbs and spirits. Club articles taken away. A shrimp with fourteen legs brought me.

"*Friday, June* 26*th.*—Sent a letter to my son in Shropshire, describing the fossils he sent me lately. Much rain in the evening.

"*Sunday, June* 28*th.*—Cold and windy. Walked up with Mr. Crafter to Clarke's garden in the evening. Heard he meant to show his seedling pink next Wednesday at the Old Prince of Orange against Mr. Collier of Stanstead.

"*Tuesday, June* 30*th.*—Went with Mrs. P. to Swanscombe and carried there to Esq. Russel that scarce plant, the lizard orchis, and chlora perfoliata or yellow wort. Walked in his garden and found him well skilled in botany, with a retentive memory; his garden having above a thousand plants in it. Found him acquainted with two botanists near London (Mr. Evans of Hackney and another) and that he had corresponded with Mr Down of Cambridge. Met at Swanscombe Mr. Fenwick, jun., of Greenwich, who I thought had been drowned.

"This day I caught a small long-bodied fly, or more properly a *beetle,* on the flower of a bramble in the chalk cliffs.

"Heard six people out of eleven were drowned in a sailing-boat off Purfleet—mostly publicans of London.

"*Wednesday, July* 1*st.*—Got some bee orchis and chlora perfoliata in Northfleet Cliffs. This day suits well to get 'eye bright' to set in a pot of sifted chalk rubbish. Flower feast at Old Prince of Orange, when Collier gained the prize for best seedling pink called 'Collier's Kentish Hero.'

"*Thursday, July* 2*nd.*—Rainy. Sent a dozen of newspapers to William Lewin, Esq., coroner, Sydney, New South Wales (a naturalist), by the ship *Spring Grove*. A storm of thunder and lightning seen about six o'clock in evening over the hills of Essex, N.W.: none at Gravesend.

"*Friday, July 3rd.*—Went on board the *Arab*, the *Spring Grove*, the *Recovery*, and *New Zealand*. (James Ferguson, the cook, promised me to collect.) Ships bound to the South Seas. Gave my cards to the stewards to collect shells and insects; found the mate of the *Spring Grove* not very civil, indeed he said he would not bring home any shells or insects, and would not let me speak to the ship's crew. Also went on board the ship *Atalanta*, bound to Jamaica, when the cook, John Rodney, said he would bring home shells and sweetmeats.

"*Tuesday, July 7th.*—Ifield Harmonic Society go out to Ifield. Heard the king died at seven o'clock this morning. A toad-fish came on the shore at the canal, Gravesend.

"*Wednesday, July 8th.*—Fine summer's day. George Pocock went to Shorn Ifield to spend the day. Heard that Banks, the sheriff's officer, was cast at law yesterday in 100*l.* damages for arresting a wrong person.

"*Thursday, July 9th.*—Mrs. Smith of Camer, Major and Mrs. Elphinstone, and Rev. Mr. Phelps of Snodland called and bought fossils; though the major and his wife bought none nor gave anything. Went to Mr. Everist in the morning to order dinner for 'Natural History Society' next Monday. Sent out letters, went in afternoon to see a toad-fish (*Lophias piscatorium*) which came on shore at the Town Quay.

"*Friday, July 10th.*—Mrs. P. and self went to

Meopham Fair, but reached only Hook Green, where we dined with Mrs. French. Got some bee orchis near Nursted.

" *Monday, July* 13*th.*—Went to Northfleet, where I was chairman of the Natural History Society held at the Leather Bottle. It was its first meeting, and attended by twenty-one persons.

" *Monday,* 20*th.*—Went to Higham by canal; then to Upnor. Saw engineers instructing men in making temporary magazines. Visited city stones there and found fault with the mason's work in spelling. Observed a halo round the sun about two o'clock. Distant lightning in the evening.

" *Saturday,* 25*th.*—Went to Grays with Mr. Geer and Arthur. Bought a mammillated echinus, the best ever seen. Very windy. The Piedmontese frigate got aground at Tilbury Fort and also in Long Reach.

" *Sunday,* 26*th.*—Went on board the *Sir William Pultney* to see Mr. Edwards, the third mate, but was not on board. Went to tea at Swanscombe. Met the 33rd Regiment just disembarked from the East Indies. Their band played excellently. The inhabitants very busy in buying rupees and pagodas from the drunken Indian soldiers.

" *Thursday,* 30*th.*—The 33rd Regiment marched out to Chatham.

" *Friday,* 31*st.*—Had some conversation with Mr. Park (surgeon of this place for the East India Company), he is brother to Mungo Park, the famous African traveller. He says the accounts related through the newspapers give nearly the true particulars of his brother's death. He has received journals of his brother's, from the last settlement

(through the hands of Government), which I advised
him to print as a benefit to Mr. Mungo Park's wife
and numerous family living in Scotland. Mr. Park,
the surgeon, is a genteel man, six feet high, darkish
complexion and middling circumference. He had
heard of me through Major Elphinstone, of the Engineers, and the Rev. Mr. Rashleigh, with whom he is
intimate.

" This day was a cricketing match at Hartley Bottom,
between Gravesend against Meopham and Hartley :
Gravesend beat. There was also a donkey race.

" *Wednesday, August 5th.*—Cloudy. First wheat
cut in Gravesend. Another toad-fish, four feet long,
taken at Gravesend Stairs : shown at the Swan Inn, twopence each for a sight.

" *Thursday, 6th.*—Read the 'Monthly Magazine' of last
month, wherein a gentleman requests (most laudably)
information on the turnip-fly or beetle (*Chrysomela
saltatoria* of Linnæus). Looked into Dr. Turton's, but
could not find any species called *saltatoria.* Wrote
to the correspondent in the magazine to know on what
authority he made use of the word saltatoria. Yesterday the judges came into Maidstone to begin the
assizes.

" *Friday, 7th.*—Heard that Captain Parr, alias Fane,
the gentleman who was taken up for offering a 50*l.*
bank note, being a forged one, was found guilty and
sentenced to fourteen years' transportation. He was
also charged with high treason, in endeavouring to form
a correspondence with the ministry of France, as appeared by his papers taken on him when seized some
time since at Gravesend. On his way to London this
gentleman, about twelve months ago, came to Graves-

end; there, by permission of the Board of Ordnance, he proved some gunpowder he had invented, but which the Ordnance would not patronize. It is supposed it made him desperate in not being encouraged, so that he was determined if possible to sell the secret to the French.

"*Saturday*, *8th.*—Had some discourse yesterday with Mr. King, a farmer, on the turnip-fly or beetle. He says the fly and beetle are distinct things. The fly destroys the turnip in its seed-leaf: the other insect he calls the negro, and will not come till after harvest; this destroys the turnip when well grown.

"Saw at Mr. Hugget's, the Duke of York, Gravesend, a King William and Queen Mary guinea. Saw Mr. Russel, of Swancombe, lately have a Queen Anne guinea. These are rarities. Offered 10*s.* 6*d.* to any person who should have a seven-shilling piece of George III. with a lion on the crown. I think they were the first seven-shilling pieces.

"*Monday*, *10th.*—Walked to Northfleet and got some stone from the cement mill.

"*Tuesday*, 11*th.*—Went to London in the *Britannia.* Visited Mr. Edwards, who had just come home from the East Indies in the *Sir William Pultney.* Visited Mr. Ball and his museum. Sorry to hear he was parting with his excellent rarities. The fanciful manner he has preserved his butterflies does him much merit. Slept in the Borough at the Talbot Inn, in the yard of which is a good painting of Chaucer's Pilgrimage to Canterbury. It is a noisy inn-yard.

"*Wednesday*, 12*th.*—Wind north, very cold morning in passing over London Bridge. Visited Mr. Jefferies' museum. He has gone into general science, and has

a great collection; but not arranged so scientifically
as it ought to be. He is a very civil man.
Visited also Mr. Pittard's museum, famous for flies
and fish. His preservation of fish and flies exceeds
every description. They are all arranged with Linnæan
names, as beautiful as life. Mr. Pittard's name in a
cipher is made of butterflies and insects; also a Mosaic
pavement is made of the flies' wings cut out in a rhom-
boidal manner, which leads to a temple or mansion.
Upon the whole they are masterly performances. Went
to Blackwall, where I got some E.I. shells and came
home in the *Duke of Bedford*, Stronghill master.

" *Thursday*, 13*th.*—Cricketing between Gravesend
and Meopham and Hartley in the Old Prince of Orange
field. Had discourse with Partridge; he says the negro
attacks turnips proceeding in straight rows, and when
at the end of a row returns again in a parallel manner.

" *Friday*, 14*th.*—First foggy morning, which turned
out a bright fine day, being the first had for some time;
in fact there has not been above seven or eight fine
days in all the year. The weather has been dull, dark,
rainy, and heavy before this day; yet corn never was
more fine. Baltic fleet arrives (Swedish); first since
the war.

" *Saturday*, 15*th.*—Fine day. Mr. Tilley called, from
Sittingbourne. He said in digging in his garden he had
found a silver spoon with a cross or mitre on its handle,
and a silver toothpick; and that in digging he had
found a new sort of earth, of a mahogany colour, and
a silver coin—which latter article he promised to give
me.

" *Monday*, 17*th.*—Walked to Chalk and observed
many small frogs crawling in the road. Got the

autumnal squill (a scarce bulb) at Chalk in bloom.
Mr. Bullock, of the London Museum, called: he is a
pleasant man. Heard the news of Lord Wellington's
victory at Salamanca.

"*Tuesday*, 18*th.*—Mr. Bullock called and breakfasted.
Sold him some shells, &c., and saw him off for Scotland. He took his passage in the *Northumberland*,
Captain Paul. He has lately been in the Orkneys,
got some eider down bolsters and pillows, young
eagles, and scarce English birds. Rev. Mr. Phelps
called and bought fossils. Shifted some pots of
geraniums, and put in them some roots of autumnal
squills. Two of the blossoms of squills were white :
very uncommon indeed.

" *Wednesday*, 19*th.*—Very fine summer's day. Dust
flies. Had one of the white jackdaws brought me dead
to stuff. It appeared to have been starved.

" *Thursday*, 20*th.*—Fine day. One Fowler was to be
hanged at Maidstone for forgery.

" *Friday*, 21*st.*—Mr. Payn, of No. 5, West Square,
Lambeth, called.

" *Saturday*, 22*nd.*—The other white jackdaw dies.
Yesterday was a hot day and I quarrelled with my
wife; also heard some of my neighbours quarrel:
perhaps it is the state of the weather. Joe Cole, a poor
man, brought me a shilling of King Edward VI.,
which he had found, with a thick gold ring and a gold
seal, on which was engraved a coat-of-arms, viz., Or,
a buck's head caboshed; crest, a bull's head issuing
from a coronet. They were found in an old chest of
drawers on breaking up. Mr. Pittard and Mr. Hatchard
called on me. Went out moth-catching : caught some
scarce moths in Singlewell Lane.

G

"*Sunday,* 23rd.—Went with Mr. P. and Mr. H. towards Thong. Caught four brimstone butterflies (*P. Rhamni*). Saw two toads (one dead, the largest ever seen by Mr. P. and H.). They were harmless and no ways poisonous, I having kept them for amusement : their mouths are not glued together as some think, but they feed on scarabæus and flies, which they take in by darting out their tongues with surprising swiftness. Mr. H. is a fellow of the Linnæan Society ; also Mr. P., the gentleman I visited on the 12th instant. They took several scarce flies and insects. With them were two lads (sons), who were well-versed in natural history ; they knew the various caterpillars and what they would turn into.

" *August* 23rd (*continued*).—Met with Mr. Smithers. Discoursed on the turnip-fly. Evidence of Mr. Smithers' nephew to his uncle is that the fly on turnips attacks on the seed-leaf appearing, and is not a beetle but a small, minute brownish fly, with long wings. They made their appearance about July 20th, since which time they had destroyed three crops of turnips. They were seen preceding the plough as it moved on, and do not fly far before they alight. They do not confine themselves to turnips only but will attack cabbages. *Dung used as manure is not the occasion of them,* because the field attacked was not dunged but manured with *sprats* in the spring. Sprats and fish have been within two or three years past much used as manure about Gravesend, and with success. Sulphur and lime (he said) was said to be a remedy for the fly—but he had not used it. The fly was not much seen when the wind blew (probably it gets under clods for shelter). The fly, which is of the same nature as the house-fly, with wings, is not the insect (which attacks the turnip in its advanced state) called the negro.

"*Monday, August* 24*th.*—Gravesend and Northfleet played at cricket at Northfleet. Walked with Mr. P. and H. to Springhead, where the gardener had found a silver piece of Severus, and an old Roman copper piece, and a Roman brick. Met with Mr. Harman's man, who told the same story as others, viz., that the fly eats the turnips when young, and rolling is the remedy used. And upon asking him what the negro was, he pointed to some aphis on the elder, as being nearly like it; but the negro was more black. Being in company with four naturalists, one belonging to the Linnæan Society, they all declared it impossible that the fly should destroy the plant, that it must be the larva of the fly. Walked to Swanscombe Wood. Found a locust or large grasshopper, and some scarce moths and insects. 73rd Regiment of soldiers, 2nd battalion, marched into town from Deal. 25th Regiment of soldiers marched out to the Tower. A cricket match between the Sociables and the Harmonic Societies, in the Prince of Orange field. The band played on the occasion. The Harmonics beat. Whilst in the field I heard (I thought) distant low thunder. Some time after I heard a noise like the cough of a lion. So it certainly was, for soon after several caravans passed by with wild beasts going to Strood Fair.

"*Wednesday,* 26*th.*—Close, warm day. Strood Fair. Rain in evening. G. and C. P. went to see Mr. Polito's wild beasts and birds. Among them were a lion and lioness, a tiger and tigress, a panther and pantheress, a leopard, a zebra, a ferocious hyena, a laughing hyena, &c., an emu, a black swan, two pelicans, &c., a cassowary, an elephant, and a crane.

" *Friday, 28th.*—Dull, windy day. Cold. Third day of Strood Fair. Jury sat on a young woman (a girl of the town) who threw herself out of the window at the Britannia, because she had been locked in.

" *Wednesday, September 2nd.*—Went to Lower Hope Battery. Saw two porpoises. Mr. Odden shot a heron and two gulls (rounded tail, black at tip). Observed many insects on the river (cimex, &c.) at the edge of the tide. Large long-leg crane gnats very numerous. A company of Marines land from Anholt Island, in the Baltic.

" *Saturday, 5th.*—Fine summer's day. Bright. Heard Lord Wellington had marched into Madrid. Baltic fleet arrived to-day here. Wind E., passing all the day.

" *Sunday, 6th.*—Fine summer's day, yet wind blows fresh. Walked to Cobham Church, where 1 heard Lord Darnley and the Lord Mayor of London had been to the service in the morning. The church has lately had a barrel-organ put up in the loft (the gift of Lady Darnley) adapted to play sundry tunes or portions of the Psalms, which have been selected and printed in a small duodecimo, this year. The church has lately been whitewashed, fresh painted and varnished, and sentences of Scripture written on the walls, which the parishioners call ' decorating ' it; but the ancient stalls and beautiful monument of Lord George Cobham with his lady is suffered to fall to decay. The antique brass plates of the ancient Lord Cobhams are half-gone, and the antiquary finds himself greatly vexed by the injudicious placement of a screen and communion-table across and over the inscriptions near the middle

of the high chancel, instead of its being at the further-
most east end which would then display the monument
of Lord George and his lady. A fine Gothic piscina
and three fine Gothic seats on the south, and a Gothic
arch in the wall on the north. The banners, flags, and
garlands, which tell of the grandeur of noble families,
have been all taken away. One helmet yet remains up in
the secluded chancel (two others were lying about, preparing for their journey from this sacred spot), which
is covered with small antique tiles bearing impressions
of fleur-de-lis, griffins, &c. This chancel was once
decorated with the arms in painted glass of the good
Duke Humphrey, and Eleanor Cobham his wife, who in
her lifetime was indicted for witchcraft and sorcery, and
obliged to do penance. But no such glass now remains,
everything giving way to the sordid and ignorant !

" A mural marble monument is lately placed on the
north side for the wife of Mr. Bligh, who died at
Funchal, in the Island of Madeira.

" The pay of the poor ' collegians ' has lately been
raised from 13s. 4d. to 16s. 8d. per month.

" Passed several fields of wheat, barley, oats, and beans
uncut, which shows the backwardness of the season.

" Met with Robinson, junior, the farmer, who says his
father had seventeen acres of very bad wheat, not fit to
harvest (nor could it be told by some if it was wheat or
rye) ; yet they had it cut, and sold it already for 5l. per
quarter, so great is the immediate demand. But he sup-
poses if it had been kept a month longer it would not
have sold for any price. Upon asking him the cause,
he says it was sown too thick, and was too vigorous at
Christmas last, being then near three feet high. He
says they have thrashed out all their corn of this year,

and sold above 1000*l.* worth; and that Mr. Smithers, his neighbour, has already thrashed and sold out every quarter he has grown this year. I never knew such exertions or demands; but this rapid industry in bringing it to market, has been owing partly to the introduction of thrashing-machines; and certainly there was a real scarcity, as the millers of Kent were obliged to go into Essex to market.

"Upon asking him about the fly on turnips, he says ants have been looked upon as a remedy, and that Mrs. Tadman, of New House, procured ants from the woods in sacks, and put them on her grounds. That some roll the ground in the night; but he knew nothing about the insect only that they attack the plant on its *coming out of the ground*, and called it the fly.

"*Monday, 7th.*—Dull. Walked to Chalk and got some autumnal squills.

"*Tuesday, 8th.*—Very fine day. Mr. Coxe and Barton went to Maidstone Gaol. The Lord Mayor of London came to Gravesend from Lord Darnley's, and went from thence to London in his barge, by water, escorted by the water-bailiff (Nelson) and the city solicitor, Mr. Newman.

"*Wednesday, 9th.*—Dull day. Mr. Eglintine brought a large-tailed wasp (I believe *Sirex gigas*) caught on the Town Quay (see Dr. Turton, p. 426). Mr. Hutton of Birmingham or Sheffield called. Mr. Hutton is a mineralogist.

"*Tuesday, 15th.*—The neat little *Peter* boat, of nine tons, lies in the canal. She has come round from Dartmouth, with Captain Ferguson (once in the East India trade) and one man, named also James Ferguson. This man promises to send me some birds, anatomized,

which is done there in twenty-four hours, by first
skinning them and then immersing them under the
water, where the sea-lice eat off their flesh presently.
A haze round the horizon in the evening.

"*Friday*, 18*th.*—Mr. Parker and a young gentleman
called on me. Mr. Parker is an antiquary: has
ascertained an accurate account of all measures and
weights from the earliest periods, deducing them as a
standard from the pyramids of Egypt. He is in search
of Roman curiosities. Mary Pocock called. Bought
of Mrs. Reding a Queen Anne halfpenny, and a brass
medal of George II., for sixpence. Mr. Reding has a
Queen Anne farthing. Mrs. Reding bought forty
hanks of fine silk, weighing one ounce and a quarter
and one dram, the produce of 300 silk-worms in 1812.

"*Saturday*, 19*th.*—Hung three and a half pieces of
paper, also three dozen and a half of border, at Mr.
Sloper's, from 11 o'clock in the morning till 9 o'clock
at night." [Paper-hanging: his other business presumably slack.]

"*Sunday*, 20*th.*—Walked to Springhead by myself.
Gathered first black grapes.

"*Monday*, 21*st.*—Had the skeleton of a starved cat
brought me.

"*Tuesday*, 22*nd.*—Small shower in morning, then fine
day. Heard a proof at Woolwich more distinct than
usual. Had a hare for dinner, sent as a present. Had
a Roman brass piece of Tiberius Cæsar, described
accurately in my folio book of coins, printed at Rome.
Rain at night.

"*Wednesday*, 23*rd.*—Master Durling, a 'simpler,'
called and showed me a root of navel-wort, taken from
All-hallows' Church. Luke Beet called and showed me

a porcupine fish (*Diodon hystrix*) which he had got
from an East Indiaman.

"*Saturday, 26th.*—An Italian gentleman called.  He
came home in the *Providence,* and brought home four
black swans for the Duke of York, and a nondescript
bird without wings.  He resides at No. 5, Swan Street,
Minories.  Another part of Glamorgan Regiment in the
town.  (Candles rise to 1s. per pound; ditto soap.)

"*Sunday, 27th.*—Mr. Kipping, from Mr. Sowerby's,
called.  Said that Nutfield, in Surrey, abounded with
sulphate of barytes; that Mr. S. paid 20s. each time
on going into the mines.

"*Wednesday, 30th.*—Attended sale of Mr. Colesary
at Northfleet.  Bought two nautilus shells."

Turning aside for a moment from the Diary, it may
be here mentioned that upon reference to the " Gentleman's Magazine " (vol. lxxxii. part 2, p. 419) of this
date, the following letter by Pocock has been found,
which affords a pleasing proof of his readiness to speak
out in defence of Hasted, the well-known Kentish
historian.  The letter is as follows :—

" Leather Bottle Inn,<br>
" Northfleet, Oct. 7th, 1812.

" MR. URBAN,—A few hours in the first week of
every month I devote to the perusal of your Miscellany,
and find the short epistles inserted by its numerous
friends have in general given me satisfaction.  This
pleasure certainly arises through the judicious selection
of your Editor.  However, among the multiplicity of
matter contained therein some are not quite concordant
to my ideas; of this nature was the paragraph signed
'Litterator' (p. 201), which cannot be passed over with-

out remarking that it is an ill-timed reflection upon the best of Kentish historians.

" If ' Litterator ' thinks that Mr. Hasted's History is deficient and unworthy of his thanks (after thirty years or more spent in the arduous undertaking), why does not ' Litterator ' immediately solicit assistance and issue forth a prospectus for an additional volume ? There is undoubtedly much to be gathered, *but not much to be gained,* by county historians."

Pocock then gives instances refuting the charge of want of variety in Hasted's History, and then finishes thus :—

" The pen is sometimes taken up in defence of personal friendship, interest, or vanity ; but L. may rest assured the writer of this article had not the happiness of ever seeing the late author, has no interest in his works, nor vanity sufficient to think this will add to his fame : yet professing an ardent desire to become acquainted with the history of his native county, he has collected already a folio MS. relative thereto, unnoticed by Mr. H., which shall be made public (if required) with the hoped for elucidation and additional aid, if and whenever he thinks proper to address himself to—

(Signed)  " THE CHAIRMAN OF THE KENT NATURAL HISTORY SOCIETY."

Resuming the Journal for 1812, it appears that our journalist, on the 2nd October, "walked to Hartley. Found a fine black mullein in bloom in the hedge of a cottage at Scotbury. Called on the Rev. Mr. Rashleigh, and took an oath that I was no freeholder.

Saw an old painting of Edward the Black Prince, at the Ship, Southfleet.

"*Monday, 5th.*—Mayor of Gravesend (Mr. Millen) chosen (Mr. Dennet went out). Had a sea-leach brought me stuck to a thornback.

"*Tuesday, 6th.*—An East Indiaman (*Marquis of Camden*), launched at Northfleet. Jurymen of Gravesend go down to the sessions.

"*Wednesday, 7th.*—Mr. DuCane called and bought some fossils. Read an advertisement from John Wells, Esq., sheriff of Kent, calling a meeting on the 13th inst. for electing county members. Sir Edward Knatchbull and Sir William Geary offer themselves. Mr. Honeywood declines.

"*Thursday, 8th.*—Received a letter from Mr. Gregson, for advice for law, although nothing done, above six years ago. It is dangerous to speak to lawyers.

"*Saturday, 10th.*—Portuguese or Spanish sailors selling port wine about the street, eighteen-pence per bottle. I bought five or six bottles.

"*Sunday, 11th.*—Heavy rain in the night near two o'clock in the morning. Saw my letter to the 'Gentleman's Magazine' in vindication of Mr. Hasted, the Kentish historian, whose works were illiberally attacked by a person signing himself 'Litterator.'" [This is the letter above given.]

"*Tuesday, 13th.*—Went on board the *Emu* storeship bound to Botany Bay, Captain Bissett, when the chief mate, Mr. John Brown, promised to bring me home an emu, &c. Lieut. Arnold's son went out in this ship. She was loaded with women convicts, and attended by Mr. Bennet. Went also on board the *James Hay*, Captain Campbell, when John Bathurst, boatswain, promised to collect curiosities for me. I gave the mate one of my cards, but had hardly any conversation with him. Sent out a dozen newspapers by Captain Campbell for Mr. Lewin. Sent my son in Shropshire a box of chalk fossils, &c., by Mr. Brown, the waterman. In the evening, Mr. T. Wallington, surgeon in the Royal Navy, called on me to see my museum. He was going out in the *Emu*, which was not expected to return for four or five years. He is a scientific person, and promises to collect for me. He had also promised Mr. McLeane, secretary to the Linnæan Society. He had married Mr. Brown's sister (the mate's), and she went out with him.

" *Sunday,* 18*th.*—Wrote to Mr. John Hunt, Norwich, in answer to his, about buying birds from abroad. George Pocock brought home some mushrooms and puff balls.

" *Monday,* 19*th.*—Wind south. Went to Northfleet. Bought several fossils, &c. Observed about a dozen martins flying to the south-west, nearly against the wind. I generally find them flying against the wind. Thought they had all gone. Beautiful double rainbow seen in the evening at Northfleet ; one end on Chadwell Church the other extended over Gravesend Hill. Heard Mr. Brown, of the *Dorsetshire,* had died at Batavia.

" *Tuesday,* 20*th.*—Mr. DuCane and another gentleman called and bought some chalk fossils, shells, &c. Went with Mr. Raspison on board the *Fortune,* ship, Captain Walker, bound to Botany Bay. The chief mate's name is Champion : gave him some of my cards. The second mate's name is Potter. They did not promise to bring me home anything, but did not refuse, the ship being in a bustle.

" Met at the Castle Inn (Mr. Jerry's) with a Mr. James Guthrie, a person who had travelled much. He said he was a master in the Royal Navy. He said he set out from Quebec with a Captain Holland of the 57th Regiment, and a party of twenty-eight men, to explore and traverse the lakes and inland country of America, so as to get to the Pacific Ocean : that when he was within some distance of it he fell in with Mr. Alexander Mackenzie and his party, just below Slave Lake, who had obtained their pursuit, and for that Mr. Mackenzie was created a knight or baronet, and he believes is now in London. Mr. Mackenzie he said was a man of considerable fortune in America—was a clerk once to Sally Hance, a person of some importance on the River Sinclair. Mr. Guthrie said that when he had got nearly to the end of his route, Captain Holland was recalled, and he, Mr. Guthrie, had the command of the party. Mr. Guthrie said that about two miles from the Falls of Niagara is a sulphurous spring, so hot that the company boiled their tea-kettle at it. That rattlesnakes are common in the islands in the lakes, and are generally avoided by a peculiar smell when near them.

"*Thursday, 22nd.*—Fish (cod) very plentiful. Sent a large one to Frances Pocock, at the school at Woburn. It cost 5*s.*, and weighed about thirty pounds. Sent another to Mr. Thomas Brewer, weighed twelve pounds, cost 1*s.* 6*d.* ! A ball this evening in the Town Hall, first this season.

"*Saturday, 24th.*—Fine day. Gravesend Fair. Fewer hogs and people than ever before. Went to it, and saw at a booth, for threepence, a large seal alive, purchased at Billingsgate about four years ago. It was then young, and not half so large as at present, weighing now, I should suppose, 60 or 80 lbs. but said in the hand-bill, 220 lbs., 4 ft. 6 in. high, and 5 ft. long. This seal is somewhat tamed, for it gets up when spoken to, and at the word of command throws its head back, then claps its sides, opens its mouth, and shakes hands, viz., put its paws together. He often got up to the side of the wooden cage and took out a small flat-fish from a pail filled with water, which he devoured whole seemingly without biting. This feeding and dipping his head in water, occasions its living, for I do not suppose they would live long without water. It has long curved nails on its fore-feet, but none on the back-feet, a short tail, and appears to me to be the *Phoca cristata*, crested seal, because on its head the hair comes down in a point or crest; or the *Phoca leonina*, bottle-nosed seal. Its head is large and long, and its nostrils are much inflated when it blows out its breath. The head not unlike a young calf. The skin whitish and somewhat spotted. If the tail or hind legs are touched, it utters a mournful tone. It brushed its fore-paw over its head and eyes, and generally sat up, almost in an erect posture. There were several monkeys and other quadrupeds.

"*Sunday, 25th.*—Fine day. The ship *Fortune*, Captain Walker, not having sailed, I sent out under the care of the second mate, Mr. Potter, another dozen of newspapers to Mr. Lewin at Sydney, New South Wales, and also forwarded a letter to Mr. Wallington, surgeon of the *Emu* ship, bound out to Botany Bay, entreating him to bring home some curiosities. Heard Guthrie had been 'pressed' and put on board the tender. Heard a meteor was seen flying westward, bout ten degrees above the horizon in the south.

"*Thursday*, 29*th.*—Had a nurse squalus fish brought me from Scotland by Mr. Man and Mr. Burton, fishermen, caught off Ferrick Head. They say it is a harmless fish. It had several worms in its intestines.

"*Thursday, November* 5*th.*—Dull day. Heard that Thomas Bowsby, a waterman, was drowned in Sea Reach on Tuesday last in the morning. Had to print a paper calling a meeting to-morrow to apply to Parliament for an act to lessen the 'poor cess,' it having doubled in seven years. My daughter Betsy burnt her leg with a serpent (firework) going out to an old Pope or effigy of Guy Faux in the street.

"*Friday*, 13*th.*—Rev. Mr. Phelps called and bought fossils.

"*Wednesday*, 18*th.*—Dull, rainy day. George, Charles, and Betsy all go to the play to see the 'Curfew and the Sleep Walker.' Porter raised to fivepence-halfpenny per pot from fivepence! I remember it threepence-halfpenny.

"*Thursday*, 19*th.*—Received a letter from Shadrach, also one from Mr. Hunt of Norwich about buying birds. Ship launched from Northfleet called the *Medway.*

"*Monday*, 23*rd.*—Bought shells of Mrs. Lindsay for five shillings.

"*Tuesday*, 24*th.*—Dry and dull day. Mr. Richard Eglintine, the waterman, died. He was a proprietor of the *King George*, tilt-boat No. 5.

"*Wednesday*, 25*th.*—Dry and dull. Mr. Johnson, the auctioneer, had four sales cried to-day,—Mr. Lewis's, Captain Fabian's, Mr. Bensted's of Milton Street, and Mr. Outred's sale in Queen Street.

"*Saturday*, 28*th.*—Assiter's sale. This man's

sale is said to arise from a debt of 6*l.*, which was run up by the lawyer's expenses to 50*l.* !

"*Sunday, 29th.*—Dull, dry day. Wrote a letter to my son Shadrach at the Coal Pit Bank near Wellington, that I was inquiring about a box I sent him not come to hand.

"*Tuesday, December 1st.*—Foggy. About this day I sent Mr. Patterden of Dover a piece of limestone, from Shropshire, with quartz.

"*Thursday, 3rd.*—Read the 'Gentleman's Magazine' containing my paragraph signed 'The Chairman of the Kent Natural History Society,' wherein I defend Mr. Hasted's 'History of Kent' from a writer in a former number who styled himself 'Litterator.'

"*Monday, 7th.*—Heard young Swarfland was attacked by ruffians last night near cross-road to Perry Street. Mr. Cooper from Chatham called, and we went to see a large frog-fish caught alive within the basin of the canal yesterday. It was about six feet long and above two feet broad. Its mouth, which was vertical, would certainly have held half a bushel : very flabby, and, I suppose, weighed from sixty to eighty pounds.

"*Tuesday, 8th.*—Heard Major Elphinstone was ordered to Spain.

"*Wednesday, 9th.*—Frosty. Wrote a letter for Mrs. Assiter to her friend, Mr. Dowling, to go to Mr. Abdy to make Assiter a bankrupt, he being in Maidstone Gaol. Received a letter from my son, R. P., saying he had met with a new acquaintance, Mr. Gilpin, who had sent Mr. Parkington near 1000 specimens !

"*Thursday, 10th.*—Frosty. Walked to Rochester to appeal about the taxes. Walked home with Mr. Haigh, a schoolmaster, who desired to have an invitation to the Kent Natural History Society. He appears to have a good method in teaching Latin.

"*Friday, 11th.*—Had some fossils brought by Captain Cole from Sheppey.

"*Saturday,* 12*th.*—Frosty. Heard that Bonaparte was killed by the Cossacks. Bought a box of Mrs. Lindsay, who said it was made of Shakespear's mulberrytree, and was her mother's (Mrs. Stevenson's) sister's. The box is a carved one, to hold a pack of cards ; had a crest seemingly of a bird holding or shaking a spear ; within it were the names of *Shakespear Wood, Sharp,* whereby it appears that one Sharp was the maker or owner, that the box was made of Shakespear wood, viz., his mulberry-tree.

"*Sunday,* 13*th.*—Frosty ; ice bears.

"*Monday,* 14*th.*—The Russian Navy fleet have been coming into the Medway for a few days.

"*Tuesday,* 15*th.*—My friend Mr. Crow of Faversham called on his way to London to get a patent for a newly contrived boat compass he has invented. He has shown it to the Lords of' the Admiralty, the Trinity Board, and has a letter of recommendation from General Harris (the famous general from the East Indies) to the Chairman of the East India Company for their approbation. The patent, he says, will cost 115*l.*, out of which 80*l.* is said to go to the Lord Chancellor for putting the seal of office thereto. He went by water in the *Sir Francis Burdet,* the wind blowing very strong from the east. Mr. Crow lately sent Mr. Bullock of the London Museum a gigantic heron, which came from abroad, and probably escaped from some ship, as it was picked up by a Faversham boat.

"*Friday,* 18*th.*—Windy. Printed a hymn to be sung

at Dartford when a sermon will be preached by the Rev. DuCane.

" *Saturday*, 19*th.*—Had a song printed of a voyage to Hudson's Bay in 1811 in the *Prince of Wales* ship. Mr. Theobald lost his gold watch last night.

" *Sunday*, 20*th.*—Rev. Mr. Davis preached Mr. Varchell's charity sermon in evening.

" *Monday*, 21*st.*—Foggy day. Mr. Park, the surgeon, called and asked me if I had Major Pasley's book on the war; I said, no, but I had seen it and thought it the most judicious and best written work I had ever read; he said Major P. was his school-fellow. I told him it did his school-fellow much credit. Mr. Park said he was sorry to find no scientific persons in Gravesend.

" *Wednesday*, 23*rd.*—Damp, foggy, dull day. George P. left Mr. Giles' school. Mr. Giles has had his picture drawn by a Mr. Medlin. A haw-finch (*Loxia cocco-thraustes*) very scarce, shot at Stanstead.

" *Thursday*, 24*th.*—The Waterford Militia marched in from Billericay on the way to Chatham or Sheerness. Talked to an intelligent private. Says that Waterford is a plain county without mountains; that he had seen the poor people about Cronebane and the Wicklow Mountains sift the sand that had come down from the hills in search of the gold found about there; that a detachment of soldiers has been placed about there since the discovery of the gold. (*Mem.* I have a Cronebane halfpenny.) The private said he had heard Sheerness was a bad place. I told him that Sheerness was noted in great plenty for four things, viz., plenty of gin, women, Jews, and sailors. Mrs. Hull of Milton called. She came to bury Mrs. Reader, her sister. Mr. P., a waterman, died.

n

He once was a great reprobate, but lately has turned very religious, from going to the new Ebenezer Meeting.

"*Monday*, 28*th.*—This evening I began to write the Life of Mr. Matthew Danson, a tailor of Gravesend, a person who has seen much perplexity and domestic trouble. He entered on board a ship the day the style was altered, viz., September, 1752.

"*Thursday*, 31*st.*—Mr. French of Shorne brought me a bittern, three feet and one inch high, three feet broad, shot last Monday at King's Well in Higham. He has been twenty years a gunner and gamekeeper, but never saw one before. Referred to Dr. Turton for a description of the bird, but it was too abstruse. Resorted to the synopsis of Berkenhout, which explained the bird exactly in a clear, comprehensive manner. Mr. French asked five shillings for it, but would not take books in exchange."

## CHAPTER IV.

He'll often stoop, inquisitive to trace
The opening beauties of a daisy's face ;
Oft will he witness, with admiring eyes,
The brook's sweet dimples o'er the pebbles rise ;
And often bent, as o'er some magic spell,
He'll pause and pick his shapèd stone and shell :
Raptures the while his inward powers inflame,
And joys delight him which he cannot name ;
Ideas picture pleasing views to mind,
For which his language can no utterance find.

JOHN CLARE.

No trace exists of the MS. Life of Danson above
mentioned, and as the remains of Pocock's Journal fail,
for a while, at the end of 1812, it affords the opportunity
of recurring to his love of botany, and of mentioning
that in and previous to the year 1815, he had secured by
gift or purchase two folio volumes of dried and preserved
plants, and had devoted no little time to the completion
of the description, laboriously noting against every specimen its Linnæan and vulgar names, with a reference
to "Withering," and the page where the description of
the particular specimen could be found ; besides which
he added to its leafy treasures numerous other ex-

H 2

traneous specimens as he had been able to secure them.

To the first of these folio volumes he has prefaced the following note : " The original plants in this book and another volume seem to be arranged according to the system of Morrison, which appeared about the year 1680.

"Other plants have since been added by me, R. Pocock, printer and bookseller, Gravesend (1815), to which I have put their Linnæan names, and inserted the volume and page where a description may be found in Withering's 'Botanical Arrangement of British Plants,' third edition, which ought to accompany these, my *two* volumes of dried specimens."

The *two* has been subsequently corrected into *three*, by pen, Pocock adding : " Because since the above was written a third volume has been added, containing mostly grasses, rushes, and suchlike sorts."

These three volumes, still extant, probably contained, before the ruinous effect of a half-century's neglect, little short of some six thousand varieties, annotated with the greatest care opposite each example, with the place and date, in many cases, of its acquisition.

But the untiring patience and unremitting perseverance of Pocock in the pursuit of his botanical collections were equal to further efforts; and accordingly we find that in or about the year 1817 he commenced a new collection of dried plants and botanical specimens, which shall be referred to in its turn.

There is ever something specially attractive in the ove of Nature for its own sake, and he who can find

solace in the simple pursuits of botany, and feel himself
rewarded in the tranquil and patient noting down of
the infinite diversities of the vegetable world, possesses
a character antecedently interesting to us and almost
necessarily gentle; but the pursuit of this study by
Pocock was not unaccompanied by many kindred
developments of his desire for accumulating information
in other paths and spheres, and for disseminating
whatever he thus acquired. We must not anticipate
what may further appear upon the botanist's love of this
department of Nature, but take up the fragments which
have been collected of his Journal for the year 1815; it
is not, however, clear to us that the March entries refer
to himself :—

"*Tuesday, March 21st,* 1815.—France. Went to the
post-office at nine, and was mortified to find no letters
returned to breakfast, and set out to make a tour of
the ramparts, which command a fine view of the neighbouring country. To acquire the better view I went
upon the highest part. When I had almost completed
my round, an old soldier, who happened to be one of
those charged with looking after the ramparts, ordered
me down. From the tone of his voice he seemed to be a
man vested with authority, and I obeyed. Approaching
him, I said in French, 'My friend, you seem to be a little
angry; but like many other animals perhaps it is
natural to you.' Swearing, he told me it was forbidden
to walk on that part of the ramparts, and that all those
whom he found there were apprehended and punished.
I said, 'Why are there not notices to that effect ? I (nor
any other stranger) know nothing of these regulations ;'
and was moving off, when he said if I would give him
a few halfpence he would let me go. I laughed at

this application, and said, 'Why take money? If I have done anything wrong, punish me.' I walked on and he was still with me, but not liking his company much I turned another way; but he said, 'You must come this way.' 'Why?' 'To take you to the *grand place*,' he replied. 'For what?' said I. 'To punish you.' I laughed again, and said, 'Certainly;' but as he was a pitiful little wasp he must show me his authority, which he instantly did. I did not yet think anything of it; I knew if he took me to a magistrate I could give an explanation as a stranger satisfactory to him; and in walking on still on my route upon the lower ramparts, I began to be merry at the old fellow's expense. I asked him the punishment for this heavy crime; not less than being shot, I supposed, in which case I hoped for some time to make my will; and in this way he became excessively angry, which I enjoyed. He made a full stand, and said if I would give him some money he would let me go. I asked him where this house of punishment was; he said quite near, and supposing I would meet with some gentleman, I would have an opportunity of making a proper apology, and I confess I had some idea of getting the old fellow drawn over the coals for exacting money from me for his own use. Laughing at him again I said, 'No; if I am to be shot, let me be shot.' Descending from the ramparts, we immediately, without going into the street or town, entered a dark dungeon of a place which was the guard-house; and here he instantly gave me in charge to the sergeant as a person who had been found trespassing upon the ramparts. I asked for the officer of the guard, but was told he was not there, and that they must obey the directions of this towns-guard man. Two soldiers were prepared with fixed bayonets to conduct me to this *grand place,* and consequently through the streets, and there I knew I would be instantly set at liberty, yet the figure I must have cut with these two personages and perhaps a crowd of persons after me would have been rather ridiculous. I still laughed and made light of it—said this was ridiculous, and what was it he required. He then said with great emphasis, ' *Nothing ;* prepare, soldiers, to conduct him.' ' Very well,' I said, ' come along; is it this way or that ? Make haste.' And coming out of the guardhouse door, he said, ' What is it you are willing to give.' This I was not sorry to hear. ' No great things, I said ; a few halfpence only;' and putting my hand in my pocket produced about threepence, which he received, and I was at liberty. I felt myself, I confess, somewhat humbled ; and after the two soldiers had retired I was asking the sergeant whether the old scoundrel had the authority to do all this, who said he must have sent me to the police if he had persisted in his charge, when seeing me speaking to the sergeant he returned very angry, and ordered me to leave the spot. ' Go that way,' he said, pointing to one street. I replied, ' No ; it is my pleasure to go that way,' pointing the contrary way. So this was the only punishment I could inflict on this nuisance. I returned home, and at four o'clock the officer called on me to go and dine with him at the *restaurateur's.* I told him my adventure, who said, however right he might have been in giving me in charge it was infamous and ought to be punished, the taking of money. But he said such subsisted with the military, for if any person is found committing the least nuisance upon the house of a general officer, or near it, the sentinel takes your hat, and you must pay him five halfpence, else he keeps it, and you have no remedy. As this is the sum the old fellow required, I rather think he also had such a permission; and in such case I too would have had no crime to charge him with. He added that there is a sort of revolutionary spirit afloat at present, and it is probable the old fellow is riding on the top of his commission. We dined together, and went to the coffee-house to see the *Moniteur;* and waiting, a party of mountebanks entered, laid down a rug up the floor and played their tricks upon the hard flags. Eight o'clock arrived, and no *Moniteur.* I took my leave of him, went home, had a good jorum of warm tea and went to bed.

" *Wednesday, March* 22*nd.*—I sent at nine to the post-office, and was again mortified to find neither letter nor remittance from Paris.

" *June* 5*th.*—The Fountain Tavern, which had been the resort of Excise tide-waiters as long as I could remember, began to be pulled down, to make room for a new building for the Excise, and the tavern was removed to the opposite side, where the Commissioners of the Excise had a house.

" *Thursday, June* 15*th.*—I set off this morning with Mr. Richard Peen on a tour to Town Malling, passing over Punish Hill, where a small cottage has this year been built which commands the finest view in Kent. The view embraced the winding Medway enclosed by hills, contracting itself to Rochester, where the arches of its bridge displayed across the river make a striking point in the picture, over which appeared Sheerness and the shipping, with the sea as an endless scene. If any person wishes to see the beauties of Kent, let them traverse the hills about Upper Malling, and they have no occasion to visit the lakes of Cumberland or Westmoreland, or any foreign countries. From Town Malling we went to Snodland, and there slept,—no, went to bed. For having passed the house (the Bull Inn) about two hours before we observed it deserted, viz., without company; but finding we could not reach home that night we returned to it late; and at that time also came a mountebank or tumbler with his numerous followers, and the villagers immediately fell to dancing, drinking, and making a noise all night long; so that we only laid down, waiting impatiently till the morning, when we gladly departed, traversing over the hills to Meopham, looking after scarce botanical plants, a few of which we found, as the deadly night-shade growing on Birling Hill, also the Orchis canopsea in great plenty.

"*Saturday*, 17th.—This day Mrs. Pocock and her three daughters went out, leaving the house open to any strangers.

"*Sunday*, 18th.—Walked with Mr. Peen to Chalk with Mr. Lamburt (gardener to Esq. Bowles, Town Malling) to see some young cabbages peculiar to Chalk as early growers.

"*Monday*, 26th.—I went with Mr. Crafter on board the *Thomas Greenville*, East Indiaman, just arrived, to see Mr. Jennings, the third mate; but he had not gone out in the ship. I carried him off some fruit, which I gave to the chief mate; and he in return gave me a large turbo greenish shell he had picked up in the Straits of Sunda.

" *Tuesday,* 27*th.*—This morning, about four o'clock, I was disturbed by a person rapping at my door, and saying the stable had fallen in. I got up ; and going into the yard I could see nothing ; and was coming in, but turning round again I observed a soldier and another man (a hostler) in my premises, whereupon I caught up a broom-handle and gave the hostler two blows across the breech ; and he was on the point of retreating over Mr. Matthew's pales, but at this instant another soldier had got over with an iron crow in his hand, and they all three attacked me and shoved me down twice. I then singled out the hostler and we had a battle in the yard. The soldiers burst open the stable-doors, could see nothing particular there, so we all went into the back street, where the hostler, encouraged by the presence of his master, challenged me then to beat him. We fell to, and I had the best of it for some time ; till by a violent fall, stepping backwards over a bundle of straw, on my head and shoulder, I was stunned, which the cowardly fellow took advantage of, running his knee into me, and beating me whilst lying on the ground, particularly by one blow in my eye which caused a handful of blood to flow out. In fact I never was so bruised in all my life.

" *July,* 1815.—At the end of this month died George Arnold, Esq. [son of Anthony Arnold, mayor in 1760], a worthy inhabitant, having been mayor of the town during the mutiny of the Nore; also when the Duchess of Brunswick arrived, and when the King of France passed through the town to take possession of his kingdom ; also upon several other extraordinary occasions and occurrences."

Cruden, in his local History (since Pocock's time), writing of this alarming mutiny, relates that "affairs wore so very serious an aspect that the delegates moored the fleet in two lines of battle to be prepared for any attempt to coerce them, and to demonstrate their determination to employ all the means in their power to obtain their demands. By this distribution of the fleet the Thames was blockaded and no ship or vessel could pass without examination and the permission of the delegates."

He mentions how "these proceedings created great alarm, and necessarily engaged the attention of Parliament;" adding that the "civil authorities and the inhabitants of the town displayed the utmost energy upon the occasion. George Arnold, Esq., mayor, relying upon the aid of the inhabitants generally in cases of emergency, provided for the preservation of the peace; and the utmost harmony was maintained between the civil and military authorities during the whole of the eventful period."

In the locality it is reputed that Parker, the ringleader, was, after being hanged on board the *Sandwich* man-of-war, buried at Gravesend at a four wentway or cross-road; but it seems that he was buried at the Naval Yard, Sheerness, and afterwards exhumed by his widow and taken to Tower Hill, when, after some disturbances, his body finally found sepulture in a vault at Whitechapel Church.

The River Thames was a main entrance for the introduction of alien enemies, and in times of war serious duties in this respect devolved upon the mayor in connexion with the safety of the state. The following letter shows the nature of such duties:—

"Alien Office, May 4th, 1807.

"Sir,—Favourable representations having been made of the alien, Smith, whom you have committed for irregularity in regard to his alien licence; it is recommended to you to consider his case, and liberate him if you see no particular cause for his longer detention.

"The Secretary of State desires me to signify to you his entire approbation of the vigilance that has lately been shown at Gravesend in watching the aliens who resort thither.

"I am, sir,

"Your most obedient humble servant,

"John Reeves.

"The worshipful the Mayor,
     "Geo. Arnold, Esq., Gravesend."

"A list of the principal families residing in or connected with the environs of Gravesend :—

### 1700.

| *Gravesend.* | *Milton.* | *Northfleet.* |
|---|---|---|
| Nynn. | Coosens | Harman. |
| Kite. | Vaughan. | Wadman. |
| Arnold. | Harison. | Le Februe. |
| Harison. | Becket. | Levett. |
| Goldsmith. | Joynes. | Birch. |
| Reed. | Lance. | Swift. |
| Brandon. | Giles. | Mackroth. |
| Wilson. | Keddel. | Kennet. |
| Tadman. | | |
| Rogers. | | |

1800.

| " *Gravesend.* | *Milton.* | *Northfleet.* |
|---|---|---|
| Arnold. | Oakes. | Rosser. |
| Wilson. | Dalton. | Pitcher. |
| Tadman. | Rich. | Harison. |
| Styles. | Brenchly. | Howard. |
| Ruck. | R. Ruck. | Marly. |
| Man. | Becket. | Whiskin. |
| Millen. | Giles. | Tadman. |
| Twist. | Woodgate. | |
| Ditchburn. | Smith. | |
| | Brett. | |

" *Wednesday, August 2nd,* 1815.—Fine day. George Pocock and myself walked to Cobham Fair.

"*Sunday,* 13*th.*—Walked to West Wood with Mr. Hatchet and Co., who caught the purple hair streak butterfly.

" *Tuesday,* 22*nd.*—A ship sailed to Botany Bay with Anthony Daffy Swinton, proprietor of the Daffy's elixir. He was the person who some years since shot Mr. George Ormerod through the body, but did not kill him. He now is sent away for being a confederate in stealing a watch.

" *Tuesday,* 29*th.*—Walked to Brompton and Strood Fair with Betsey Pocock, and called on Mr. Hoar of Brompton (who gave me a piece of the rock of Elba), and drank tea with Mr. Wright, of Best Street, Chatham.

" *Friday, September* 1*st.*—This day I first became acquainted with Mr. Haviland of Sussex, who came into my shop with his two sisters going out to settle in Russia, on the borders of the Black Sea. In discourse

I found Mr. Haviland an architect of some abilities.
He was grave, and seemed to possess a general knowledge of literature and science. He knew Mr. Dallaway,
who wrote a portion of the ' History of Sussex.' Said
his aunt, who had married in Russia, had sent over
for them to advance their prospects in the world;
that his uncle in Russia was the person who had
buried the great Mr. Howard (the philanthropist), and
had been mentioned by Dr. Clarke in his travels.
His uncle has a house in Moscow, and has 500 slaves,
and his aunt says in her letters they must be treated
as slaves otherwise the master will not be respected
among the higher class of Russian nobles! When I
hinted to him the prospect of gain through his abilities
as an architect, he said, No; his aunt had told him that
business is not thought of nor mentioned in the higher
classes; nothing but the army is supposed to be
honourable, and nothing but a war with Turkey is ever
desirable. He wished to correspond with me by
giving his direction to Admiral Mordwenoff's, St.
Petersburg, who was waiting at that city for their
arrival. I then requested he would, when there, go
to Count Orloff's, who resides about two miles from
St. Petersburg, and inquire for William Macpherson,
botanic gardener to him, begging he would let me
hear from him. ' Ah, sir,' said he, ' who could think our
Government could receive Count Orloff as an ambassador at our court, when it was known the *Count had
murdered his own father ?* '

" *Sunday, 3rd.*—This day I received a letter from
Dr. Gerelius, M.D., physician to the household of
the King of Sweden, saying on his arrival in London
he lodged in Aldgate, which he found too filthy,

next in Cornhill, which was too noisy, and next in Wellclose Square; but he wished to reside in or near Gravesend : that he liked the country of England better than the people. Mr. Crafter, Mr. Pittard, G. Pocock, and myself walked to Luddesdown, where we heard the iron furnaces in Kent, at Barden, were heated with charcoal alternately laid with iron ore. Went to Birling Hill to take a view of the country, and dined at a small cottage of a wood-reve erected in 1815 by Government for the purpose of taking care of 236 acres of woodland lying in the parishes adjacent. The wood-reve said the magpies often kill and eat the young partridges. St. Paul's said to be seen from Holly Wood. In this day's journey, passing over a stubble-field about nine in the morning, the sun suddenly shone from behind a cloud, when instantly there began a concert of stubble music, which grated the ears with a crackling noise somewhat like a field of stubble burning.

" *Tuesday*, 5*th.*—Walked to find and see the old Dane holes in Hangman's Wood, between Chadwell and Stifford, described by Camden, the antiquary, and Dr. Derham.

" A very loquacious lieutenant in the navy, a native of Barbadoes, says that island is the most healthy of any in the West Indies. Is not hotter than in England; never has the yellow fever or other disease unless brought there from the other islands ; and is always the receptacle of invalids from them.

" *Wednesday*, 6*th.*—An English officer put into Gravesend Gaol for the night's security, having been brought as a prisoner from the continent. Said to be a

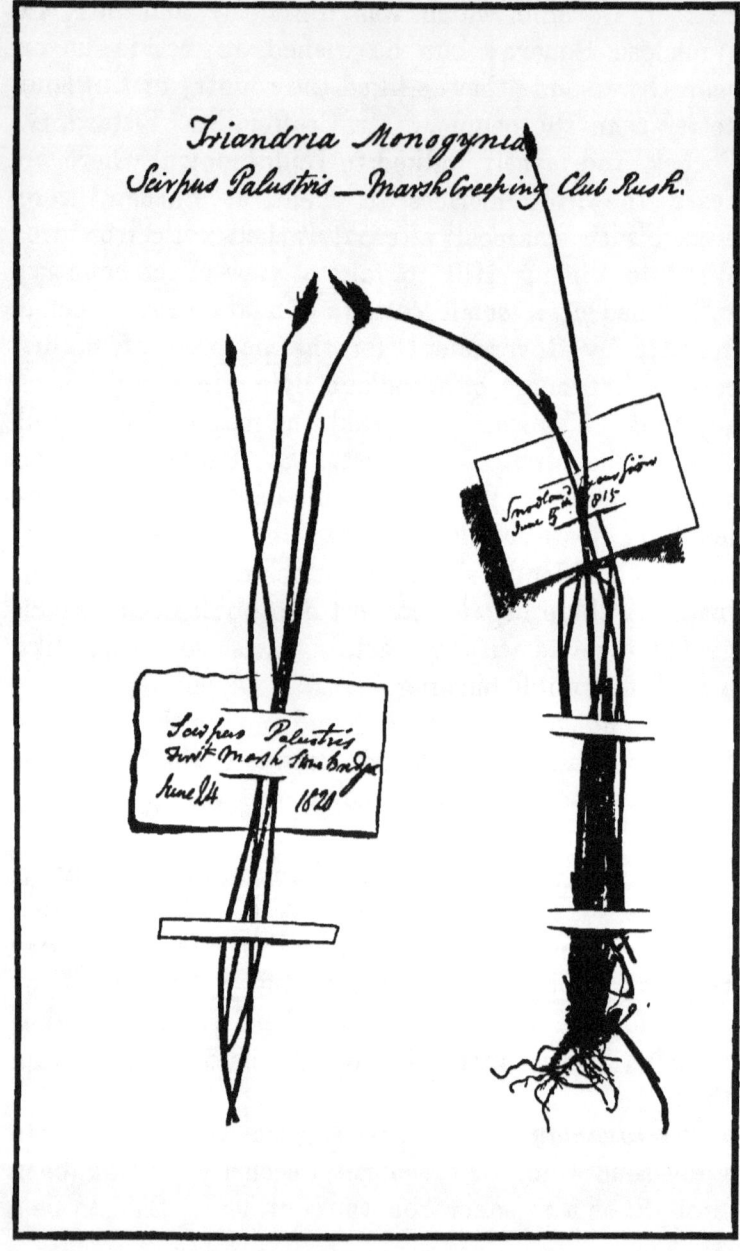

spy and cashiered from the English service. Thursday the officer went from Gravesend to London."

It was mentioned (at an earlier period of this work) that in or about the year 1817, Pocock began his new collection of dried plants in five quarto volumes, each volume containing about 600 pages.

This work was the source of great delight to him, and the accumulation of its contents the aim and object of many a long piece of pedestrianism in the neighbourhood of Gravesend and the more distant parts of the county of Kent.

If he had been able to have completed the collection, they would probably have contained some 5000 specimens, divided in the following manner :—

The first volume containing classes 1 to 5 ; the next, 5 to 9 ; the third, 9 to 15 ; the fourth, 15 to 20; and the fifth, ferns.

The following (p. 114) is a reduced *fac-simile* of the title-page which Pocock prefixed in his own hand to the first volume, and in the records of his many receptions of naturalists and other friends it would seem to have ever been a prime pleasure to him to produce his "Hortus Siccus ; " while on the preceding page (112) is shown a reduced drawing of one of its leaves, showing his mode of annotating the specimens :—

*Hortus Siccus*
*Magnæ Britanniæ:*
*or*
*A Dry Garden*
*of*
All the Indigenous Plants
*in*
*Great Britain*
giving
Their Class, Order, Genus and Specific Name
From the latest Authority
viz
Dr. Smiths Compendium Floræ Britannicæ.
Published in 1816
Together with
Their Time of Flowering, Duration, and Place of Growth,
in
*The County of Kent,*
For which it is
*A Botanical Directory;*
Collated not only from Authors of authority
But
From actual Observations and frequent Perambulations
within and around the County,
By Robert Pocock, Printer, Gravesend, Kent.
1817.

In the following year, 1818, Pocock lost his second wife, Frances, who died in the month of July at his shop in the High Street, and was buried at Gravesend (the place of interment of his first wife Ann) on the 23rd of that month, at the age of fifty-three years.

Becoming thus a second time a widower, he never accomplished a return to the " holy estate :" probably the absence of his frugal helpmate had its baneful effect upon his steadily declining pecuniary fortunes.

## CHAPTER V.

A president, on butterflies profound,
  Of whom all insect-mongers sing the praises,
Went on a day to catch the game profound
  On violets, dunghills, violet tops, and daisies, &c.

DR. JOHN WOLCOT.

"*Wednesday, January, 2nd,* 1822.—Mr. Henslow of Rochester and his son from Cambridge called to view my ' Hortus Siccus,' &c.   The son is a botanist.

"*Thursday, 3rd.*—Miss Loft (daughter of the slop-seller) married at Gravesend to Mr. Handville of the Hudson's Bay ships.   It is said his father, Captain Handville, went *fifty-two* voyages there.   He is now about eighty.

"*Tuesday, 8th.*—Had an imber goose (so called in the north of Scotland) brought me.   Authors are deficient in its description, as it is not a goose.

"Mr. James, the author, gives readings on Shakespear in the Town Hall, which is a novel thing among the *non-literati*.   Mr. Edward Fuller called and said there were snipes in the marshes.

"*Wednesday, 9th.*—Fine.   Mr. Coosens of Margate called, and said he had given Mr. Deputy Nichols MSS. enough to form an extra volume to Hasted's

Kent, and that he had found out 2000 mistakes in that work, which he had communicated to the author, but no notice was taken of them, because Mr. H. said if he did it would show his inattention. I said I had found many. Mr. C. said it was Mr. Bridges of Wales who found fault with the Kentish history in the 'Gentleman's Magazine' which was defended by me (R. Pocock). Mr. Coosens said he had found in a wood near Chilham a Roman station; and that the site of Stonar Church was lately found. Mr. C. is well versed in Kentish history and antiquities, having published a work from the monumental inscriptions in East Kent. He is a pleasant man; has a daughter married and settled in Essex.

"*Thursday,* 10*th.*—Mr. Russel of Swanscombe called, and said he had found Roman works in Swanscombe Wood.

"*Friday,* 11*th.*—Dull. Mr. Lakes, a young gentleman from the University of Cambridge, and nephew to the Rev. Mr. Rashleigh of Southfleet, called, and I sold him eight rare English insects.

"*Monday,* 14*th.*—Fine, sunny. In company with Captain Rosbrook, a fisherman, who said he had taken a willock (a bird) out of a cod; and another fisherman said he had taken out of a cod a stone as big as his fist; and Mr. Rackstraw said he had seventy-five stones; all of which came out of one cod! Such stories may appear fabulous or untrue, but Captain Rosbrook does not, I am sure, wish to lead me into error, as it is well known the cod will swallow many strange substances, I having heard it said by many different fishermen.

"*Wednesday,* 16*th.*—The Rev. Mr. Rashleigh and

Mr. Lakes called and brought some more insects. Said there was no stag-beetle in Cornwall, and that Mr. Seymour of Dorsetshire was a collector.

"*Friday,* 18*th.*—Fine, sunny. Sent a letter to Mr. Spencer of Chatham (he having laid claim to a great estate of the Selby family in Bucks) with all the names of Selbys in Blome's ' Britannia,' a folio work.

"*Sunday,* 27*th.*—Sunny in morning ; dull in afternoon. Radishes sold three bunches for a penny, so mild and forward are the vegetables. Most of the autumnal flowers are in bloom, and yesterday was brought me in bloom the bean, Antirrhinum rotundifolium, primroses, barren strawberries, violets, &c. ! Jupiter and Saturn have been in conjunction some months, and the evenings exhibit beautifully the starry wonders of the celestial world. I am told my daughter, Sarah Pocock (although a woman), has been christened at Gravesend Church by the Rev. Mr. Gray. Witness to this unusual circumstance, Mr. Covus, a shipwright, Mrs. Roach, a shopkeeper, Miss Covus, the daughter, and Mr. Tyler, son-in-law to Mr. Covus.

"*Tuesday,* 29*th.*—Fine and dry. Bells ringing at six and fort guns fired at twelve for the king's accession. Mr. Peen brought me a list of sixty-two British plants in bloom the second week in January, 1822 ! Sent a letter to Mr. Elliot at Hobart's Town, Van Diemen's Land, by a young man from Frome in Somersetshire, who says Mr. Shepherd's black cloths are the best. Received the ' Cambridge Guide ' from Canterbury. I forgot to say Mr. Shepherd has a daughter well skilled in natural history, having a good collection.

" *Sunday, February 3rd.*—In evening a man called on me for information about Hume, the ropemaker, who lays claim as the presumptive heir to the earldom of Marchmont.

" *Monday, 4th.*—Dull, but fine. Settled with John Hobcraft. Heard the *Thames*, East Indiaman, was lost near Eastbourne, in Sussex: very sorry to hear this, as the principal owner, Mr. Blanchard, is a worthy gentleman, an acquaintance of mine. Settled with Mr. Thorowgood's Rider, and spent the evening at the New Inn.

" *Tuesday, 5th.*—Clear morning ; windy in night. In evening Mr. Stevens (the dean of Rochester's brother) and a Mr. Smith called to know if I could give them any account of the old Mr. Hume's papers (which are lost), by which it is said the younger Hume is kept out of his estate and title to the earldom of Marchmont ; but as they would not pay me for my trouble in searching over my papers I declined looking for them, observing to the dean's brother that as Hume, the claimant, was borrowing money from many persons and spending it lavishly among the watermen at Billingsgate, and riding about the country, I thought I might have some for my trouble as well as his throwing it away so profusely. They left me Hume's pedigree.

" *Thursday, 7th.*—Fine, sunny. Heard that Mr. George P. was dead in the workhouse. He had long been very poor, and had been in the gaol of Maidstone, where it is said he refused money sent him from his brother, as his proud spirit would not brook receiving any from that quarter, since he said his brother unjustly withheld what he was entitled to.

"*Friday, 8th.*—Fine, mild, sunny. Saw in the paper that the ship *Abberton*, Captain Gilpin, had arrived in Madras Roads September 24th last. In this ship went Charles Pocock, my youngest son (as baker).

"*Saturday, 9th.*—Fine day. Mr. Millen (the mayor), kindly offered to be my friend (in case I could find a friend). Some author has observed a man may think himself happy if he finds six friends in his life. I have often said I keep three books: a little one for my friends, a large one for my acquaintances, and a small one for my customers. My late wife used to say our acquaintances were so numerous that we kept a public-house without profit. The best sentiment to give in company is, 'From injudicious friends, good Lord, deliver me.'

"*Sunday, 10th.*—Fine. Mr. Matthew Buchinger called and dined and spent the day. He is a plain, stout, blunt man, grandson of the famous Buchinger, born without hands or feet in Germany. He lays claim to the estate of the late George Arnold, Esq., in this parish, lying to the south of Wilson's garden, and extending from the Fair Field Road (now Bath Street,) to Princess Street, so now called. At four o'clock George Powell (having been conveyed to the Odd Fellows' Hall, where he laid in state) was buried in Gravesend churchyard, aged sixty-four, escorted thereto by the society of which he was a member. And no person enjoyed himself better than George, when he had money and spirits! He once imported West India produce, as sugar, pepper, &c., and was a member of that useful scientific society, formed some years since by the writer of this article, and the

dissolution of which evidently hurt the happiness of
many of its members.

"*Monday*, 11*th.*—Delightfully fine. Buchinger
went home to Dartford. Made an exchange with
Mr. Pierce, the tailor, for his book, Chamberlayne's
' State of Great Britain,' for a blank book or ' Seaman's
Journal,' of about 2*s.* 6*d.* value. Mr. Pierce has a
better idea or knowledge of astronomy than any man
in Gravesend, in fact he possesses abilities above many.

"*Tuesday*, 12*th.*—Rather foggy. Mr. Manning of
John Street, Adelphi, called and said his son would give
me any account of arms in heraldry, &c. Mr. Bullock,
jun., of Egyptian Hall, Piccadilly, called on his way
to Lapland, going there for some more reindeer. He
gave an account how his father, with Mr. Allan Burn,
got at and examined the shrine of St. Mungo in Glasgow,
and took a model of St. Mungo's hand in wax. The
great church in Glasgow is dedicated to St. Mungo,
where he appears to have been buried, never to have
been disturbed, as an immense large stone is placed
over his grave, and on which were built the pillars to
support the edifice ; but these two curious gentlemen,
when about giving up their pursuit by reason of the
pillars and huge stone, were agreeably apprised by
the resurrection-men they had employed, that an
entrance to the coffin had been effected by entering
into an adjoining vault and breaking through into
that of St. Mungo !

"*Wednesday*, 13*th.*—Fine day. Mr. Manning, jun.
(the herald), called, and the evening was spent at the
New Inn with Mr. Keene, late a clerk at Bow Street,
whose son had married into Mr. Manning's family.

"*Thursday*, 14*th.*—Mr. Manning employed in

making extracts from the ' Reg. Roff.' of the Manning family.

" *Friday,* 15*th.*—Fine, sunny. Mr. Bullock sailed for Lapland, and Mrs. Manning for the West Indies.

" *Sunday,* 17*th.*—Rather dull. Frances Pocock walked to Ash and back, nine miles. A woman and child drowned last night by one of the Gravesend boats running over the sculler, said to be Pullibank's boat as master.

" *Monday,* 18*th.*—Sunny. Recollect Mr. Manning, jun., greatly recommended Hudson's Bay *minions* at five shillings per hundred, as the best for writing, to be had of the law stationers. Heard that young Ridley, one of our fishermen, went out in the *Hecla*, bound to Baffin's Bay on discoveries. I am to look out for this ship or its companion, as Mr. Fisher, the surgeon, and author of the former voyage, promised me gifts.

" *Friday,* 22*nd.*—Lady Darnley visits the charity children of Gravesend.

" *Saturday,* 23*rd.*—Fine day. Mrs. W. (late Miss Mary Gladdish of Chalk), wife of Mr. W., came through the town in grand procession in a hearse and two mourning coaches, &c., to Chalk Church to be buried (where her father, Mr. Townsend Gladdish lies). This was the most decent funeral I have seen some time past, or recollect, at Gravesend; but it was not by a Gravesend undertaker. The *Thames*, East Indiaman, lately wrecked on the Sussex coast, arrived in the Reach towed by two steam vessels.

" *Monday,* 25*th.*—National School children treated with dinner.

" *Thursday,* 28*th.*—Fine, sunny. Walked to North-fleet to John Theobald's, who made his will (by Mr.

Southgate the attorney) leaving his freehold and leasehold property to Mrs. Goodewe. The witnesses to the will were Mr. Southgate, Mr. R. Pocock, and Mr. Southgate's clerk. At this house was a man who said he had had a violent bruise from a shower of stones which fell from the sky near Northfleet Green; and I was given two, but on looking at them, I found them not the sort of stones which fall from the sky, which are called meteoric stones, and all of which abound with much iron. Such wonderful stones may be seen at Mr. Sowerby's, in Mead's Place, Southwark, and in other museums. I think this man's name was Goodewe, and that he told me a lie.

" *Saturday, March 2nd.*—Fine day. Mr. Millen paid with my money the rent to Christmas.

" *Sunday, 3rd.*—Fine day. Tortoise-shell butterfly seen, and I hear that young robins fledged were flying about Knockholt on February 14th.

" *Monday, 4th.*—Fine day. Employed in printing bills for sale at the Globe Auction Room.

" *Tuesday, 5th.*—Fine day. Went to London by coach and visited Mrs. Saxter, called at the Egyptian Hall, and slept at the Black Bear, Piccadilly, where I met with Mr. S. from Eton Wick, who knew well a Mr. Pocock residing thereabouts, and promised to lend me books about paintings in the vicinity of London.

" *Wednesday, 6th.*—Wind S.W. Rainy day. Settled with Mr. Langdon: visited Exeter Change. Drank with Mr. Giles in Clare Market, and heard of a remarkable low tide this day, when a man walked across the river. Slept at the Bull Inn, Holborn.

" *Thursday, 7th.*—Rainy, wind strong west. Left a jaconot and two other birds with Mr. Ryals, but to have two back preserved. Came down by the boat from Billingsgate at eight minutes past three, and arrived at Gravesend at five o'clock. (*Mem.* The quickest passage I ever had.) Walked to Southfleet to put in the way to Sundridge, Alexander Hall, the captain's steward of the *Canning*, East Indiaman (with another young man going out as baker to Bencoolen), who both promise me curiosities, &c. In this voyage down was an intelligent person of the name of Avan, who appeared, by a letter he produced from Messrs. Cowtan and Co., Canterbury, as a good politician. I found him an agreeable companion and a staunch ' minority man,' which made me remark he was a disciple of Lord Sondes and Thanet, to which he nodded assent.

" *Friday, 8th.*—Heard the tide on Wednesday last was forty-one feet beyond the stone causeway or bridge at Gravesend ! Work at Tomlin's job, being for a new coal concern.

"*Monday, 11th.*—Work at Brewer's, Newman's, and jobs of printing.

" *Wednesday, 13th.*—The new coal company began (Everist and Co ) by having a vessel in canal and selling coals 36*s.* per chaldron.

" *Sunday, 17th.*—Dull. Heard Roe, the ferryman, was dead. Drank tea at Mr. Crafter's, where my friend Mr. Pittard and his acquaintance were. The two latter may be deemed butterfly merchants, and Mr. C. a pupil, whilst I myself am somewhat tainted with the disease, for want of better employ. Mr. Pittard says he has hired a house at Eynsford, where he intends residing.

" *Tuesday, 19th.*—The 41st Regiment passed through. In evening at eight o'clock a fire broke out in Denton, and burnt a straw stack. It made a great alarm, as it could be seen from Highgate to Southend. Engines came from Rochester and the three towns, and a man got hurt by jumping from one, which passed over his body.

*Wednesday, 20th.*—Lent Mr. Rackstraw a volume of old magazines.

"*Friday, 22nd.*—Sale at Layton's of his stock. Walked with Mr. Walton to view where the fire had been at Denton. Remarked that if the wind had been N.E., probably the barn and stacks, and even the house, would have been in danger, or all consumed. Went to Wombwell Hall and found there a good painting of the ruins of Rome, the amphitheatre, &c., probably by Panini, and another painting of Venice by a capital artist. There was the painting of a shipwreck (apparently modern), and in the garden were two low shrubs of the cornelian cherry in bloom, like unto the tree growing a few yards to the westward of the Bathing-House, which bears fruit at Christmas of a long, oval form ; but it is very scarce, as I never remember but once in my life seeing the fruit on it. The gardener would not have it as bearing that name, but the Virginia dogwood, showing me another shrub, not in bloom, as a cornelian cherry : however, I would not give up my opinion. I am told there is a large tree of this sort at Mr. Treadwell's, a farmer at Hartley ; the one near the Bathing-House appeared indigenous. In the green-house is a Barbadoes cherry; otherwise it contained only a small collection of plants. In the evening a gentleman (foreign) bought a chart of the river, having come home in a ship from Lima (where he had resided some years), and brought from thence, as merchandize, a great quantity of gold and silver in bars, supposed half a million as it filled several of our short ferry-boats, and Mr. Little's great boat took it and him to Calais in France.

"*Saturday*, 23rd.—Fine. Walked with Mr. Peen to see the lizard orchis we had transplanted towards White Hill and found it only with one small weak leaf, which shows it will not blow this year, although we put it there so long ago. On my return I found a parcel (to my great surprise) had come from Miss Lousada containing many scarce plants. I had supposed this lady was dead, having heard her name was in the newspaper, and had grieved much about the loss of such an agreeable correspondent; but upon my opening her letter found it was her mother. I have been married twice and lost relatives, but none of them affected me so much as the supposed loss of this amiable lady.

"Heard a grampus whale (*Delphinus orca*) had been found dead in Northfleet Hope, and taken to London by Luke Beet, when it was ordered away under threat of taking him into custody for the nuisance, as it stunk intolerably.

"*Sunday*, 24th.—Rain in morning. The afternoon occupied with Mr. Peen and Crafter in looking over the plants sent me yesterday, and talking about the grampus which had floated down to Denton coal-wharf, where Mr. C. took a drawing and measured it. Its length was eleven feet.

"*Monday*, 25th.—Mr. Nayler of Rochester called. Says he has some very ancient deeds, and will give me copies. He has a small collection of coins, &c.

"*Tuesday*, 26th.—Received by post a letter from Chas. Pocock, dated Madras, October, 1821, saying he had been well shaved when crossing the line, and that it was a fine day's sport. This ceremony is greatly enjoyed by all seafaring men. Mr. Crouch, a conchologist, called, and saw me the first time, and bought a few specimens. Mr. Grundy, sen., died.

" *Thursday*, 28th.—Frances goes money-hunting for me to Dartford.

" *Tuesday, April 2nd.*—Wind north. The winds since Saturday have cut the vegetation and parched the leaves as if burnt. This is the first check we have experienced all the winter. Mr. Grundy buried. Lent Mrs. Pitt one volume of White's 'History of Selborne.'

" *Wednesday, 3rd.*—Mr. Barlow called and says that Mr. Vigors and Mr. Eversfield are to be the joint collectors of land tax for Gravesend, as he declines. Yesterday Mr. Hubble and Mr. Gladdish, the two new overseers, called, and ordered some parish printed receipts to be done with their names. Buried this day Mrs. Etherington—Robert Oakes's child, &c.

" *Thursday, 4th.*—In the night some thieves broke open the house of Mr. Sothers, the grocer—getting in the back way, making use of a centre-bit to bore holes in the pannel of the door—and stole bank-notes, checks, gold and silver, &c. I went to Dartford. Waited on Mr. Fooks, the solicitor [grandfather of Edward J. Fooks, Esq., solicitor, Hillside, Gravesend]; and on my return met with Robert Okill, who paid me five shillings for a printing job. He had just returned from Maidstone, where five men had been executed, viz., four smugglers for wounding officers at Margate, and one man for robbing Dr. Pigot at Mereworth.

" *Good Friday, 5th.*—Sent two notes (one pound each) to Mr. Simmonds.

" *Saturday, 6th.*—Lent Mr. Peen second volume of White's 'History of Selborne.'

" *Easter Sunday, 7th.*—Some thieves taken up for

robbing Mr. Styles, and on suspicion of robbing Mr. Sothers. Two years ago this day I went to North-fleet Church, and heard the Rev. Mr. Whittaker preach his first sermon.

" *Monday, 8th.*—Some suspicious men taken up with a cart, having in it saddles and bridles, &c. In the after-noon Mr. Turner and Mr. Kemp, I believe is his name, and brother-in-law called, and bought some spiders, haliotes, &c. Frances gets a new situation and goes.

" *Monday, 15th.*—Mr. Peen walked to Boxley in search of plants, and found growing in Boxley Street the golden saxifrage, a scarce plant, noticed by Mr. Jacobs as only growing in Judd's Wood, near Ospringe: it is the Chrysoplenium oppositifolium of Withering, and has bristles on the leaves, which circumstance authors have omitted, and by its taste and brittleness appears good as a salad. Evening, rain.

" *Tuesday, 16th.*—Received a letter from Cambridge to send Mr. Lakes, a student at Clare Hall, four or five butterflies by name, they being not about Cambridge, and to make him up a dozen of scarce sorts, as he is making a calendar of the lepidoptera, and wishes for Papilio comma, Papilio polychloros, Phalena hexa-dactyla, Phalena caja (great tiger moth), Phalena fagi, &c. Two young men taken up on suspicion of being thieves, and discharged.

" *Wednesday, 17th.*—A young man named Marchant, about twenty-four or twenty-five, going out in the *Defiance,* Captain Barker, promises to collect.

" *Tuesday, 23rd.*—Officers demanded lamp and pave-ment tax due. 71st Regiment, with a very fine band of music pass through for Liverpool. Old Mrs. Beale buried.

" *Wednesday, 24th.*—The 3rd Regiment of Guards marched up the road, and in the afternoon the Regi-

ment of Buffs marched into the town, going down.
Saw the first swallow flying against the wind.

"*Thursday*, 5th.—The Regiment of Buffs marched
out to Chatham. Mr. and Mrs. Paul and their son,
Mr. Paul, a youth about twenty, with Mr. Bradley, all
passengers going out to settle in Van Diemen's Land,
called, and promised to send me home shells and curiosities. The ship *William Shand*, in which they go out,
is now here with eighteen passengers. I gave them
directions to several gentlemen in the colony who
have before promised me and not kept their words, or
have forsaken me.

"*Saturday*, 7th.—Mrs. Paul and son came to take
their leave.

"*Sunday*, 8th.—Mr. Paul, jun., comes on shore,
having given them a cat and my 'Everlasting Song
Book' to remember me, and the ship *William Shand*
sailed in the afternoon.

"*Monday*, 9th.—Yesterday a sailor called and said
he left my son Charles well in the East Indies, that he
had given satisfaction to the ship's officers, and that he
had bought a monkey, and would be home in a month.

"*Tuesday*, 30th.—Mr. Dadd of Chatham called and
bought some minerals, &c., and said he sold his bar-
nacle goose flint for 2s. 6d. (worth a guinea) to Mr. Bright,
a Member of Parliament; which was very wrong, as it
was a great if not an unique specimen and rarity! In
the afternoon Mr. Francis of the post-office, Rochester,
called, and wanted to be instructed in the printing
branch, having a thought of commencing that trade.

"*Wednesday*, *May 1st.*—Boughs of the white-thorn
in leaf put up at a few houses, but not in bloom yet. I
have seen it (a flower bloom) brought by Mr. Peen,
who, I believe, has forwarded its bloom. Colonel

K

Landman, of the Engineers, called to see me with seemingly much freedom, at which I was rather surprised, he not having ever been my acquaintance. He inquired after my son George, who had been some time in his office; but not having been paid by Government, viz., the Ordnance, he left it, and is now settled at the Clarendon Press in Oxford, where Colonel Landman said he had been, but did not see my son because he was ignorant of his being there. Colonel Landman seems now to be fond of natural history, and wanted a spined echinus, &c.

"*Thursday, 2nd.*—Saw the second white butterfly. In the afternoon Mr. Peen returned from a journey to Wormshill and Throwleigh, &c., having found a species of stonecrop (*Sedum reflexum*) growing on the churches of Bobbing and Bredgar. He had before observed the same on the wall of Trottescliffe Court.

"*Friday, 3rd.*—Walked down the sea wall to Shorne Battery, and found mousetail in bloom, but could not find my spider orchis (*Ophrys araniflora*) on the hillocks, which I had planted a year or two before. In my walk only saw five gulls, two or three pairs of tit-larks, two pairs of pewits, and two or three reed sparrows, with as many wagtails. I think the easterly cold wind prevents many birds appearing.

"*Saturday, 4th.*—Went on board the *Onyx* ship, just returned from the River Bellise, Bay of Honduras, after a passage of thirteen weeks. Heard the church there, which cost 15,000*l.*, was finished except the spire, and that the Rev. Mr. Armstrong was the minister. Saw on board a beautiful tortoise, black and yellow. I think it was the terrestris, although the people said it was caught, as they supposed, in the river. I bought a few shells, viz., six false argus shells, which the natives called mangoo; a pair of pink conchs; a pair of bull's mouth conchs, called by some the king conch; a shell harp volute; and some small shells, among which were a cowrie with a raised ridge in the middle, but more likely a bulla, a cowrie with three brown bars across it (cyprea), an orange murex with black lines across it and white within, a few olives, and other small washed shells.

" *Sunday, 5th.*—Received letters from my son, Shadrach, at Wellington. Heard yesterday that the Duke of Bedford and Duke of Buckingham had had a duel, and that the Duke of Bedford had behaved with much humanity in not firing at, nor trying to kill, the Duke of Buckingham. All duels are a species of murder or manslaughter, which nearly amounts to the same. My friend Crafter called and showed me copies of letters he intended to send to Lord Darnley and Colonel Christie at Chatham to endeavour to get him re-established as clerk of the works or some other appointment.

"*Monday, 6th.*—The king's yacht towed down the river by a steam-boat to the Downs for Prince of Denmark. About eight this morning saw and heard the first ' swift.' Birds I think all come in storms or bad weather, which prevents persons seeing them; for we know little about the migration of birds or their habits. Mr. Dadd of Chatham called and bought a piece of Shropshire limestone.

" *Tuesday, 7th.*—Had part of a 'cat-fish' fried, which is very fine eating.

" *Wednesday, 8th.*—Mr. Pottinger, a gentleman at lodgings at Mrs. King's at the Hill, called to have a gossip. He is a Radical in politics. He has visited France and Switzerland, Jersey, Cornwall, &c., but never made any remarks, and owns he is very ignorant.

"*Thursday, 9th.*—A young man of the name of Alfred Gardiner (bought song-book), going out in the *Mediterranean*, Captain Ross, for the South Seas, promises to collect curiosities. He says they eat and make puddings of the terrapin's eggs, which are quite round. His father is captain of a South Sea ship, now out and expected back soon. In the evening Mr. Blanchard called, who was with me when we went to Cobham Hall on an inclement day of snow, cold, and wind : the day when many great personages were visiting there, and one got wounded—I think he was the Archbishop of York's son : and I think Lord Wellington was there. Mr. Blanchard was the managing owner and met with loss by the *Thames*, East Indiaman, getting on shore in Sussex. Heard Mr. Heathorn, the brewer, was dead.

"*Friday, 10th.*—Mr. Pottinger called and left me Cobbett's ' Register ' to read, which I skimmed over. It did not suit my taste, being deficient seemingly in the subject and editorship. A fishing-boy brought me eight shrimps with fourteen legs, having the appearance of longish shrimps, probably the Cancer linearis of Linnæus, but Berkenhout says it has only twelve legs. Its antennæ were as long as its body. It may be a new species.

"*Saturday, 11th.*—Fine day. A woman applied to me for a pair of patella shells to cover the nipples of her breast, which she said were of infinite use in sore breasts. It is not the first time I have heard of this remedy, and I sold her a pair in exchange for a pair of spotted cowries.

"*Monday, 13th.*—Dull. Sent off a letter I had wrote to Mr. Walcot, sen., Clifton, near Bristol, to collect some plants for me about the rocks; and sent also a letter to my son in Shropshire for the same.

" *Thursday,* 16th.—Bright. The king's yacht came up the river again. Mr. Peen set off down into Kent. The stationer called, and took twelve dozen of 'Jobina' and two dozen of 'Youths' Amusements' on account. Heard the Queen of Denmark passed through yesterday in a coach with six horses, but it made no noise.

" *Friday,* 17th.—Printed some bills that Mr. Notley of Stone Cottage had lost 'a small gold watch, chain, and seal,' with reward of five pounds.

" *Sunday,* 19th.—Walked with Mr. Jones to Thong and Shorn lfield, and caught the argiolus, a beautiful blue butterfly with black tips and margin, certainly scarce, never having met with one before. Got also the grizzle or brown fritillary, which is not plentiful. Found a neat small nest, in a holly-bush, built of moss and lined with feathers, with one very small egg, likely a tom-tit's nest; it was about six feet above ground.

" *Tuesday,* 21st.—A regiment of soldiers (white jackets) came into the town from Essex on their route to Chatham. Mary Ann Pocock came from Shropshire, having been deserted by an old unfaithful clergyman of the name of B—, who having solemnly promised marriage, and named the day and prepared all things requisite, went and married another who had formerly been his maid!

" *Wednesday,* 22nd.—Warm. Mr. Peen called, having come back last night from his journey through Kent, in which he collected some scarce plants, viz., the stink weed of Thanet Isle, found on dry ground a few miles inland from Deal or St. Margaret's. It appears not yet particularized and may be a new species, as botanists differ about it. It belongs to the class Tetradynamia, order Siliquora, the genera Sisymbrium or Erysimum. However, on the authority of Mr. Peen, who may be relied on, all the leaves are alike, the segments of the leaf being wing-cleft : its smell is very disagreeable.

"*Thursday*, 23rd.—Windy clouds, wind easterly. Wrote to Mr. Gray to name a moss found in the River Stour, near Chilham.

"*Friday*, 24th.—Wrote to Mrs. Amhurst, a widow lady at Ore, near Faversham, for leave to visit her garden, which contains a great variety of flowers.

"*Sunday*, 26th.—Went with Mary Pocock to Rochester Cathedral to divine service, in hopes of hearing Rev. Mr. Stevens the new Dean; instead of whom an affected clergyman preached who lost his words and voice at the end of each sentence, so that we left, neither made better nor instructed. Mary was not pleased with the mode of chanting. On coming out met with my acquaintance, Mr. Spencer, by appointment, having given him a friendly challenge to meet me there. Went to my cousin Reuben Fletcher's, at Rochester, to dinner, and better pleased with his roast beef and plum pudding than with the sermon or preacher. Drank tea and spent the evening with Mr. Spencer's family.

"*Monday*, 27th.—Went from Chatham by coach to 'Upper Blue Bell,' and had from the top of the house an extensive view, as we saw the road (plainly) going up Shooter's Hill (about twenty-four miles distant), and Lord Petre's house, near Brentwood, Essex (thirty miles off), the towns of Southend and Leigh in Essex (about twenty-five miles), the town of Sheerness with Minster in Sheppy, the Nore and ships sailing down the Swin; to the south Cox's Heath; and south-west a fine prospect of a campaign valley, with the hills of Surrey. Yet this delightful prospect did not equal, Mary said, the view of *Wrekin Hill in Shropshire*, where an extent of seventy miles round may be seen distinctly. Then walked to Maidstone (four miles) and saw several benefit societies parade the town with bands of music, having gone to church as an annual treat and paid the parson for preaching. Afterwards walked through several hop-gardens to Barming, and drank tea with the Rev. Mark Noble, whose wife and daughters I found good botanists, and their garden I reckoned the second for variety of plants in Kent (Mr Russel's of Swanscombe being the first). The old clergyman was happy to see us (although the first interview), and I was surprised at the clearness of his manuscripts, for he told me he never made a drop or wrote from a copy. His collection of books was nicely arranged, and his manuscripts numerous. Here we met with Mr. Cresswell, a gentle-man going to the bar, who related an anecdote or two not much to the credit of the law; viz., that a lawyer ran a poor man to seventy pounds and upwards in expenses in prosecuting him for five pounds only. Hard enough! and in our walk by the tow-path (side of the River Medway) found a scarce Scirpus sylvaticus, not having met with it before. Maidstone Palace, Church, College, and Bridge, as we approached, made a fine picture, and must give great pleasure to any anti-quary who may visit them. Here also we found boys fishing, who had caught some bleak, dace, &c., and were told that there were pikes, eels, and some others. Called upon my cousin Champion, who is a *greasy* relation, as he sells hams and keeps a cook-shop. Slept at the Swan Inn.

"*Tuesday, 28th.*—Breakfasted with Champion, who was vain enough to read to us some of his poetry about

Allington Castle, on which old fabric his head seems to have run wild.   Took our leave and walked by Allington Castle to Mr. Milner's, where we saw the largest barn in England, fifty-five paces long and about sixty feet high, having a date at the end, over a window, of 1102, and the initials T. C., which are those of Thomas Colepepper, and his arms quartered with a chevron. A similar date is on a building on the opposite side of the road, but those buildings do not agree with the date, as the figures made use of there are said to be much more modern.   An old woman who had lived above forty years in the parish had never heard of these curious buildings.   Passed over Aylesford Bridge, on which grows wall rue (*Ruta muraria*). Visited the churchyard, where there is an old yew-tree. Visited the Friars, once the seat of the Carmelites. Here we met with a very civil (wished to be polite), ignorant young man as gardener; treated him, and walked to Boxley Hill, and then rode to Chatham in a caravan which goes weekly to Rotherfield in Sussex. Proceeded to Strood to the turnpike, where at the Angel Inn we could get no refreshment because the landlord would not change a Wellington note, and so obliged to walk to Gravesend, very much fatigued, and to our mortification obliged to sleep at the Nelson Inn, having been shut out either by accident or design, not having ever been treated so before as I always have the key in my pocket.

"*Wednesday, 29th.*—Fine.   Received a fine present from Edinburgh of dried Alpine plants, and engaged all day with Mr. Peen in putting them away.   Mrs. Jones brought to bed yesterday of a boy, being my first grandchild.

" *Thursday, 30th.*—Engaged again with my plants. Walked in the evening to find my 'lady's slipper' I had put out in the marsh; but could not find it. It must have been taken, as I certainly did keep the place of planting sufficiently secret.

" *Friday, 31st.*—Engaged in printing bills about indecent bathing, by order of the mayor. Supped with Mr. Blanchard (brother to the East India captain), at the Falcon Inn, on veal, green peas, &c.

" *Saturday, June 1st.*—Mr. Blanchard, myself, and daughter Mary went to Cobham College and Church, where Mr. Blanchard read with much facility the ancient French and Latin monumental inscriptions in the church to the memory of the Cobham families, &c. Spoke to Mr. Pemble about the ancient helmets in the chancel (as the chancel is belonging to him). Mr. B. wished to make an equivalent to the poor of the parish for the same; but Mr. Pemble did not grant the request. Went to visit Cobham Hall, where we were refused, because Lord Darnley's daughter Mary was going to be married that day in the hall by special licence to her relation (I believe, cousin), Mr. Brownlow, and the house was full of company. Visited Chalk Church to see the two figures on the porch, likely enough made to perpetuate an obit or drink ale day. The Hudson's Bay ships fire their guns : an annual custom at Gravesend, where their officers and owners dine, and have green peas for dinner, which this year have come most early.

" *Sunday, 2nd.*—Walked with Mary Pocock to drink tea with old Mr. Fletcher of Claphall. In the morning we rambled through the chalk cliffs of Northfleet, and found in bloom Orchis latifolia, &c.

" *Tuesday, 4th.*—Went to West Wood in search of

plants.   Found there a bee orchis, but not in bloom.
Anthropophora in bloom—nearly out.

" *Wednesday, 5th.*—Got orchises from Northfleet
Cliffs for Mr. Neil of Edinburgh.

" *Friday, 7th.*—Put orchis roots on board the *Forth*,
Captain Stuart, for Leith, this morning about five
o'clock, for Mr. P. Neil, Secretary to the Wernerian
Society.   My daughter Mary returned to Woolwich.
Went over to Dartford to Mr. Brewer.

" *Saturday, 8th.*—Mr. Peen said he went yesterday to
Wanstead in Essex, to see the house and gardens, and
near 4000 persons there to see this fine place, now put
up for sale, by thirty days' sale.   The catalogues were
sold at five shillings each, which admitted three persons
to view the first ten days' sale, and again the same for
the second and third divisions.   [Wellesley Pole.]

" *Tuesday, 11th.*—Busy all day in ' setting ' Mr.
Tolhurst's   bill   for   leaving   the   Prince   Regent.
Heard at night, at eleven o'clock, the death watch for
the first time this year.   A county meeting held this
day at Maidstone for a Parliamentary Reform.

" *Friday, 14th.*—Heard  Samuel  Johnson,  an  old
shoemaker, was dead.   Went to Gravesend Church
and stood godfather to my daughter Elizabeth's (Mrs.
Jones') child, by naming it Shadrach Edward Robert.
The curate's name I understood was Owen, but I had
never seen him before.   The child's name was to please
all parties : first  Shadrach, because my grandfather
Pocock's name was such, and also my eldest son, now
settled at Coal Pit Bank, Ketley, Salop.   The second
name was to please the family of Jones, and the third
name is my own.   Bought some skeletons and medical
book and plants.

" *Saturday*,15*th*.—Busy in 'composing' bills for sale of estates, &c., at Wigzell Row, St. Mary Cray.

" *Sunday,* 16*th*.—Frances visited me from Kingsdown, and told me the storm at Kingsdown on Monday last was there at three o'clock, but no four distinct loud claps. Cobbett mentions this storm in his *Weekly Register*, describing his tour to Maidstone to attend the county meeting, when they petitioned for a reform in Parliament, &c., on Tuesday last.

" *Tuesday,* 18*th*.—Frances returned to Kingsdown, and took a French book on paintings to translate for me. Printed 200 cards for Mr. Chipperfield, who removed to No. 17, Gee Street, Clarendon Square, Somers Town, saying Gravesend market had ruined the town; meaning nobody but strangers were encouraged.

" *Wednesday,* 19*th*.—Mr. Mac Murdie, from Epping, called, and I gave him five shillings.

" *Thursday,* 20*th*.—Prof. Henslow, from St. John's College, Cambridge, called on me, and bought a piece of crystallized slag from Salop. He said he caught nearly fifty swallow-tail butterflies in a meadow near Cambridge one day (P. Machaon). We have none in Kent ! Mr. H. certainly is a pleasant young man and worthy his professorship.

" *Saturday,* 22*nd*.—Professor Henslow called, and I gave him a list of British plants wanted to complete my 'Hortus Siccus,' and he promised to send some scarce ones growing about Cambridge.

" *Monday,* 24*th*.—Busy all day in printing particulars of seven houses in Wigzell Row, St. Mary Cray, to be sold by auction.

" *Tuesday,* 25*th*.—Harmonic Society take their usual annual excursion to Ifield, attended by a band of music.

I walked to Twelve Step Stile, and found the pyramid orchis in full perfection in bloom, and the lizard (which I had transplanted from near Wilmington) in the height of bloom, having had, this first year of its bloom, above fifty flowers on its stem!  In my short route I caught the swallow-tail moth (*Sambucaria*), the marble (*Galatea*) butterfly (first seen this year), the brown-eyed (*Hyperanthus*) butterfly, the Barnet moth, &c.  The large stag beetle flying in the evening.

"*Thursday*, 27th.—Heard the *Abberton*, Indiaman, had arrived (wherein was my son Charles) in the River Thames.  Mr. Curd, the bricklayer, buried in a very deep vault, dug on purpose in Gravesend church-yard : and it is said the rector, Dr. Watson, claimed ten pounds for breaking the ground without his leave.  A vestry held to know if Mr. Owen could be the lecturer, he having been appointed as curate by the rector.

"*Friday*, 28th.—Mr. Gardner from Chatham takes the Nelson Inn.

"*Monday, July 1st.*—The Free Masons of the county walk to church (dinners each 14s.) for the benefit of the White Hart.  The band of the Welsh Fusileers played (not very well).  At night at ten, saw rather to the south of Purfleet a fire from Mr. Hazard's end of the town.

"*Tuesday*, 2nd.—The Sunday-school charity children have an afternoon's recreation in a field near the hill.

"*Wednesday*, 3rd.—Received letter from my friend Mr. Blanchard, saying he had given directions to the commanding officer of the *Thames* to employ Mr. Jones, my son-in-law.

"*Thursday*, 4th.—Walked yesterday to Randall Wood

in search of insects; but most surprisingly found none
among the brakes (*Pteris aquilina*) nor saw any
moths but what were small; and in the course of the
afternoon I took only three or four butterflies (*Papilio
comma*), which are scarce, and only one of the
marble (*P. Galatea*), which I found in the grass field
adjoining the lodge at Thong, where I had met with
them before on the 2nd day of August,—generally on
that day plentifully there. Counted whilst at Thong
above 750 rooks going towards the rookery in the park
to roost at sun-down, likely distributed in the day in the
marshes. During my walk yesterday the Rev. Mr.
Rashleigh called, and took away the ' Reg. Roffense '
he lent me. Lord Darnley to-day gave a silver cup
among his troop for the best horse-racer, and many
persons went to see the performance. Mr. Lloyd, a
lecturer on astronomy, gave out a prospectus that if
he could procure fifty at 9*s.* each for three lectures he
would begin. I am told he is not equal to Mr. Walker.

" *Friday, 5th.*—Sent Mr. Pearse to the hall to
answer to Mr. Toovey's debt of 2*l.* 3*s.* 5*d.* Having paid
him before 1*l.* and a 5*s.* It must be paid before this
day month ! Heard the *Abberton,* East Indiaman,
was in Bengal in February last, wherein Charles
Pocock went. Mr. Baker of Chalk began harvest by
cutting a field of oats !—the earliest known.

" *Saturday, 6th.*—Mr. Crafter tells me he is re-
established as clerk of the works, and also has his
father's place, who is pensioned off.

" *Sunday, 7th.*—Dick Simmons, my boy, did not
come this day. Three gentlemen called and bought
some books for 12*s.* One was a fossilist, and the
name of another was Fitzroy. Said they were going to

Cornwall; and the fossilist said he would call again. This day I wrote a copy from a slate of a letter I sent to Mr. P. Neil of Edinburgh, when I sent him the plants last month; and this copy, with his letter, I have put by with Mr. Scott's letter from Edinburgh (now dead). The carpenter and armourer of the *Thames,* East Indiaman, bound out with my son-in-law Jones. They said they would bring some shells and curiosities from the East Indies for me.

" *Monday, 8th.*—Fine and warm. Dick Simmons returned. J. Tolhurst paid, having been abused by Mr. Brenchley, jun., at Milton Church whilst I was present. Mr. Bowdler returned from Ramsgate (having called on Mr. Coosens of Margate, who has promised me some plants procured by a friend of his). Mr Bowdler brought me some plants from Thanet, but nothing new. The 10th Regiment of Foot marched into the town from Woolwich. The Odd Fellows of the Britannia lodge, with a band of music, enjoy a day at Wombwell Hall, with the church bells ringing. Mr. Chipperfield, the baker, died this day in the hospital, London.

" *Tuesday, 9th.*—Mrs. Dominy, an old inhabitant, called and drank tea. A person from Chatham, known to Mr. Dadd of the Arcade, Piccadilly, called and looked over my fossils, &c.

" *Wednesday, 10th.*—Meopham Fair, when Meopham played against Gillingham. Jerry Tolhurst put in gaol for abusing Mr. Brenchley, jun., although Mr. Brenchley gave him sufficient provocation for so doing last Monday morning. Mr. Eversfield, jun., undertakes to play the part of Macbeth at the Gravesend Theatre, being his first attempt !

"*Thursday,* 11*th.*—Three gentlemen going to Brussels called—one, a mineralogist, bought some minerals. Employed in printing about a prepared wheaten food for infants, by Jas. Hards of Dartford.

"*Friday,* 12*th.*—A young gentleman of the name of Fletcher (a student in medicine, and nephew, so he said, to Mrs. Graham, who wrote a pleasing and learned account of the East Indies) called in my shop, and informed me he was going to St. Petersburg, and the interior of Russia, to travel for some years, and would think of and write to me on natural history, &c. By him I sent my compliments to Mr. Etter, mineralogist to the Emperor of Russia. He said he promised Mr. Brooks of Blenheim Street to collect for him.

"*Monday,* 15*th.*—Paid Mr. Wilson his bill of 5*s.* 6*d.* In the afternoon a rowing match for a skiff of 10*l.* value, given by the players; and it was won by a waterman named Dixon. In the afternoon walked to Dartford : called on Mr. Nottley and Mr. Brewer. Found Mrs. Nottley died of the same complaint as Mrs. Pocock, and that Mr. Beaumont, surgeon, of Gravesend, predicted the death of both (a judgment which is sufficient to establish the reputation of Mr. Beaumont). Came home in a return chaise, wherein was a Mr. Knell of Cuxton, a wheeler and carpenter, who informed me he had lately, by command of the parish, buried (or put under-ground) Miss Coosens who had lain *above*-ground in the church ; the particulars of which, with her family, may be seen in the ' History of Gravesend.' No rain to-day, although it was St. Swithin's Day; but great show of it.

"*Tuesday,* 16*th.*—Yesterday, in my walk to Dartford, saw the first wheat began to be reaped, and also beans,

which show this is the most forward year I ever remember ; it being also very heavy and fine. In coming
home last night I saw a glow-worm shine brightly :
they appear about July 10th. In the evening Mrs.
Colepepper (wife of the elder Mr. Colepepper) called—
who claims to be, and who I believe is, the heir to the
Leeds Castle estate, late in possession of Martin and
Fairfax, and now in possession of a Mr. Wykeham—to
know what information I could give her respecting
deeds and other papers belonging to the family ; but
five or six years ago, when I could have given much,
her husband, in an abrupt manner, said he wanted none
of my assistance ! for he had employed an attorney,
who now appears to have done nothing !

" *Thursday*, 18*th*.—Fine and warm. Innumerable
numbers of Irish labourers about, more than I ever
remember, owing to their great distress for want
of food in Ireland. Mr. Preston's Rider called, and
I gave him an order, the music to be sent on sale
or return, and he is not to call for a twelvemonth.
The *Partridge*, East India ship, returned home and
passed the town. Heard a child of Mr. Childs, carpenter, Northfleet, fell down a well and was killed.

" *Sunday, July* 21*st.*—Mr. and Mrs. Leadbetter and
family (the famous animal stuffer) called on me, and
said Lord Darnley had a condor, or large vulture, which
he stuffed for him, and that the large horn owl was
worth three guineas. Lord Darnley bought one last
week of Macdonald, a fisherman, for about half the
money, which was bought by Macdonald for fifteen
shillings out of a smack from Norway.

" *Monday,* 22*nd.*—Mr. Lloyd gives a lecture on
astronomy in the theatre house—to about fifty auditors.

" *Tuesday, 23rd.*—Mrs. Willatts bought shells.

" *Thursday, 25th.*—Walked to Dartford with Mr. Peen, and got Mr. Brewer to accept a note for 8*l.* 10*s.* 6*d.*, payable at two months, drawn in favour of Mr. Charles Amherst. The harvest has become very general as some of the wheat has been carried.

" *Friday, 26th.*—Paid Mr. Amherst, in presence of Mr. Peen, his half-year's rent to Midsummer, 12*l.* 10*s.* ; viz., by giving him Mr. Brewer's note-of-hand, dated July 17, 1822, at two months for 8*l.* 10*s.* 6*d.*, which was made payable at the Bull Inn, in Leadenhall Street, and at the same time I gave him cash 3*l.* 17*s.*, and there was also owing for a book 2*s.* 6*d.* ; in all making up the amount; but for which he gave no receipt until, he said, he had received the money from Mr. Brewer.

" *Monday, 29th.*—Many martins flying about at five in the afternoon, apparently foreboding a storm, or about congregating.

" *Wednesday, 31st.*—Warm. Taken very ill with the colic and cholera morbus.

" *Thursday, August 1st.*—Warm. In bed with the colic all day : very ill.

" *Saturday, 3rd.*—Sally goes for me to Dartford, and Frances called and said she was going to Dartford Fair, and thence to Kingsdown. Heard the lightning and thunder had done damage to Hoo Church yesterday. And that at Brandts-hatch was a great fall of hail. It is remarkable that on August 2nd I have known it often thunder and lighten, with violent storm. It was on that day, about fifty years ago, I remember seeing the mill-post of Shorne Mill, with the mill, all shattered to pieces. The miller's name

L

was Billboe, one of whose sons lived and kept a public house at Northfleet a few years since.

"*Saturday*, 10*th.*—Many genteel persons in the town in expectation of seeing the king, &c., pass by in his voyage towards Scotland. Saw a curious printed bill for a cricket-match to be played this day at Shorne Common, for 10*l.*, taken from a list of fifteen persons of Shorne named Botting, against fifteen of Cobham named Baker! The Bottings beat by six runs. About six in the evening, the king in his yacht passed by, when the bells rung and the guns from the *Flamer*, "alien vessel," moored off the town, and the guns from Tilbury Fort alternately fired to make up a royal salute. The day was quite calm, and the yacht was accompanied by the Lord Mayor's barge, which went as far as the Round Tree, when it returned. On this occasion two regiments came from Chatham who stood with their bands on the sea-wall extending below the canal entrance, which must have had a pretty appearance from the water. The king's yacht was towed down by a steam-vessel and passed the town with rapidity.

"*Monday*, 12*th.*—Heard the king sailed yesterday morning, between four and five, from the Nore, leaving all the pleasure-vessels to follow, some of which returned, not well pleased. (*Mem.* The guns at the Nore heard at Gravesend, a distance of above twenty miles.) Heard this morning that Lord Castlereagh died suddenly.

"*Thursday*, 15*th.*—A report that Lord Wellington was killed by Marshall Ney's son. This proved false.

"*Saturday*, 17*th.*—Heard Sir Samuel Achmuty was

dead. His family by marriage was related to Colonel Montresor of Whitehall, near Faversham, who died in Maidstone Gaol.

"*Sunday*, 18*th.*—Matthew Buchinger from Dartford called and dined, and said some suspicion had fallen out about Lord Castlereagh's death, and that a further hearing was to take place yesterday. To-day the *Charles Grant*, and two other East Indiamen, *Lowther* and *Kelly Castles*, arrived off this place. This afternoon, as my daughters were walking down the canal, a man was found drowned, and very likely murdered, having many bruises and cuts about him. He was taken to Chalk for the coroner's inquest to sit on him. He was pulled out of the water by Mr. Jones, my son-in-law, and appeared a navigator or labouring-man, by his Guernsey jacket, in which was 1*s.* 6*d.* and a farthing.

"*Thursday*, 22*nd.*—Heard a death-watch very plainly, which I suppose is one of those small insects called 'wood lice.' It was in my bureau. I think they are only heard in warm weather, because I heard one in July, 1818, at the death of Mrs. Pocock. Some think them a beetle; but I am convinced the wood lice have this power of ticking, which I have proved in two instances. Mr. Pewtress called, and I settled with him by a bill at two months. [Wholesale stationer.]

"*Monday*, 16*th.*—Went down to the Hope, to the *Abberton*, Captain Gilpin, to see my son Charles, whom I found well. Squally wind, S.W. He sold his fat for 2*l.* 16*s.* per tierce (five tierces to Mr. Cooper). The ship had three Persian cats on board belonging to General Forbes, who came home in her with Major Frazer, &c.

"*Wednesday, 28th.*—Warm.   Charles came home (not very sober).   He sent home a Madras monkey, which differs from those of Bengal.   Walked over again to Northfleet to Mr. Theobald's, who made another will, which I signed as witness.

"*Thursday, 29th.*—Windy.   Horse-races at Chatham Lines for a plate of 50*l.*, when it is said 20,000 persons assembled, and where a poor woman was killed by a horse and cart going over her.   Charles P. went out, but did not come home all night.

"*Sunday, September 1st.*—Pleasant.   The king returned about twelve at noon in his yacht, towed by a steam-boat, and followed by another.   The guns fired a salute from the *Flamer* and the fort, and Mr. Rodmell's son had his hand injured by the explosion of a gun.   Hand was cut off by Dr. Rogers and Sanders. Mr. Lee, a gentleman (special pleader), of the Inner Temple Lane, called on me.   (*Mem.* He is well skilled in Latin and many sciences, and a good botanist and companion.)

"*Tuesday, 3rd.*—Warm.   Busy   papering   Mrs. Rhodes' room (the blacksmith).

"*Wednesday, 4th.*—Fine, sunny.   Mr. Bennet, surgeon, of Edward Street, London, called (a good botanist), and we walked over to Cobham Hall gardens, and on our way caught some fine butterflies (the admiral) on the elms at Parrock and oaks on Randall Heath.   We go after them again this day.   Saw many curious scarce plants and trees : among them was the willow-leaved oak from North America, not far from New York, where there it is also scarce.   Another scarce tree, about four feet high, from Chili, with branches shooting horizontally, and leaves like butchers' brooms, said by Mr. Wilkinson, the gardener, to be a species of fir. It is the *Araucaria imbricata,* or the Sir Joseph Banks pine, from Chili, introduced into this country in 1796. I left Mr. Bennet to sleep at Cobham, and returned home.

"*Monday, 9th.*—Young cuttle-fish, half an inch long, brought me.

"*Tuesday, 10th.*—Received letter from my son George at Oxford. Mr. Arlis, the publisher, called, and I gave him an order for 10*l.* worth of books.

"*Wednesday, 11th.*—Bought a new tea-pot of Barnaschina's boy for 3*s.* In afternoon, Captain Weddle, of *Jane* brig, bought some books. He told me he was bound out on the South Sea fishery, and that he had been twice to New South Shetland, lately discovered ; but that it produced no tree, shrubs, or vegetation, except a short grass which grew sparingly. He had brought home several specimens of stones and minerals from thence ; but I did not find by his discourse any to be of value. It is singular, I showed him a piece from the same place lately given me by a sailor, who said it was gold ore, but to me appeared only as yellow copper ore.

"*Thursday, 12th.*—Wrote a letter for Mrs. Currie to Manchester to a young man, her favourite. This woman partly told me her name was not Currie, and she was determined to leave him. A young man, with his coat all torn and mended, came into the shop, and left 5*s.* deposit for a book to read. I found him a good Latin and Greek scholar by his ready translation ! Learning appears not to produce wealth ! but Mr. Arlis, on the 10th, said 'a writer of original matter for the new "Monthly Magazine" (edited by Dr. Campbell) gets from six to eight guineas per sheet.' A gentleman and lady called from Deptford, who had passed through the tunnel at Higham (where lately three men lost their lives by the chalk falling in), and found a very large alcyonium on which were nodules of sulphuret of iron! It was the largest I ever saw, with an opening in it, or a gash. Martins come to their nests to-day.

"*Friday*, 13*th*.—Busy in printing for the mayor, J. Millen, Esq., 100 bills, being an abstract from an Act of Parliament made in the 56th of George III., enforcing a penalty of five pounds on the driving of carriages at a furious or improper rate.

"*Saturday*, 14*th*.—Windy, strong at east. Major Groves, the storekeeper, carried yesterday to Hampstead to be buried there. Finished yesterday and to-day some bills for Newman, stating he had reduced the fare to London to eight shillings inside and four shillings outside.

"*Sunday*, 15*th*.—Heard Mr. Bryan, of Swanscombe, had had his leg cut off by Newman's coach breaking down on Thursday last.

"*Monday*, 16*th*.—Walked to Dartford with Mr. Edward Helloit, who is quite a philosopher, although a waterman. We went through Greenhithe and by the fields to Dartford, and both were struck with the delightful picture the Phœnix Flour Mills of Mr. Wilks afforded. On the east side, one field off, several tall drooping willows, planted on small islands in a large pool of water, added much to the delight; in fact, I never saw such high beautiful willows nor such a charming scene. Called at Mr. Hurst, surgeon, to see Mr. Bryan, but was refused by the surgeon seeing him, who said his own sister had been refused, as quietness was necessary to a cure, and that his life was in critical danger. Mr. Brewer paid me 8*l.* 10*s.* 6*d.* for a bill due. On coming home we could see a fire blazing to the westward, which we conjectured was about Plumstead, or east of Shooter's Hill.

"*Wednesday*, 18*th.*—Sun very fine. My acquaintance, Mr. Rider, called with his wife, and praises the steamboat much.

"*Tuesday*, 24*th.*—Printed cards saying G. Simmons had succeeded Loft Raspison in his business of mast, oar, and pump maker.

"*Friday*, 27*th.*—Generally cloudy. Packed up twenty-four scarce moths, butterflies, &c., for Mr. Lakes, Clare Hall, Cambridge.

"*Saturday*, 28*th.*—Walked and rode to Dartford. In passing through Northfleet there was a burial of Miss Chapman in the church, said once to have lived in this parish, near the river-side, but now no resident there knew the name or family, and two gentlemen with the hearse (likely they were administrators) were making diligent inquiry. Waited on Mr. Hubbard, a new auctioneer at Dartford, and found his mother-in-law, Mrs. Munns, of Palace Street, Canterbury, a pleasant woman.

"*Sunday*, 29*th.*—The mayor, J. Millen, Esq., walks to church in procession. Sent a letter to Mr. George Pocock, about Dartford.

"*Monday*, 30*th.*—Fine day and fine evening, being full moon. This day Mr. Medhurst Troughton was chosen mayor. Walked in the morning into Clark's garden and found in bloom antirrhinum, Michaelmas daisy, &c.; but saw no butterflies, except a white one, although a fortnight since the Atalanta were so numerous. In the afternoon went down to East Tilbury in a boat (lately there established by Mrs. Smith) in search of dwarf elder, said to have been seen in the chalk pits, but found it the common elder.   Between the coal wharf and church saw abundance of Typha latifolia, or reed mace, the heads of which are worth gathering for beds, &c.   So is the down of corn thistles, and down of plowman's spikenard, which grows in abundance in the chalk pits here.

"*Tuesday, October 1st.*—At home.   My left knee seems not well, as if swelled; but I know not what has made it.   It rather affects my walking.   Read letters from Mr. Walcot and Frances Pocock.

"*Wednesday, 2nd.*—Wrote letter to John Walcot, Esq., Highnam Court, near Gloucester, saying I could supply him with the set of bound Botany for 10*l.*, or for 5*l.* he should have a set of my duplicates; but for particular plants from sixpence upwards.   I have found the Mr. Walcots very civil gentlemen, except a younger son who went to the East Indies.

" This afternoon Charles Pocock went out in a ship or brig to Smyrna, in the *Sultan,* Captain Christopher Yeoman.   Had a new pair of shoes of Mr. Worsly, which did not fit me, being too little.

"*Thursday, 3rd.*—The stuffed 'lump fish' becomes moist.   This I have observed before, and suppose it annually is the case.   It is worth remarking again. When I was at Dartford last week a poor woman, Mrs. Bax's daughter (the simpler), told me she had been bitten by a mad dog, and that day found herself very unwell, and had been persuaded to try the Birling medicine as an antidote !   She said she would rather die than be dipped in the salt water !   I packed up a parcel for Frances Pocock of writing paper and a cyphering book to transcribe some French therein.

"*Friday, 4th.*—Mrs. Cabamell of Coburgh Theatre bought a pink conch. Her husband is the architect, and will give a ticket of admission.

"*Sunday, 6th.*—Sunny, fine ; rain at night. Heard that last Friday morn at daylight an immense quantity of hirundines were seen flying towards the moon. She at that time was about westward. I have said before they come and go in a storm.

"*Monday, 7th.*—The *Royal Sovereign* yacht went past last Saturday with the Duke and Duchess of Clarence on board.

"*Tuesday, 8th.*—Wind strong, W.S.W. Rain at intervals. Crafter's paragraph appeared in the *Rochester Gazette* about the market provisions, &c., &c.

"*Wednesday, 9th.*—Received a letter from Mr. Walcot, Highnam Court, near Gloucester, for plants, stating his son, who went to the East Indies, died there. Captain Vanburgh died.

"*Thursday, 10th.*—Fine, windy, clear. The bishop comes to Gravesend, and confirms there. He is blind. Took refreshment at Dr. Crawford's.

"*Friday, 11th.*—Fine. Employed all day in sorting my dried plants. Young Tadman buried. This young man bade fair to be an excellent artist, as he showed by a drawing of the ' Round Tree,' near Gravesend, well done. This remarkable tree was at its highest prosperity about 1800 ; then being about sixty feet high and spreading above forty feet. It was injured, as so many shots were fired into it during the war, and since that time has been going visibly to decay.

"*Saturday, 13th.*—Settled with Mr. Cooper, the milkman, by his paying half-a-crown as balance. Received letter from Miss Lousada.

"*Monday, 14th.*—A new newspaper announced for to-morrow, to be called the *Kent and Essex Mercury.*

"*Tuesday, 15th.*—Cloudy. Captain Vanburgh buried at Milton. Mr. Hawkins, the waterman, died yesterday on board the boat. If the cap fits me, there has appeared, by the Rev. Mr. Durham, a severe epigram (in the Rochester paper) against my person and knowledge.

"*Thursday, 17th.*—Rain all last night. Sent off a letter to J. Walcot, Esq., Highnam Court, near Gloucester, saying plants had been sent him by Newman's coach to Bull Inn, Leadenhall Street.

"*Monday, 21st.*—Bill Taylor, at Mrs. Taylor's, butcher, had his leg broken by a horse. Miss Rashleigh called and desired the parcel to be forwarded to Mrs. Lakes, having paid 6s. for it.

"*Tuesday, 22nd.*—Went to Dartford, and called to see Mr. Bryan who had the accident to lose his leg when Mr. Newman's coach broke down on Dartford Brent. Met with Mr. Lee, the botanist. Saw on the road the admiral (red stripe) butterfly.

"*Thursday, 24th.*—Gravesend Fair. Mr. Reuben Fletcher and son Reuben called. Two gentlemen (one a botanist) called and bought some fossils, &c. At night, rain. A grand collection of wild beasts, viz., an elephant, a lion and tiger (so tame as to suffer the keeper to be in the den), a nilghau (like a horse) with two horns, &c., and many other rarities, being the largest fair known.

"*Wednesday, 30th.*—The dulness of the day appears

to have made me very sleepy, and this symptom has affected both Mr. Durham and Mr. Crafter. I think the same was so last year, and it is worth remarking next year. The skin of the lump fish is yearly moist, and when it begins to be so is a good guide, as the atmosphere ought to be more looked to.

" *Thursday, 31st.*—Went to London by boat and spent the evening at Mr. Bennet's, Edward Street. Mr. B. and his brother are excellent botanists and naturalists. Slept in Oxford Street.

" *Friday, November 1st.*—Saw two elks from North America at the Egyptian Hall, Piccadilly. Visited Mr. Brook's museum, Blenheim Street, where I saw a fine hippopotamus and a great collection of curious anatomical specimens. Spent the evening with Mr. Clark, the antiquary, who promised to return me my folio book and to give me some manuscript matter for my intended ' History of Gravesend.' His daughter is an agreeable girl and an excellent player on the pianoforte—the best I ever heard ! He has a son an excellent painter of landscapes.

" *Saturday, 2nd.*—In bed resting, having been all night on the water.

" *Sunday, 3rd.*—Mr. Brooks from Blenheim Street, London, with a lady, called to see my collection.

" *Monday, 4th.*—Two Atalanta butterflies taken.

" *Wednesday, 6th.*—Read the *English Chronicle,* or Whitehall newspaper, and thought it the best I had ever read, being full of amusement.

" *Thursday, 7th.*—Minute white moths in Clark's garden.

" *Friday, 8th.*—The barbers say lice are numerous with disease following always at this time !

"*Monday,* 11*th.*—Fine. Mr. Spencer, sen., called (from Chatham), and said his son William, with Mr. Vinall, had given Mr. Nugent Bell, the Irish barrister, a large sum (between two and three hundred pounds) to make search for pedigrees, &c., and to proceed in recovering the Selby estate from Mr. Lowndes, the possessor; but that Mr. Bell had died the day a verdict had been given against him in a cause wherein he took more money than the law allowed.

"*Tuesday,* 12*th.*—Mr. Pitcher bought my curious China jars.

"*Wednesday,* 13*th.*—Dull at intervals. Walked in Clark's garden, and found the Silene armeria in bloom. It is scarce; has a pink blossom, and crowned or fringed in the crown. Look for it again next year.

"*Thursday,* 14*th.*—Sun. Mr. Brown of the *Ogil Castle,* East Indiaman, going out November 14th, 1822, promises to collect shells, &c., and to write to me when the ship arrives in the Downs. Old Mr. J. Sherrass died this day in the poor house of Gravesend. His daughter married Mr. Spencer, of Chatham Dock-yard, whose son lays claim to the Selby estate of Buckinghamshire, now held by Mr. Lowndes, a member of Parliament. Many gulls in the river.

"*Tuesday,* 19*th.*—Received a letter from Miss ——, the intelligent and rich Jewess.

"*Wednesday,* 20*th.*—Mr. J. Finch (grandson to the famous Dr. Priestley) called upon me, on his way to America. He is going out in the *Acasto,* bound to New York. He bought some paper, and I informed him that when his grandfather was going out to America he also bought some paper of me, at which he wondered, and we got into conversation. As he was known to Mr. Hamper, the antiquarian of Birmingham, to whom I am known by name, and from which place he had come, and was going out by recommendation of Dr. S. James Smith, the famous botanist, we entered into the subject of those sciences, and soon became intimate acquaintances. At night Mr. Pottinger called to bid me farewell, and took my letter to Mr. Clarke, the lecturer on botany at Islington.

"*Thursday, 21st.*—Mr. J. Finch called again, and I sold him 300 chalk fossils (on credit) for one guinea, which sum he promised to send over from New York!

"Sent two cards of compliments to Van Diemen's Land (yesterday) to Mr. and Mrs. Paul, Mr. Bradley, Dr. Arnold, and Mr. Elliot, by the *Avon* (they are all respectable persons), desiring they will collect me the curiosities of the island.

"*Friday, 22nd.*—At sunrise the clouds bore a fine pinky tinge, and I thought before I was up there would have been a fine scenery. Mr. Crafter called and told me a sloop had arrived from Quebec in twenty-one days, the quickest passage known. Was only sixteen days coming from land to land. Said they made the Scilly Islands, and came at the rate of nine miles per hour!

"*Saturday, 23rd.*—This day Mr. Peen found a peziza in perfection, south side of Gally Hill; but by Mr. Withering's vol. iv. p. 357, it is Nidularia campanulata! It is very curious.

"*Sunday, 24th.*—Read Mr. Fuzzell's tour through Kent, and found errors, having placed some verses which stood at the Hermitage, near Gad's Hill, to Swanscombe. Yet it contained some good criticisms and judicious remarks ; but it appeared written prior to the tour, or perhaps no tour at all.

" *Monday*, 25*th.*—Young Taylor, the butcher, who had his leg broken about three weeks since, has this day had it cut off by Mr. Park, brother to Mungo Park.

" *Tuesday*, 26*th.*—Young Barnard brought me yesterday to see a coleoptera insect, which had eaten through a roll of (twenty-two yards) sarcenet and penetrated into the wood ! I remember going on board an East India ship, Captain Birch, about five years ago, and he showed an insect which had turned into an aurelia, taken out of the mast of a ship ! This Captain Birch had a brother an engineer at Gravesend.

" This day a gravestone, weighing 6 or 700 hundred-weight was found in the old churchyard field (described in the ' History of Gravesend,' page 61), with two others of a square form. All of them were Bethersden marble, and of high antiquity ; for of such stones we find the columns of our ancient ecclesiastical buildings made, being a turbinated greyish stone, composed of small shells, capable of taking a good polish. The heaviest stone, being six feet three inches, was evidently placed there for an ecclesiastic, as on it there was the sign of a cross, and made not exactly square, but narrower at one end and grooved with two deep concaves at the edges. I think it was placed there prior to 1587 as conjectured in ' History of Gravesend,' p. 66.

" *Wednesday*, 27*th.*—This morning, about three o'clock, a fire broke out at Mr. Murrell's, Perry Street, in the nursery, which it destroyed ; but the children of Mr. Robinson, a clerk in the Tower, escaped with difficulty by the activity and perseverance of a person at the hazard of his life. The market-bell was rung and the town alarmed, when two engines were sent over, but the fire was extinguished without them.

" *Thursday,* 28*th.*—Men digging to trace the ruins of the old Gravesend Church.

" *Friday,* 29*th.*—Miss Tucker and Miss Rashleigh called and brought some shells and fossils. Miss Tucker is a botanist, and informed me the spiral orchis grows about Wingham. (*Mem.* There never has been a spiral orchis in Scotland yet : 1822.)

" *Monday, December* 2*nd.*—Walked to old churchyard [St. Mary's, Gravesend], and brought away paving tiles with greenish glaze upon them on one side. They carried somewhat the appearance of Roman bricks or tiles, but were not so long and broad, nor thick, so we may date them of the date of the church.

" *Tuesday,* 3*rd.*—Preparing chalk fossils for London.

" *Wednesday,* 4*th.*—Bought two whiting pouts with flat-fish.

" *Thursday,* 5*th.*—Sat up last night and counted Gravesend clock striking twelve, and from five to ten minutes after I heard some distant clock strike, which surprised me, as I have read that the church of St. Paul's, London, was once heard about the same distance, viz., twenty-two miles. How was the wind last night ? Sent yesterday evening a box of fossils to go by Newman's coach to Miss L.

" *Friday,* 6*th.*—The Berwick ship sailed for Van Diemen's Land. To-day made many small boxes to pack fossils in.

" *Saturday,* 7*th.*—Frances Pocock came to see me,

and in the evening repeated a poem from a newspaper about the mermaid to be seen in London, which was very witty and laughable. Heard the *Thames*, East Indiaman, was lost a second time, at which I am very sorry, as it belongs to my friend Mr. Blanchard.

"*Sunday*, 8*th.*—Mr. Povey of Northfleet brought me a golden-crested wren, knocked down in North-fleet. I never recollect seeing one before, and it must be a scarce bird, although I have heard they are about Farningham.

"*Monday*, 9*th.*—Mr. Moore, a clerk lately in the Bank of England, brought me (he said) a great curiosity, which he said was a calf's head, or dog's head, petrified, which he got from Greta Bridge, in Yorkshire; and he set a good value on it, saying if I could dispose of it I might have half. But on my examining it, I knew what it was, and told him he had better not know what it was as it would lessen its value; yet if he would read Van Helmont's works, a Dutch physician, they would tell him! This Mr. Moore is related to the Rev. Mr. Moore, of Kendall, an antiquary: I believe it is his uncle. I had to-day two left-handed whelks brought me, taken at Whitstable, for which I gave sixpence each, being very rare shells.

"*Tuesday*, 10*th.*—Fine sun. Received a letter from Miss Lousada, thanking me for a box of fossils, and saying they were the best she ever saw (except Mr. Mantell's, of Lewes, in Sussex). Mr. Bullock's daughter married.

"*Thursday*, 12*th.*—White frost first observed this year. Frances Pocock returns to Kingsdown by way of Maidstone. Sent by her Mrs. Mark Noble's tin botanical box. Wrote to Miss Lousada for her kind offer, and expressing thanks. Young Taylor died at the work-house after losing his leg, although Mr. Park was the surgeon.

"*Friday*, 13*th.*—Mr. Amherst buried at Milton. Last night, one Barnet, a biscuit-baker, died. Received present from Miss Lousada.

"*Saturday*, 14*th.*—Paid Mr. Salcote 2*s.* for two sheets of paper written out, which he thought reasonable, and which I thought was too dear ; yet to him it was a charity. This afternoon I was called on a jury at the Town Hall, and appointed foreman thereof, to inquire about the death of a young man, George Polley, who fell from the masthead of a ship, bound to the West Indies, and was killed, his brain being injured and his skull dreadfully broken. Mr. Park, the surgeon, attended at the Custom House Tavern, where the body lay; and the jury brought in accidental death. The young man was taken to London by his father, who came down on this sad accident. Golden wren shot.

"*Sunday*, 15*th.*—Received letter from Shadrach Pocock, Ketley Bank, Salop, saying beef was 1½*d.* to 2*d.* per lb. ; mutton, 2½*d.* to 4*d.* ; flour, 7*s.* per bushel ; eggs, eight a groat ; fowls, 2*s.* per couple ; and that the weather was so mild that wallflowers, cloves, stocks, carnations, and primroses were in bloom !

"*Monday*, 16*th.*—Miss Man's sale. She was called an old maid ; but she said, ' It is not my fault, no person has asked me to marry.' This she said in my presence (R. Pocock, Gravesend). At this sale a sword was sold for 6*s.* which belonged to Mr. Israel Harrison, storekeeper at the blockhouse, who said it was given to him by the Duke of Marlborough when

M

fighting by his side! Bought by Mr. Crafter, and sold to Mr. Brett for 14*s.*

" *Tuesday, 17th.*—General cloud. Sent a letter to Mr. S. Pocock, in answer to his of the 8th inst. Young Taylor (butcher) buried in the Princess Street Chapel ground, attended by the Comical Fellows' Society. Sent a letter to Mr. Lakes of Clare Hall, Cambridge.

" *Wednesday, 18th.*—Settled with Glover for all cesses due to this day. A blind worm brought alive.

" *Thursday, 19th.*—Professor Henslow from Cambridge called and left me some dried plants.

" *Saturday, 21st.*—Alarmed this morning about four with the market-bell ringing for a fire at the Prince Regent Public-house, Town Quay. Soon extinguished. In evening Mr. Crafter brought a golden plover, shot at Tilbury Fort. There were forty or fifty in a flock which, alighting on the ground, all separated, so that two could not be shot together. This bird does not seem to be so well described as it ought.

" *Sunday, 22nd.*—Sent a letter to Miss Lousada with thanks for former favours, and sent her six fossils.

" *Monday, 23rd.*—Had brought me by Neil, waterman, the smallest tern, which weighed three ounces (*Sterna minuta*), shot at Gravesend.

" *Tuesday, 24th.*—Sent my tern and a golden plover to Mr. Ryall's to stuff. Decided a wager by Walker's Gazette, and found it wrong, by stating that Sunderland was only 204 miles instead of above 290!

" *Wednesday, 25th.*—Mr. Jerry C— died. This man was on board the *Preston,* man-of-war, when the English fleet fought the Dutch. He had been a Gravesend waterman, and once kept the Dundee Tap in Wapping. He was noted as a reprobate character, viz., a swearing, dissolute person; but for two or three years previous to this had turned an enthusiastic follower of the Methodists or Dissenters. Wild fowl about.

" *Thursday, 26th.*—Paid Mr. Harris, executor to Mr. Amherst, a quarter's rent to Michaelmas, 1822. Had a bat with long ears brought me alive. It flew into the linendraper's shop.

" *Friday, 27th.*—Miss Beechy buried. Had two long-tailed titmice brought me. Employed looking over my plants, and selected out thirty-one to give Professor Henslow of Cambridge, because he gave me sixteen which he had selected for me.

" *Saturday, 28th.*—The Rev. Mr. Durham, full of Greek and Latin questions, visited and puzzled me, by asking me who the father of Joshua was; when he said the answer was *Nun*.

" *Sunday, 29th.*—No gossipers to-day !

" *Monday, 30th.*—Mr. Lakes, a student from Cambridge, called and bought some butterflies.

" *Tuesday, 31st.*—River at London frozen. In afternoon the first snow."

So closes the Journal for 1822, from which, amidst its varied information, the reader has gathered (pp. 87, 148, 149) evidences that Pocock's versatility was equal to combining the business of paperhanging and the profession of correspondence-writing with his other manifold occupations, and these we know included the arts of bookbinding and type-founder !

## CHAPTER VI.

I saw from the beach, when the morning was shining,
  A bark o'er the waters move gloriously on :
I came, when the sun o'er that beach was declining,
  The bark was still there, but the waters were gone.

Ah ! such is the fate of our life's early promise,
  So passing the spring-tide of joy we have known :
Each wave that we danced on at morning ebbs from us,
  And leaves us, at eve, on the black shore alone.

THOMAS MOORE.

THERE is yet another year's diurnal extant, the
final, and the most complete portion which has
come down to us; and in perusing it for the period
it covers, viz., the whole of 1823, it will be obvious
that some entries have been retained less on account of
their general than their local interest, and for the purpose of more fully exhibiting the author in his daily life,
views, and sentiments,—his business and his pleasures.

It is scarcely probable that journals of such fulness
as those for the years 1822 and 1823 would not have
been preceded, and, for a time at all events, followed
by compilations of the same method; but these which
are now published are all that have been discovered,
and all that are supposed to exist.  They have been

given more fully, as they constitute at this distance of time one of the best means of estimating the man, and this the more as it may be most truly said of those who laid him to rest as well as of those who followed after,—

> We carved not a line and we raised not a stone,
> But we left him . . . alone—

The entries in the Journal for 1823, amidst the desirable information which they confer, serve a less pleasing office, since they reveal that having sold his patrimonial house and shop he dispenses with a composing-room in order to save some 3*l.* yearly rent, reduces his printer's wages, disposes of surplus furniture, and unsuccessfully appeals for time to the tax-gatherer : all ominous of the future troubles which, already impending, began, like other " coming events," to "cast their shadows before."

### JOURNAL FOR 1823.

" *Thursday, January 2nd,* 1823.—Professor Henslow of Cambridge called, when I gave him about thirty plants in exchange for his. Heard that Mr. Bedingfield, the lawyer, was dead, and that another lawyer had run away !

"*Friday, 3rd.*—Bills stuck about for the sale of Town Clerk Mr. John Mills Evans' goods ! Mr. Evans not seen lately. Heard another young lawyer was not of the best principle. Had Mrs. Thorpe's son from North-fleet to work this day.

" *Monday, 6th.*—Rev. Mr. Durham called and informed me that Nicholas Gillbee, Esq., late of Denton, was dead. So he died a poor gentleman, from being among the first men of credit in the county, leaving by his second wife an infant child. Mr. Gillbee was once an officer belonging to the West Kent Militia, and his father was a man of considerable property; but it is very remarkable that all his relations, both male and female, have, within a few years, been insolvent.

" *Tuesday, 7th.*—William Brean, a printer (from Dublin), came to work at 3s. 6d. per day, giving me the secret how to make composition balls, viz., 1 lb. of treacle, ½ lb. of best clear glue, ½ oz. of bee's-wax, ½ oz. of Burgundy pitch, and a tablespoonful of Venice turpentine, with sometimes a small quantity of oil. I afterwards made a new ball of this composition.

" *Wednesday, 8th.*—In afternoon two gentlemen waited on me; one, Mr. Dunbar, said he was a relation to the Gordon family of Boley Hill, through his marriage, and entitled to landed property in the vicinity of Shorne, which had been in Chancery eight years. The other mentioned his name (Rev. Mr. Radford), and said he was very partial to history and topography. Both promised to call again; and Mr. Dunbar said he would lend me any peerages or baronetages I may want. Had a sparrow hawk brought me.

" *Friday, 10th.*—Walked to Northfleet; met with a Mr. Russel from Rolvenden, who said the church floor of Rolvenden was often covered with water, and was so when the Rev. Mr. Durham preached to a large congregation; and that a relation of his came twenty-two miles to hear him; and that Russel's brother, now at Greenhithe, had some old pieces of silver found in Hastings, when a bushel was found and kept by Sir Godfrey Webster. At night Captain George Phelan of the 92nd Regiment, lying in Jamaica, called in, and bought some paper previously to his going out in the ship, Captain Popplewell. He promises to collect curiosities for me.

"*Saturday,* 11*th.*—Two brent geese brought me, shot in Burnham River, Essex. They cost 2*s.* 6*d.* the couple. Length two feet, breadth three feet six inches. Sally's sweetheart, James T., with all his religion, very drunk!

"*Sunday,* 12*th.*—Sally's sweetheart called to make an apology. I heard he was drunk at the meeting! So much for his religion! Four wild swans seen.

"*Monday,* 13*th.*—Heard that Mr. Parker had been brought down from London and buried at Milton. This man kept the Prince Regent, and before it the New Tavern, which his father had kept.

"*Tuesday,* 14*th.*—Had a beautiful duck brought me, shot at Lower Shorne : it was called a *Merganser,* otherwise in the books a sheldrake ; weighed 2¼ lbs., length 2 feet, width 2½ feet. It breeds in Sheppy Island. In the year 1820 this day was the coldest.

"*Wednesday,* 15*th.*—Mr. Evans' sale began, where I bought a mattress for 10*s.*, and ten cloths for 2*s.* 6*d.*

"*Friday,* 17*th.*—Mr. Evans' sale continued and ended. His whole effects raised above 704*l.*, which was more than supposed by 200*l.*

"*Saturday,* 18*th.*—Snow on the ground. Fetched my lots away from Mr. Evans' sale to the amount of 4*l.* 7*s.* 6*d.*, and among them found one printed by Franklin, at Philadelphia, 1744. The 'Encyclopædia Britannica' of Edinburgh, in twenty volumes, fetched 17*l.* 17*s.* from Mr. Barber, Gravesend. Hasted's twelve vols. 8vo, with Views in Kent, the folio plates, 8*l.* 2*s.*, purchased (I believe) by Mr. Harvey, calico printer, Crayford; and all other books were equally high, especially law.

"*Tuesday,* 21*st.*—Not so cold as yesterday. Last night sent a letter to Mr. George Pocock at Oxford, and one to Mr. Spencer, Chatham, telling him all Mr. Bell's effects (the barrister) were to be sold, and now lying about his house in confusion. So Mr. Crafter heard at Mr. Evans' sale. Received a letter from Frances Pocock, saying she met a friendly reception at the Rev. Mark Noble's, where she was introduced to the company of Colonel Sims, Mr. Dominicus (a gentleman fond of flowers), Miss Noble, Mrs. Noble, and Mrs. Cresswell (her daughter); and that Mr. Woodward of Kingsdown wishes much for me to come, as he says he will introduce me to a lady of great antiquity and pleasant *singularity!*

"*Wednesday,* 22*nd.*—A meeting in the hall, when a subscription was raised for relief of the poor; at which Lord Darnley gave 20*l.*, Dr. Crawford, 10*l.*, Messrs. Brenchley and Son, 10*l.*, Mr. Dennett, 5*l.*, Mr. Wade, 5*l.*, and others, to the amount of 114*l.* 15*s.*; and Mr. John Hooker, baker, in lieu of subscription, gave forty quartern loaves, and Mr. William Turner forty pounds of meat.

"*Thursday,* 23*rd.*—The ships and vessels running on shore to avoid the ice. Many birds have died from the frost, particularly bullfinches. A vestry held at Milton Church to choose a vestry clerk. Candidates, Cruden, with Southgate and Pearson, attorneys.

"*Friday,* 24*th.*—Printing club articles for Green Street Green, three and half sheets. Seventeen wild swans flew (over the town) up the river yesterday.

"*Saturday*, 25*th*.—The frost has now lasted from the 9th instant, and is very severe.

"*Sunday*, 26*th*.—River filled with ice right across to Tilbury.

"*Tuesday*, 28*th*.—Had two scarce birds brought me, called bramblings, shot at Cliffe, about the size of chaffinches. A few visit Kent yearly, from the eighteenth to the end of the month.

"*Wednesday*, 29*th*.—Earl Darnley's troop dine at Gravesend. Received 1 lb. of printer's ink (two shillings) from Pewtress and Co.

"*Thursday*, 30*th*.—Received a hare from Frances, and a napoleon. Had a bald-coot given me by Mr. Hawkins. Coals are one shilling and sixpence per bushel, they having risen six shillings per chaldron since the frost! Had in half a chaldron from Tomlin's.

"*Saturday, February* 1*st*.—Read in the paper that a snow bunting had been shot this last week in Sussex.

"*Tuesday*, 4*th*.—Bright sun, which is a glorious sight after such severe weather. Walked to Southfleet and Green Street Green to take home one hundred club articles, 3*l*. 14*s*., which were paid for. Heard that two uncommon birds were shot at Southfleet, about three weeks since, with strong beaks; one the Rev. Mr. Rashleigh had, the other Mr. Garland had. I suspect them to be bramblings. Bullfinches are plenty in orchards, the old birds having the finest colours.

"*Wednesday*, 5*th*.—Heard a wild swan was shot, and that Mr. Hugget had bought it for ten shillings. A merganser or sheldrake shot by Mr. Gladdish.

"*Thursday*, 6*th*.—Miss Fuller called and had some books. Mr. Simmons the stationer's rider called, and

I paid him the balance of a note given, which he returned. Heard that a wild swan was worth twelve shillings at a furrier's for skin only, but the body is not very salable in Leadenhall Market.

"*Friday, 7th.*—Rain. Sally went to Skib's Cottage to work; and I went to Greenhithe, when Mr. Forrest paid through Mr. Watson. Heard that my baskets with fish had lain three days at Gravel Hill—most likely spoiled.

"*Saturday, 8th.*—Received an 'Oxford Guide' from George P., who said nine compositors had been discharged from the Clarendon Press, and that no works were of value, except Aldus, Wasse, Wesselingius, Ricobius, or others of great repute, and that the writing on the long leaves which I gave him was Malabar! He appears depressed in spirits. My man, the printer, is employed in printing papers for the Rev. Mr. Woolmough, a dissenting minister, in order to form a society for visiting sick members and praying to them.

"*Sunday, 9th.*—My journeyman printer went from me this day, having been employed since the 7th of January last, at three shillings and sixpence per day, whereby he has got a new suit of clothes, of which he is deserving, as I found him very steady.

"*Monday, 10th.*—Went to Mr. Trezise, Commercial Tavern, and offered him a bedstead and furniture for 7*l.* 17*s.* 6*d.*, which twelve months ago cost 11*l.* 11*s.*

"*Tuesday, 11th.*—Mr. Thorowgood the letter-founder's rider called, and I paid him for what I had had since last journey.

"*Wednesday, 12th.*—Agreed with Mrs. Teasdale for sale of a spinet for two guineas; one of which she is to pay down to-morrow on delivery, the other at the return of Mr. Teasdale from his voyage (on the cod-fishery) in about three weeks.

"*Thursday,* 13*th.*—The Rev. Mark Noble, Mrs. Cresswell, her daughter, and Miss Noble paid me a visit, when I gave Mrs. Cresswell a reversed whelk from Whitstable, which is a great rarity, and a Bernard crab, and an Helix pomatia (found in Sir John Dyke's park on May 1st, about five years ago). Mr. Noble bought Fussel's 'Journey into Kent,' octavo, and a 'Biographical Peerage.'

"*Friday,* 14*th.*—Valentine's Day. Two gentlemen (unknown) called on me to buy a 'History of Graves-end' (but they did not), when they said that a Mr Illingworth of the Record Office, Tower, would give any information in that office on liberal terms.

"*Monday,* 17*th.*—Sold Mr. R—, assistant at Mr. Beaumont's, surgeon, Homer's 'Odyssey' and 'Iliad.'

"*Tuesday,* 18*th.*—Employed in "composing" an account (additional), of the subscribers for the relief of the poor of Gravesend, when this second amount was 52*l.* 2*s.* 4*d.*, making with the first amount a total of 166*l.* 17*s.* 4*d.* distributed in and among the towns-folks, &c.: thus there were relieved 680 families, and 2330 persons in the greatest distress, by 2741 quartern loaves of the best wheaten bread, 1313 pounds of meat, and 24½ chaldrons of coals! I cannot close this paragraph without mentioning the name of Mr. James Wade (of Ash), who gave liberally five pounds; and at every such subscription he gives handsomely, not for-getting his native town of Gravesend, where his father was Mayor.

"*Wednesday,* 19*th.*—A gentleman in the shop whose features so resemble Mr. Blanchard (part owner of the *Thames*) as to induce me to think he is his brother.

" *Thursday, 20th.*—Worked off the committee's job about the poor. Heard Miss Walsh was married to a Mr. White of the East India House.

" *Friday, 21st.*—My birthday, having completed the sixty-third year of my age, being born February 21st, 1760, and, thank God, retaining my general good health, and having outlived most of my enemies, and seen them fall.

" *Saturday, 22nd.*—A lady called—Mrs. Browne, No. 41, Edgeware Road, Paddington—and bought two conch shells for four shillings.

" *Sunday, 23rd.*—Perused Mr. Charles Clarke's quarto pamphlet on ' Ancient Seats, Sinks, and Remarks on Chalk Church, Kent; ' but found he had not been quite correct with the inscription on one of the bells in Chalk Church, by mistaking a letter, and giving in Roman capitals what ought to have been in old black capitals.

" *Monday, 24th.*—Heard that a young man was drowned from a fishing-smack belonging to Mr. Fletcher on the Terrace.

" *Tuesday, 25th.*—This day Mr. Dill, surgeon of H. C. S. *Atlas,* out-bound, called and said he would bring me home a bird's nest from China, made by a species of swallow from the foam of the sea, so said, and used in China as a favourite dish or soup.   He also said if I would call at his house, No. 37, Devonshire Street, Queen Square, London, I might have a bird's-nest in the form of a bundle of hay, and if not at No. 37, then try No. 43 in the same street.

" Mr. Peen called, and found the ship Charles Pocock

'(my son) went out in was the *Sultan,* Captain Christopher Yeoman, bound for Smyrna, which sailed from Gravesend on the 3rd of October, 1822.

" *Thursday, 27th.*—A person called on me with beads to sell, and said he was in the employ of Mr. Mawe the mineralogist, and that Mr. Mawe was in London when it was thought he was in the Brazils! This person seems to understand minerals, &c., and takes, he says, great delight in music as a composer. The *Kellie Castle,* East Indiaman, sails from Gravesend.

" *Friday, 28th.*—Had a dog sent from Mrs. Taylor of Higham Hall, to get stuffed, because it was a favourite dog, which will cost above a guinea. The son is a miller, and has Gravesend Mill on a lease. Sent the dog by Newman's coach.

" *Thursday, March 6th.*—" Composing " a card for Mr. Ashdown's niece, Dartford. Mr. Ashdown lives on Bexley Heath, and is a good bird-stuffer. Election in church between Glover and Gladwell, for assistant overseer.

" *Friday, 7th.*—In the evening two gentlemen called. One was P. C. Banks, Esq., of the Honourable Society of the Inner Temple, author of the ' Dormant and Extinct Baronage of England,' ' Honores Anglicani,' &c., whom I found a very intelligent, pleasant person, being about to publish in two volumes octavo, boards, price twenty-eight shillings, ' Regalia Curialia ; or, An Historical Account of all the Grand Solemnities and Public Ceremonies ; as also of all the high offices, hereditary or temporary, appertaining to the Royal Court and Crown of Great Britain : the whole replete with a variety of novel, curious, and interesting Remarks, Notes, Annotations, &c.' The other gentleman,

I think, must be a German or Danish quaker, and dumb, as he never spoke a word, sat with his hat on, and spat on the carpet !

"*Saturday, 8th.*—Paid T. Harris my rent to Christmas last, when he talked about taking away the large composing-room. Bought new gridiron of a poor man for 1s. 2d., from Deptford.

"Composed a bill, to print 500 copies, that a sermon will be preached in the Parish Church of Gravesend, on Sunday, March 16th, 1823, in aid of the funds of the Incorporated Society for the Propagation of the Gospel in Foreign Parts, by the Rev. Samuel Watson, D.D., Rector. Prayers will begin at eleven o'clock. Yesterday, came into the shop a woman who lives at the Dover Castle, about three miles from Gravesend, who said her mother was alive at Ash, and 108 years old! having been born in 1713 at Bexley parish, and for some time worked for Lady Fermanagh at May Place, near Crayford; that she had been married three times, and that her maiden name was West, and she would die a West (her first husband was Vaughan, second Woodman, and third West); that her appetite at present was very good, and she could walk well (which I know she did, two or three years ago, coming from the Dover Castle to Gravesend); but now her eyes begin to fail, and she is getting blind, but she did not want for plenty of victuals, as Mr. James Wade, of Ash (well known for his repeated charity to the Gravesend poor people, where he was born), assisted her.

"Printed off the 500 bills announcing Dr. Watson's sermon for next Sunday, as said yesterday. Heard Mrs. Evans was dead. She was the mother of the town clerk, and her maiden name was Mills.

" *Tuesday*, 11*th*.—A man playing or chiming on the bells of Gravesend Church many very pleasant tunes, as ' Oh, dear, what can the matter be ? ' &c., &c. The mode he took was to tie tight all the bell-ropes near him in a circle, and pushing from him the ropes very quickly, made the bells strike.

" *Wednesday*, 12*th*.—At night Mr. Crafter brought a foreign round fruit, as big as a man's head, full of prickles; and it resembled a hedgehog rolled up, so exactly that I was some time (at first) before I thought otherwise. On looking for its name in my botanical books, I could not find it out exactly, but I believe it ranks as a cactus.

" *Friday*, 14*th*.—Heard that a great fire had been at Canton, and all the tea burnt. Mr. Crafter brought an old almanack, made by twelve pieces of wood, cut out in Runic characters.

" *Monday*, 17*th*.—Heard few persons gave anything at Dr. Watson's sermon yesterday.

" *Tuesday*, 18*th*.—Brenand, my late journeyman compositor, returns from a journey through Kent, and I set him to work this morning.

" *Wednesday*, 19*th*.—Printed this morning twenty-five posting bills ' for petty officers, carpenters, sail-makers, and able seamen to enter on board the *Albion*, Captain Sir William Hoste, Bart., K.C.B., now lying at Portsmouth.' He is brother to Sir George Hoste, chief engineer at Gravesend, Tilbury, and Purfleet.

" *Saturday*, 22*nd*.—William Brenand, my journeyman printer, left me for London. The assizes ended.

" *Monday*, 24*th*.—Cleared out of the composing-room, in order to have my rent lowered three pounds per year, from twenty-five pounds per year.

" *Tuesday*, 25*th*.—Employed in placing my printing types and frames in the upper room.

" *Thursday*, 27*th*. — Settled with Mr. Glover, the assistant overseer, by his paying me twelve shillings and sixpence balance—my bill being 2*l*. 14*s*. 6*d*., and his cesses, one church and two poor, 2*l*. 2*s*.—when he told me they got about ten pounds for Dr. Watson's sermon last Sunday. Mr. Pewtress, stationer, called.

" *Good Friday*, 28*th*.—Hawkins, the waterman, with a gentleman, called to see my collection of curiosities.

" *Saturday*, 29*th*.—The new butchers' shambles occupied by the butchers the first time.

" *Easter Sunday*, 30*th*.—Walked up Northfleet Cliffs and saw the first white cabbage butterfly, as well as a yellow with red spots, and a small tortoise-shell. The common bee on the bloom of coltsfoot, which this day first expanded. Got two orchis roots. This may be said to be the first fine day towards summer.

" *Monday*, 31*st*.—Mr. Crafter brought me yesterday a small brass counter of Queen Anne's, with her head well raised, and the words 'Anna Dei Grat.' On the reverse was the queen standing, and with her right hand pushing back the arm of a seeming courtier, who is seen kneeling, with his left hand touching the queen's knee, and holding his hat in his right hand. He has a long beard, and his dress reaches nearly to his feet, like a woman's gown, and at the bottom are the words, 'All for love.' Now I cannot recollect any part of the English history that alludes to or mentions any lover Queen Anne had, except her husband, the Prince of Denmark.

"*Tuesday, April 1st.*—Busy in "composing" Mr. Penman's card for his fishmonger's shop near the market; and also Mr. Crafter's card for his new cookshop near the Fountain.

"*Wednesday, 2nd.*—Went to Wilmington, and got five or six roots of the lizard orchis, all of which must have grown in the two last years, as when I was there in 1821, in March, only one root was left. (*Mem.* I killed a viper there; which I have done every time I have been there; although to-day it was so cold.) Came home in a caravan with a young man, about twenty-seven or twenty-eight, of the name of Hunt, of Borden, a farmer.

"*Thursday, 3rd.*—In my walk yesterday I saw in bloom besides primroses, violets (white and blue), veronica ivy-leaf, alder, hazel, and a garden flower in full bloom (white), I believe an arabis; but the season on the whole is very backward, there being no blackthorn in bloom. The common willow was in bloom, but not the elm.

"*Friday, 4th.*—Read the 'History of Glasgow,' an octavo, and found in it that St. Mungo and St. Kentigern were one and the same person! I found also that Oliver Cromwell, and several other gentlemen therein named, readily signed their names towards the relief of the inhabitants of Glasgow, who had suffered much by a dreadful fire which happened there a short time before, viz., on June 17, 1652. This document, as it appears in the appendix, p. 317, of the 'History of Glasgow,' proves that Oliver Cromwell was possessed of some charity and well disposed. And I have somewhere else read that when the Bible (I believe the polyglot) was printed, the paper

N

being had from abroad, Oliver permitted it to be imported *free of duty*, which may be called a good trait in his character ! Wm. Brenand, the printer, returned.

"*Saturday, 5th.*—Went to Northfleet, to Mr. Locket's, when Mr. Higgins paid me 12*s.* for printing 200 bills for contracts. Got some Orchis anthropophora (?), and observed many blackish efts busy in the water, which water I have observed rises in the spring-time higher in those chalk pits and more full than at other times ; nor can I conjecture from whence those black efts originate, for they are not found in the autumn. Much rain in evening. The *Duke of York* ship came up from the East Indies.

"*Monday, 7th.*—At night I settled with William Brenand by paying him 2*s.* 4*d.*, which made up his wages of Saturday and to-day, and he is to stop with me at 3*s.* per day, until I get something that will pay well. Miss Cooke, the blacksmith's daughter, married, and also some others, at Gravesend Church.

"*Tuesday, 8th.*—Not a pleasant day yet; except Easter Day. My man William began setting my Chronology in brevier. William had a shilling.

"*Wednesday, 9th.*—Paid Wm. at noon 6*d.* Walked with Mr. Peen and put out four lizard orchis. The first two at or near two holly-trees, about fifty yards to the south of the turnpike road, in the hedge leading to West Wood; and the other two in the same hedge, a quarter of a mile up, where the militaris orchis grows about. Mr. Crafter gave him a shilling at night.

"*Friday, 11th.*—Walked to Dartford, when Mr. T. Brewer paid me in full, 14*s.* and 7*s.* 6*d.*, and saw Mr.

Ashdown of the Calico Print Grounds, who says any Saturday noon he is at leisure, and will go down the marshes to botanize. In my journey I met many coaches loaded with persons going down to the ship launch at Chatham to-morrow, of the *Prince Regent* a beautiful first-rate with a round stern, being the first on that principle. Gave William 2*s.* 6*d.* out of Mr. Crafter's money. Paid Niel, the waterman, a shilling for putting on board the *Comet*, bound for Leith, half a firkin of plants for Mr. Patrick Niell, printer, of No. 10, Old Fish Market, Edinburgh. Sent by post a letter to Mr. Niell, saying the plants were forwarded; and in the firkin was a list of what rare plants I wanted.

" *Saturday,* 12*th.*—The ship launch at Chatham of the *Prince Regent*—the largest ship, I believe, yet made with a round stern. Heard a person by accident was there killed. Paid William, my man, 9*s.* at night on his leaving me. Frances Pocock came.

" *Sunday,* 13*th.*—Frances returns. Put out two lizard orchis in the Claphall Road; one stout enough to blow this year, and the other with only one leaf, as if only one year old; so that I suppose it will not blow till 1825 (*watch it!*). Heard first nightingale.

" *Monday,* 14*th.*—Went by boat to London. Waited on Mr. Simmonds, and gave him a new bill; but the old bill was not returned. Waited on Mr. Pewtress, my stationer.

" *Tuesday,* 15*th.*—Went to Paddington, and much pleased with two new churches I saw on the road. I believe one was Marylebone, and the other St. Pancras. Slept in Bedfordbury.

" *Wednesday,* 16*th.*—Wet, uncomfortable. Sold old

type to Caslons, of Chiswell Street; but did not like their price or behaviour. Found all the founders in one mind, as if in combination. Mr. Figgins said printing was only six months old! Bought the 'History of Rochester,' and some other books. Came home.

"*Friday*, 18*th*.—Miss Brenchley married last Monday or Tuesday to Dr Day of Maidstone.

"*Saturday*, 19*th*.—Season very backward. Mr. Brown called and paid 10*s*., being the balance for his cards.

"*Sunday*, 20*th*.—The 5*l*. lottery club which I belong to, by my number eleven, viz., the eleventh week from the beginning, is to be found by my day-book when I am to receive it from Mrs. Jones.

"*Wednesday*, 23*rd*.—Walked to the boundary-stone in Shinglewell Lane, marked MP, for Milton Parish (although placed on the Gravesend side, viz., west side of the road); and there I planted (about nine feet from the said post marked MP), on the west side of the hedge, a lizard orchis to remain as a breeder, which root I had brought from near Roe Hill in Wilmington. Those roots are very scarce, and I want to propagate them.

"*Thursday*, 24*th*.—Matthew Buckinger (grandson of Matthew Buckinger *born without hands or feet*), having been to Mr. Southgate, the attorney, to relate his claim to two estates, one the house wherein Pierce, the coppersmith at Dartford, lives, and the other the Arnolds' estate at Gravesend, returned back to Dartford.

"*Friday*, 25*th*.—Heard it was the *Hebe*, brig, bound to Antwerp with shot and shell, which had foundered off Margate, about November last, with Bentley, the pilot, on board.

"*Saturday, 26th.*—Mr. Crafter opens his cook-shop.

" *Sunday, 27th.*—Began my MS. book, 'Errata in Past; or, Mistakes of Authors,' observed by myself in the perusal of books; noticing my own 'History of Gravesend' first. In the evening visited Mr. Crafter to see his new toy and cook-shop at New Tavern, which I prognosticate will not answer, but get him in debt.

"*Monday, 28th.*—Appears the first fine day this year. Old Mr. Spencer from Chatham called, and I gave him a direction to Mr. Manning, to inquire for his son (I believe a special pleader) who is very fond of heraldry, and who has made a search after the family of Selby of Bucks, of which family young Mr. Spencer thinks he is heir !

" *Wednesday, 30th.*—Bought four pink conchs for 5s. of Ogleby.

" *Thursday, May 1st.*—Elm-tree just in green, but leaves not expanded. Heard that Mr. Miller, living at Bristol, near the river, was a collector of shells.

"*Friday, 2nd.*—A gentleman called (I believe a clergyman), who said Mr. Streatfield (I believe the late high sheriff) is making a collection for the 'History of Kent,' by illustrating Hasted with portraits, MSS., &c. The gentleman is fond of fossils, minerals, &c.

" *Saturday, 3rd.*—Received a letter from the Rev. Mark Noble of Barming, with an enlarged pedigree and notes of the Robinson families, now of Denston Hall, Suffolk, and formerly of Gravesend, Kent. Also a letter from Mrs. Noble to thank me for some orchis I sent her, among which was a lizard orchis now rare in Great Britain.

"·*Sunday, 4th.*—Had a sad cold and inflammation

at the nose, with every sign that I should be ill. Stayed within doors, and read over two or three times the letter and communications of the Rev. Mark Noble on the Robinson families, which have taken several branches; and his research for names has been most laborious. He is a valuable friend, and has kindly promised me his assistance in any of my literary pursuits. Mrs. Sarah Noble, his wife, is fond of gardening and botany. So is a daughter of theirs, settled in Staffordshire, a complete botanist. Another daughter is a Mrs. Cresswell, a widow with two children. Colonel Sims's wife, and a daughter unmarried.

"*Monday, 5th.*—A gentleman from near Tunbridge called, and bought a chalk fossil, and confirmed that Mr. Streatfield, near Bromley, was collecting and making illustrations for Hasted's Kent, as before mentioned.

"*Tuesday, 6th.*—Received a letter from C. Clarke, F.S.A., saying he had made a collection of MSS., for my 'History of Gravesend,' and requesting me to come to town for them on Thursday next, to Nassau Street, Oxford Road. He said the *Cottonian MSS.* contained nothing about Gravesend. Mr. Dunbar of the Middle Temple called, and promised books. Wrote letter to the Rev. Mr. Noble, Barming, to thank him for his pedigree of the Robinsons, and to Mr. C. Clarke, F.S.A., saying I would meet him in London on Thursday. Mr. Crafter called and said a serious charge had been made against him (by Wm. Webster) to Major Kelly; all of which appears to arise from malice by Mr. Webster, a shopkeeper, because Mr. Crafter has set up a shop next door to him. I have always found Mr. Crafter ready to do good.

"*Wednesday, 7th.*—Mr. Crafter called, and said Mr.

Webster had delivered to Sir George Hoste, the engineer, a written charge against him; when I told him not an instant should be lost in trying to make friends and stopping such a serious accusation, and I was willing, if any good could be done, to act as a mediator and to go directly to Mr. Webster; which I did, but Mr. Webster said it was too late, as the proceedings were before the Board. I did all I could on this occasion, staying with him till past twelve o'clock p.m.

"*Thursday, 8th.*—Overslept myself by staying out later than usual last night, and so lost the boat. Got on board the *Sally*, an oyster-vessel, from Queenborough, employed with three others in bringing upon an average about 300 bushels from that place, the grounds of which extend from near Sheerness to King's Ferry. Oysters they said were four years coming to growth. The young are brought from the westward, as few of the natives live! Met Mr. Clarke, who gave me my books and MSS.—one of which related to Shorne—and also an accurate drawing of Gravesend Church, which I shall have engraved in my intended second edition. One of Mr. Clarke's sons is a good landscape painter, another a surgeon, who went a voyage in 1822 to Greenland, and another afflicted with St. Vitus' dance. Mr. Clarke has also two daughters.

"*Friday, 9th.*—Heard the *Thomas Coutts*, East Indiaman, had got aground coming up the river yesterday. Waited on Mr. Coreton and sold him an ancient gold coin, when he offered me good Roman copper at 3s. 6d. per pound! Visited Mr. Manning, of John Street, Adelphi,—Mrs. Saxter, a distant relation,—and Mrs. Cross of Exeter Change, who gave me some of

the best Scotch ale I ever tasted, and commissioned
me to buy (if possible) two New Zealand heads at
three guineas each, for Mr. Norman, for a museum in
Dublin, there being some about Gravesend! One
was lately sold in a sale for thirty shillings.

"*Saturday*, 10*th.*—Visited with Mr. George Manning the library of the Inner Temple (about ten
o'clock), which is the neatest, best, and most elegant
I ever saw. Made some extracts from Sir Henry
Chauncy's 'History of Hertfordshire'—a very scarce
work, and most valuable!—and from others. Stayed
two hours, but not a person came into the room, except
the under-librarian, and the librarian, who passed
through, saying, 'I hope you gentlemen have found
what you wanted.' Returned home by the boat from
Billingsgate, by John Creed, and found my cherry-
tree had been dug up and taken away.

"*Monday*, 12*th.*—Fireworks in evening in the field
opposite the Globe, or Ordnance Field. Mr. Crafter
called, and said on Thursday morning last he went
over to Major Kelly, and brought a note from him to
Colonel Sir G. Hoste, purporting that it was not the
wish of Major Kelly to proceed with any charge
against Mr. Crafter, and that Sir George Hoste had
returned to Webster his charge against him!

"*Tuesday*, 13*th.*—Windy. Waited on Viggers
about the taxes due, 34*s.*, who behaved very violently,
saying he would not give me any indulgence!—no,
not an hour! Walked over to Northfleet with
some parish receipts, but came away without the
money.

"*Wednesday*, 14*th.*—Sale at White Hart of the
property. Got some bills to print about young Francis

Jewiss, drowned yesterday off the town. May ready but not expanded in bloom. Young Jewiss found. Walked to Northfleet.

" *Thursday,* 15*th.*—Walked on the hill, and found on south-west side corn salad in bloom, with the small scorpion grass and serrated leaf veronica, in the road to the Blue House. The leaf resembles the Veronica chamedrys, but is not so large, and is in seed-pod this day, while the V. chamedrys has but just come in flower.

" *Friday,* 16*th.*—An East Indiaman (the *Clyde*) expected, wherein is the daughter of Dr. Scott, of Twickenham. This gentleman is a descendant of a Scott family of Kent, and also of Fair Rosamond. He has been high up in the interior of the East India territories—to Nepaul and Almorah—and has seen the long range of snowy mountains whose heights are much above the clouds. I first met him in Mr. Prall's shop, the chemist, where he related many anecdotes. One was of Admiral Pocock, whose son having married a Miss Long, was, at the dinner, handing her to the chair at the top of the table; but the old gentleman said ' Stay,' and seated himself in it to the great discomfort of the lady—who (Dr. Scott said) was much given to gaming; to the hurt of the family. I think he said she was a clergyman's daughter; but this does not agree with my pedigree, it being there as Miss Long, daughter of Edward Long, Esq., of Wimpole Street (?). Dr. Scott related many curious anecdotes whilst we were in the shop : one was that the late king going into a mill, and the miller opening a trap-door above him, got his clothes all over flour, which the miller perceiving came down and tried to clean off. The king, so far from being angry, called Lord Chesterfield and another lord (I think Goldsworthy) to come and look up at the place, when the king desired the miller to open it again, and down came much on them, to the sport of his Majesty! Another time a Mrs. Scott, nurse to Queen Charlotte, lay in an adjacent room, whilst nursing his present Majesty, King George IV. The king, who loved a joke, slipped out of bed, and took away from the nurse, unperceived, the child to his own bed, much to the wonderment and dismay of the nurse, of whom the queen was jealous,—perhaps not without some cause.

"*Saturday*, 17*th*.—Mr. Pache from Mardyke, Hotwell Road, Bristol, called and bought some shells, &c., 11*s*. Mr. Watts, a gentleman (from, I believe, Northamptonshire), called and bought some shells, and said his sons were botanists.

"*Sunday*, 18*th*.—Mr. Chambers and Mr. Johnson called, and I went with them botanizing to Thong and Shorne. They both were good draughtsmen, and wanted plants only to draw. We found in bloom at Shorne Rabbit Warren the Narcissus poeticus; and on the verge of a chalk pit, one field south of Shorne Workhouse, going up Gad's Hill, the Orchis fusca, hitherto called Orchis militaris; on the bank under a broom in flower, viz. about three feet off. In the field above, being the west side of Gad's Hill Wood on the south side of the Dover road, I planted a spider orchis as a breeder. On the north side of the turnpike road, in a small wood, or part of a wood, called Chapel Wood, we found the Orchis fusca, the bird's nest, the oxslip, the cowslip, and other scarce plants. Caught the grizzle butterfly in Thong Lodge Field.

" *Monday, 19th.*—Mr. Fitz Strathern (Mr. Hume's lawyer) called about the Marchmont title and estate; when I told him that some years ago I bought of old Mr. Hume a piece of magnetic iron-ore, when I believe he at that time related a story, that he supposed himself entitled to an estate and title. This Mr. F. said he went from Edinburgh to Stronsa to see the sea-snake, which had two spinal piths, or marrow,—an uncommon thing in nature,—and that it was fifty-five feet long, and its mane or bristles shone very much. He was sent from Edinburgh by order of the College of Surgeons there. I told him Miss Jane Burgess, of St. Margaret's, Hope, had sent me a drawing of it; which surprised him as he knew the young lady, whom, he said, had married a Mr. Calder, a surgeon, who used her very ill; but that they were now both dead.

" *Tuesday, 20th.*—A regiment of soldiers marched out. Busy in printing some bills for the sale of 'Prall's superior ginger beer.' This sort of drink has only come into fashion within a year or two.

" *Wednesday, 21st.*—Betsom Fair. Paid Mr. John West yesterday 8s. 6d. Settled with Mr. Prall, chemist, by paying him for the pill boxes, and he for my printing 200 bills for ginger beer.

" *Thursday, 22nd.*—Walked to Southfleet with Mr. Simmonds, coast inspector in the Customs, and saw the private and mourning coach of Rev. Mr. Rashleigh (aged 77) returning from Boxley, having been there with Mr. Rashleigh, senior, and his son, Mr. Rashleigh, minister of Horton Kirby, and a Mr. Brookes, an acquaintance, as mourners; to deposit there Mrs. Frances Rashleigh (aged 67), who died on the 14th. She was a Miss Barville, an heiress, and has left one son and two daughters. Mr. Peter Rashleigh, senior, is of Cornwall, having a brother, Thomas, of Blackheath, a barrister. Another lately dead, Charles, an attorney. Another a merchant; and another possessor of a valuable collection of minerals, at Menavilley, in Cornwall. Charles Rashleigh, lately dead, Mr. Simmonds said was very unfortunate by being involved in a lawsuit, the expense of which, he thinks, cost above 20,000*l.*!

"Mr. Simmonds was much delighted with the prospect and variety of scenery in our walk; and coming near to Scotbury, in the road from Southfleet, in looking to the north, a beautiful scene presents itself of Northfleet Church, Fiddler's Reach, and part of Essex, worthy the attention of the artist!

"*Friday*, 23*rd.*—Grays Fair. Mr. Fitz Strathern called about Hume's business, and I made a deposition that when old Mr. Hume sold me a piece of magnetic iron-ore, he said that he was entitled to an estate in Scotland. I made this deposition before the justice of Gravesend, Mr. Thomas Johnson (aged 76), in presence of Mr. Fitz Strathern, and have a copy left with me.

"*Sunday*, 25*th.*—Mr. Dadd from Chatham called, and bought some fossils and minerals. He is collecting the minerals of Kent. Walked to White Hill and found burnet in bloom.

"*Monday*, 26*th.*—Young John Whitbread came to do anything about the house. Mr. Scoones called and said Colonel Dalton had travelled in Russia and Italy, and been introduced to the high persons there." [This gentleman, Col. Dalton, believed to be a native of Gravesend, was colonel of the West Kent regiment of militia, and held office as Equerry in the Duke of Gloster's household. He built and resided in Parrock House, now used as an industrial school, in Milton.] "Mr. S. has an elder brother, an attorney, and said that it was his great-grandmother, Mrs. Whatmore, who was drowned in the tilt-boat. His sister married a Mr. Crawford, an engineer, and he has a brother, an attorney, and two dead. Mr. Warren's rider called, and I paid him 17s. for blacking.

"*Tuesday, 27th.*—Mr. Scoones called and bought two chalk fossils (5s.). Bought of Mr. Prall, spirits of salts, 7½d., in exchange for clam-shells.

"*Wednesday, 28th.*—Bought crescent oyster of boy Penman for 2s. A gentleman at the New Inn cut his throat in two places, but by my assistance recovered!

"*Thursday, 29th.*—Charles Pocock, my son, has just arrived in a ship passing the town from the Mediterranean. I hope he will be more grateful than he was on his return from the East Indies. Received a nosegay from Mr. Russel, Swanscombe, containing 200 varieties of flowers. Bought some chalk fossils at Northfleet.

"*Friday, 30th.*—Walked into Greenhithe Marshes, and coming home bought some chalk fossils, among which were teeth of fish. Bought shells and cement stones of Mrs. Bennet, Stone Bridge Hill. Received a letter from Mrs Roe, Woolwich, saying her brother wanted 2l. worth of chalk fossils and shells.

"*Saturday, 31st.*—Sally received a letter, post paid, from Harwich. Mr. Champion from Maidstone called

to show a MS. of his on Penhurst. Charles Pocock
came home from sea, dirty enough! Shameful!
Sent a letter to Mr. Robinson of Denston Hall,
Suffolk, about his family, by Mr. Champion, my
nephew."

It is scarcely necessary to announce that Pocock
was never able to realize his hope of publishing a second
and improved edition of his " Gravesend," for which he
had obtained the additional materials mentioned at
pp. 155 and 182—183 above, and at p. 220 post.

# CHAPTER VII.

Can gold calm passion, or make reason shine ?
Can we dig peace or wisdom from the mine ?
Wisdom to gold prefer, for 'tis much less
To make our fortune than our happiness

.        .        .        .

The man who consecrates his hours
  By vigorous effort, and an honest aim,
At once he draws the sting of life and death :
  He walks with nature, and her paths are peace.
                    EDWARD YOUNG, 1780.

THUS have we accompanied Robert Pocock through
the first five months of the most complete of his
few and fragmentary Diaries which remain extant,
namely: that for the year 1823. In the following
pages it will be resumed and carried to the close of
that year. Its entries will afford the reader many
salient opportunities of judging of his character, its
defects and merits.

It may be thought that these diurnal entries, following each other throughout the year, are tedious in
perusal as they are necessarily detached and broken up
in subject; but upon the most careful considera-
tion it has been felt, as indeed has been previously
observed, that where the means of exhibiting the course
of life, character, and occupation are so mainly to be
derived from the few written remains which have sur-

vived, and which have been here with difficulty gathered, it was on the whole the more faithful work to set them forth and to let the reader judge of the man at first hand, rather than for the author to have compiled a diagnosis of his own, and to have withheld, as would then be excusable and even necessary, a great part of the data upon which his appreciation or depreciation had been based.

" *Sunday, June 1st.*—Wrote a letter to Mr. Spencer, junior, Chatham, that the Manor of Hertingfordbury, in Hertfordshire, in 1700 was in the possession of — Selby, Esq., of the Inner Temple, to whom he pretends to be the right heir.

" *Monday, 2nd.*—Wrote a letter to Mr. Thatcher, No. 51, Newman Street, London, saying I could supply him with shells and curiosities. Also to Mr. Miller, near the river, Bristol, saying I could send him 100 specimens in chalk for a guinea—I mean a pound note. Sent a love-letter to Mrs. S., at Mrs. D., wishing for an interview. Mr. Aldersley, with a Gent well versed in reading, called and read MS. of Cobham Hall.

" *Tuesday, 3rd.*—Bought a palate of a fish in chalk, single, but to be perfect they ought to be conjoined, and a series of them.

" *Saturday, 7th.*—Settled with a poor, honest woman of Northfleet by giving her a shilling.

" *Sunday, 8th.*—Mr. Peen returned from a journey to the Isle of Oxney, having found some scarce plants. Drunken Millingham from Greenwich (called Tipsy Austen) and his friend refused seeing my curiosities.

" *Wednesday, 11th.*—Mr. Hally, nurseryman, Blackheath (Sir Gregory Page's), called and offered to show nursery and garden.

"*Thursday,* 12*th.*—Professor (Henslow) of Mineralogy from Cambridge called, and I gave him some plants, and he promised some from Cambridge. I introduced Mr. Peen to him.

"*Friday,* 13*th.*—Mr. Warwick, dealer in shells, called from a voyage in Van Diemen's Land, &c. He was sent out by the British Museum to collect shells, &c. He is here waiting the arrival of the *Castle Forbes,* as he left the ship off the Land's End ; and now has bought of me a left-handed whelk, and two purple oysters from Scotland. His residence is in Roebuck Place, Great Dover Road, London. Monsieur Noddgeriezn Pfefferkorn (pronounced Peppercorn) called, wanting old armour, weapons, &c. He is captain and *aide-de-camp* of the second brigade, Dantzic. Has an acquaintance, Heidegger, colonel, knight, and consul in the service of the Emperor of Russia, wanting Greek and Roman medals.

"*Saturday,* 14*th.*—Sent last night letters to Mr. Marshall, druggist, Vauxhall Walk, and A. B., there to be delivered by Mrs. Hanson. Walked to Green Street Green, and waited on clergyman at Swanscombe.

"*Monday,* 16*th.*—The sturgeon brought up alive by the *Favourite* smack is ten feet long, and weighs about two hundred pounds.

"*Tuesday,* 17*th.*—Sam Mud (an almost idiot) lies dead, through bite of Mr. Brenchley's dog.

"*Thursday,* 19*th.*—Went to Hole Haven with Mr. Peen and Mr. Brown, and drank tea with Captain Kelly, on board the oyster-vessel; and ón shore Captain Webb gave me a piece of peacock copper-ore.

o

I walked near three miles in the island, but did not find the common stinging-nettle. The island not favourable to botanical excursions. Saw there only the mustard in bloom, with the scarlet vetch, not 200 yards from the house in the high road. Narrow-leaf typha to eastward of house, two miles off. Heard from Captain Kelly that the water in the harbour gets of a reddish colour, which rain dispels ; and that when of this colour it is not good for the lobsters. This colour (the cause of it) is to be inquired into. Was only one hour and two minutes coming from Hole Haven. The landlord of the public-house always has been represented as an uncouth, disobliging man ; but I found him, though something of an ignorant man, more civil than I expected.

"*Friday,* 20*th.*—Mr. Daniel Mackintosh, a young gentleman, with another (lately attending Dr. Corpue's lectures), of Port of Spain, Trinidad, West Indies, promises to collect and send me butterflies, humming birds, &c., for part of a woman's head I let him have. Write to him in three or four months for his promise.

"*Saturday,* 21*st.*—Spoke to Mr. Gowers, of Essex, whose female relation (Miss Baldwin, of Grays, Essex) I went to court thirty years ago (viz., prior to my marrying my second wife), and would have had her ; nor did she object, but for some secret reasons best known to herself. Hence, the more I wanted to be married, the more she prolonged the time, and at last suddenly left Grays much in debt, which accounted for her behaviour, for if she had been so disposed I should have been ruined by such marriage; and for this conduct I have often said she was the most honourable woman I ever met with. I have not seen her since; but was surprised to hear she was alive, and now at Shorne, as Mr. Gowers thinks.

"*Monday, 23rd.*—Bought two puffins of a boy found on Faro Island, near Holy Island, sitting on the egg, which is white, and one only. They would not get off their egg, but suffered themselves to be taken by the hand.

"*Tuesday, 24th.*—A young gentleman from Derbyshire, a mineralogist and botanist, called with a lady, who said she had some bills printed by me a few years ago, when she was at Gravesend, with a reward, to find her father (who had strolled away, he being of weak intellect) and found him; but he is since dead. Bills handed about for forming a new association at Gravesend for protection of property, on the dissolution of the Northfleet society. The lady (my confidant) whom I intrusted with a letter to make inquiry for Mrs. A. B., at Mr. Marshall's, druggist, Lambeth Walk, returned, saying she had seen him, and the lady whom I sought for had been married very well above a twelvemonth. So here ends my hope of happiness with her. It is a good lesson not to lose an opportunity when in your power. Mrs. Angles paid me a visit: she is an agreeable woman.

"*Wednesday, 25th.*—Lord Darnley's daughter, who married Mr. Brownlow, I hear, lies dead.

"*Thursday, 26th.*—Walked in Clark's garden and gathered specimens.

"*Friday, 27th.*—Drank tea with Mr. Galton, at Northfleet (a young botanist), and his aunt, Miss Golding, whose brother married Miss Pitcher.

"*Monday, 30th.*—The first fine summer's day this year. Returned Mr. Lamburn his books and Mr. Rackstraw his magazines.

o 2

"*Tuesday, July 1st.*—Fine. Grand dinner at New Inn for eighty people, ladies and gentlemen, who danced on the bowling-green  Went into Essex and found the flowering rush in bloom; also the yellow iris.

"*Saturday, 5th.*—Visited Mr. Scoones at Parrock. Saw Colonel Dalton's library : only Hasted and Fisher's edition of ' Rochester ' belonging to the county.

"*Sunday, 6th.*—Found in bloom yesterday the Vicia crassa, going to West Wood by Denton's Fields (*alias* Baker's).    Also    common    cow-parsnip (*Heracleum spondylium*).

"*Monday, 7th.*—Walked to Kingsdown.    Found in field next Ruffet's, towards Southfleet, the Campanula hybrida; and took two brassy-thighed insects, feeding on a flower.

"*Tuesday, 8th.*—Walked to Knole, through Kemsing and Seal.    Saw at Kemsing a most curious house, ornamented with box and yew, worth seeing again. Found growing between Kemsing and Seal, water dropwort (*Œnanthe fistulosa*), in road and footpath, near a place called Noah's Ark.  Saw the paintings at Knole House, and greatly admired the portrait of Countess of Desmond, and a painting of the present Duchess of Dorset. The eyes of the Countess of Desmond are done admirably, and the elegant figure of the duchess is lovely. The number of rooms took up two hours in showing, and the collection was greater than I supposed.    Called on Mr. Morris, an attorney, in Sevenoaks, and returned to Kingsdown, by Kemsing, where we had tea in a miserable public-house, and not much civility.    Found the pomatia snail, going to Kemsing.

"*Wednesday, 9th.*—Walked to Otford, a better place for accommodation than Kemsing.  Called on Mr. and Mrs. Waters, who lay claim to the estates of Waters, at Gravesend, but for want of money are likely to lose them. Heard at Otford that Mr. Pain, who once lived with Lord Frederick Campbell, was alive at Westerham. Went there, and found him just returned from a journey out of Lancashire. Drank tea with him, and viewed the church of Westerham, where we saw General Wolfe's monument ; but it wants a much better one for the credit of the person and town. Found the road from Brasted to this place the best, and the country also, it being one continuation of a delightful spot. The like before I never witnessed— nothing but gentlemen's seats, fine farming, and de- lightful shrubberies. Returned to Kingsdown.

" *Thursday, 10th.*—Walked to South Ash, to see the pinks and flowers of Mr. Hodsoll, a very ancient family in the parish, who lived in a very ancient house (now being modernized, with marble chimney-pieces and furniture, because Mr. Hodsoll, junior, had married a Miss Kettle, from Wateringbury, with a fortune).

" *Friday, 11th.*—Tired with walking yesterday, so placed my plants in paper. At a court burghmote this day Mr. Matthews was chosen town clerk. Lord Darnley was present, and much opposition prevailed against his Lordship's interest.

" *Monday, 14th.*—Walked to Southfleet, and drank tea with Rev. Mr. Rashleigh, his son (Rev. Mr. Rash- leigh of Horton), and his two daughters (the youngest of whom is a good botanist), who gave me two speci- mens of Sibthorpia Europea in bloom, brought by themselves out of Cornwall. They were going to visit Sir Howard Elphinstone, settled near Cox's Heath, and then to Worthing. Mr. Townsend, from Herald's College, called about a picture of Gravesend, 1692.

" *Wednesday,* 16*th.*—Dull, windy. Among the paintings at Knole, which I saw last week, the fine painting in the hall of the procession of the Lord Warden (Lionel, Duke of Dorset) after taking the oath of office, at a court of Shepway held on Bredenstone Hill, exceeded for grandeur all the others ;—therefore Haydon is right that historical paintings should rank above portraits, and be the chief aim of the artist ; but pursuing this opinion has got Haydon into a gaol, viz., the King's Bench ! But if one portrait excelled another, it was her Grace the Duchess of Dorset's, whose full length, easy style, and beautiful figure were the admiration of the writer.

" *Thursday,* 17*th.*—Sent letter to Rev. Mr. Rashleigh, Horton, that reeds for thatching were sold at 40*s.* per 100.

" *Friday,* 18*th.*—Went to Mr. John Rackstraw's burial (son of Gaynam), aged seventy-four : buried in Gravesend Churchyard

" *Monday,* 21*st.*—Walked through Swanscombe Wood and drank tea. A Rider fond of fossils, &c., called ; dealt in tea.

" *Tuesday,* 22*nd.*—Mr. Kemp's son-in-law, Mr. Turner, called and bought some shells. Walked into Clark's garden and saw the carrion flower in bloom (*Sterculia hirsuta*). It stinks abominably, and appears to be fly-blown, as it is said to breed live maggots. It comes from the Cape of Good Hope.

" *Wednesday,* 23*rd.*—Walked with Mr. Turner to the mausoleum in Cobham Park. Saw the great chestnut-tree (not horse chestnut), said to be thirty-two feet in circumference. Saw a kingfisher bird about the pond, in the poultry-yard. Saw a heron on its nest in the park, the others having bred and gone. Heard Lord Darnley's daughter, Mrs. Brownlow, died in child-bed, and that the child was living at Cobham Hall; but that Mrs. Brownlow was taken to Ireland to be buried. At Shorne a great storm of thunder and lightning, with a beautiful rainbow.

"*Thursday*, 24*th*.—In our way through Shorne called on old Mr. Chipps, who had been twenty-five years in Lord Darnley's service as poulterer, but had left him.

"*Friday*, 25*th*.—Lord Mayor of London at Rochester, having been to view the city bounds, gave a ball.

"*Sunday*, 27*th*.—Heard Tilbury Fort was in the Duchy of Lancaster, a jury having sat on the body of an infant found dead in a closet there!

"*Monday*, 28*th*.—Wrote a letter and sent a list of British plants wanted to Mrs. Smith of Camer, saying I intended to publish a volume of Kentish botany.

"*Tuesday*, 29*th*.—Paid Mr. Holderness eighteen-pence, balance due to him for a pair of breeches. Mr. George Pocock from Oxford came last night." [He had a printing employ at the Clarendon Press.]

"*Wednesday*, 30*th*.—A jury sat on a child found drowned in the Swan Inn well, the child was supposed to have been stolen. The mother had travelled from Manchester, where the child had before fell down a well and cut a gash in its eyelid: otherwise it was a very pretty child. Walked into Northfleet Brooks, where I found growing the yellow loosestrife, a beautiful tall plant.

"*Thursday*, 31*st*.—Charles Pocock going to Sierra Leone in Africa, but could not fetch the ship.

"*Friday, August* 1*st.*—Mr. George Pocock returned from Woolwich.

" *Saturday, 2nd.*—Charles Pocock goes out as baker to New South Wales in a ship called the *Asia*, Captain Lindsey. He is to have 2*l.* 5*s.* per month; but if he comes home in the ship then 2*l.* 10*s.* Witness to this, Mr. Richard Raspison and Mr. Eliot, waterman.

" *Sunday, 3rd.*—Mrs. Cleveland buried from the Compass.

" *Monday, 4th.*—Rainy. Walked to Ivy House and first saw the field opposite laid out as a garden in plots of ground, with canary-beet, &c. &c." [Now part of the grounds of Milton Hall.] "In evening, 200 swifts flying about (high).

" *Wednesday, 6th.*—Horse-races at Chatham Lines.

" *Saturday, 9th.*—Walked to Dartford with George Pocock, and took home 300 club articles to Mr. Allchins, the Two Brewers, Lowfield, who paid me 4*l.* 10*s.* for the same.

" *Sunday, 10th.*—Mrs. Rowe, my daughter, came from Woolwich.

" *Monday, 11th.*—Fine. Went to Cobham Hall with Miss Fuller, Miss Couves, Mr. George and Kezia Pocock from Oxford, and Sarah Pocock, my daughter; when we found the days of viewing the hall were Tuesdays and Fridays; but upon my writing a note to Lord Darnley we were granted permission, and hurried over the rooms by the housekeeper, who was glad enough to accept of 2*s.* 6*d.* for ten minutes' haste ! Drank tea in the college at the room of Mrs. Grant, who by the polish on her goods shows she is a good housewife.

" *Tuesday, 12th.*—Went with Mrs. Rowe in a boat from Northfleet to Long Reach Tavern, and put her on shore on the other side of Dartford Creek to walk to Woolwich. In this voyage we lost our oar.

" *Wednesday,* 13th.—Printed some bills to find the oar lost yesterday by George Pocock and myself.

"*Friday,*15th.—Attempted to reach Dartford, but got no farther than Greenhithe with George Pocock.

"*Saturday,* 16th.—Cherries 1½d. per pound in the market.

" *Monday,* 18th.—Fine. Walked to Dartford by way of Greenhithe, and fell in company with Mrs. Backley, or Bagley (whose husband is of Apothecaries' Hall), who related a remarkable story of her child, about seven years old, falling down a well at Northfleet last year, and in falling pulled the well lid down, and so was hid in the well about two hours, until a woman came to draw water, when the child cried out, 'I am in the bucket, draw me up;' but when nearly up the rope broke and he fell to the bottom again, where he remained until a new rope was got and a person obtained to go down, who brought the child up. The child is now alive at the same house, behind the India Arms, where the accident happened last year !

" *Thursday,* 21st.—The walking-man Wright, aged fifty-eight, is passing through. He has a shuffling walk. He starts from the Montpelier Gardens, Walworth, through Gravesend to the twenty-third mile-stone, and returns to the above place ; thus making fifty miles a day at fifteen hours per day for fourteen successive days.

" *Saturday,* 23rd.—Dull; close. My stuffed fish gives out moisture. It does so yearly. Mr. Turpin, an acquaintance of Mr. Elliot, New Road, called and bought articles.

"*Monday, 25th.*—Very hot. The first sunny harvest day. Walked with my son George to Mr. Baker's, Orsett, and there saw an ancient bedstead made of thousands of pieces, and I believe the identical one which Queen Elizabeth slept in when she visited Horndon and slept at Mr. Rich's. Now if Mr. Rich was ever in possession of those premises it will confirm the idea. Mr. and Mrs. Baker behaved with great civility, and gave us a general invitation. On our way called in at the Cock, where Mr. George Pocock showed how two ovals could be made out of a circle or round table without wasting any stuff; viz., make a circle half the diameter of the other and cut each in four parts, when the smaller four pieces will exactly fill up the vacancies of the larger.

"*Tuesday, 26th.*—A fine, red, beautiful fish brought me, with large scales all over; the dorsal fin 18 rays, the caudal fin 20 rays, the ventral 9 rays, the pectoral 14 rays, and the anal 6 rays. It was caught off the Town Quay this day, and appears to be the Cyprinus nilotus. None of the fishermen at Gravesend knew it. Its length was 7 inches; breadth 3 inches.

"*Wednesday, 27th.*—Walked to Dartford with George Pocock, and settled with Mr. Samuel Elliot. Saw a man whose hands and arms above elbow were full of large blisters by weeding, he said, or pulling up May-weed and wild parsnip in a marsh near the Powder Mill Creek and River Thames (Long Reach); but not seeing the weeds I cannot tell the identical species. He was put under the care of Mr. Hurst, an apothecary and surgeon, who asked the man if he felt any pain under his arm-pit, and seemed to say if the blisters broke there would be a sore, and it was a dangerous case! Wasps numerous.

" *Friday,* 29*th.*—George Pocock goes to Southfleet, to meet Frances Pocock.

" *Saturday,* 30*th.*—Frances and Mrs. Jones go to London; George Pocock to Dartford with Mr. Brett, to take a house there.

" *Sunday,* 31*st.*—Mr. Brett came, and quite abused me, because I would not give the staff out of my hand!

" *Tuesday, September* 2*nd.*—George goes to London.

" *Sunday,* 7*th.*—Walked to Luddesdown by myself.

" *Monday,* 8*th.*—George and Kezia go to settle at Dartford in the printing line.

" *Thursday,* 11*th.*—Walked through Swanscombe Wood with Mr. Martin, and found a scarce grass in field opposite Spring Head Lane (*Polypogon monspeliensis*).

" *Friday,* 12*th.*—Fine. Wright, the pedestrian, walked (from twenty-second to twentieth mile-stone) fifty miles in twelve hours, nearly losing by about seven minutes.

" *Tuesday,* 16*th.*—A young man (of the name of Wickham) walking fifty miles in twelve hours (from twenty-second to twentieth mile-stone), which he did in eleven hours and a quarter! I walked to the Telegraph in Swanscombe and drank tea.

" *Saturday,* 20*th.*—Heard Mr. Christopher Pottinger had died at Canterbury. He was a singularly pleasant man; friendly to Cobbett's works, and an enemy to most of the proceedings of the Government! an acquaintance also of Capel Loft. The early part of his life he spent in hunting and shooting. He had travelled in France; and was in general well informed.

"*Tuesday,* 23*rd.*—Fine. A hornet brought me, and a monk fish.

"*Monday,* 29*th.*—Printed bills—'Beer 4*d.* per pot at the White Hart.'

"*Tuesday,* 30*th.*—Sally leaves me, to live at Woolwich.

"*Saturday, October* 4*th.*—An insect from a water-butt, with a pair of oars or long legs and two black eyes, and hairy under the belly in rows, was brought me to name.

"*Monday,* 6*th.*—Choose Mayor Day, when Mr. Medhurst Troughton went out of office and Mr. J. Dennet was chosen mayor. The court was near seven o'clock before it broke up, never known so late.

"*Tuesday,* 7*th.*—Mr. Oakes and Cruden had a quarrel.

"*Thursday,* 9*th.*—In the night died Mrs. Cruden, Mrs. Pattinson, Mrs. Cleverly, Mrs. Eglintine, and Mrs. Nash of Chalk; with Mr. Smithers of Parrock Farm, who some years since was footman to Mr. Dalton of Gravesend (now Colonel Dalton).

"*Friday,* 10*th.*—Miss J. Rashleigh sent me two dried plants, viz., the Cornish heath (*Erica vagans*), and the sea-pea from Walmer Beach, near Deal. Busy to-day in printing 300 bills (fcap. size) for the mayor (J. Dennet, Esq.), about violation of the Sabbath by publicans suffering tippling on the Lord's Day.

"*Saturday,* 11*th.*—Last night Mr. Nicholson, shell-dealer, No. 110, Strand, called and bought 170 chalk fossils, at one penny each, and a flute.

"*Monday,* 13*th.*—Rain. Wrote a letter last night to Frances Pocock, saying I had had a quadruple dinner—viz., one sausage, one potato, one piece of apple-dumpling, and one piece of damson-pudding—by myself, and quarrelled with no one, because no one was near me to quarrel. In afternoon paid Mr. Washer of Northfleet five shillings for his oar which I lost overboard when with George Pocock, &c., going to Long Reach Tavern, through fear of the steam-boats running foul of us !

"*Wednesday, 15th.*—Mr. Smithers buried : Colonel Dalton attended. The corpse came from the meadow down King's Lane, and Pennycoat Lane [1] into the road opposite the Globe, and so to Milton Church. At Gravesend was buried Mrs. Cruden, aged sixty-four : Mr. Harman of Croydon attended.

"*Friday, 17th.*—Mr. C. Clarke, F.S.A., called, on a tour in France, from Boulogne, where he had resided three months, and had made some drawings of the ancient churches, &c., in the neighbourhood. He witnessed a young woman, about twenty-five, taking the black veil (with much sanctity) for a period of five years, assisted by some nuns who pinned into her head-dress a few artificial flowers, as roses, &c. Mr. Clarke observed that the English at Boulogne did not associate so much together as might be expected, most of them retiring there for economy. A French woman called Boulogne 'Little England,' or Little London, as the inhabitants imitate the Londoners. At Boulogne they are in politics Bonaparteans ; at Calais Bourboneans.

"*Sunday, 19th.*—A louse seen, with black eyes !

"*Monday, 20th.*—Fine. Heard the discovery ships, *Fury* and *Hecla*, had arrived, and were coming up the river ! They went out about May 1st, 1821.

"A flock of wild fowl seen flying up past the town.

---

[1] These thoroughfares meet opposite South Hill Bank, the residence of Charles Chadwick, Esq.

A gourbill fish brought me picked up near Cleverly's Wharf.

"*Tuesday,* 21*st:*—Heard the discovery ships are near Hull. But in the afternoon they both (*Hecla* and *Fury*) passed Gravesend in good order: I went on board the *Fury,* and the commanding officer (Mr. Henderson) be-haved with much civility; but the *Hecla* proceeded so fast with the easterly wind that I could not overtake her, whereby I lost the opportunity of seeing Mr. Fisher, the surgeon of the *Hecla,* who promised to bring me home some curiosities. Saw several large Esquimaux dogs alive on board. Mr. Henderson said they had discovered about 600 miles of coast, dragging their ships along and proceeding about forty miles per day.

"*Thursday,* 23*rd.*—Busy printing 200 bills to prevent gaming and holding the fair after half-past eleven at night, by order of J. Dennet, Esq., mayor.

"*Friday,* 24*th.*—Gravesend Fair. Very fine sunny and dry day. This day is generally very disagreeable weather. I remember it snowing on this day, and fre-quently raining.

"Mr. Storbuck, pilot of the *Hecla,* discovery ship, called and said he had the following account from the officers on board her; viz., that the ships were frozen up the first winter from October 6th, 1821, to the 2nd of July, 1822; and the second winter from the 24th of September, 1822 to the 12th of August, 1823,—and that they saw the wrecks of two ships, the stern of one and part of a cask or staves from another; but the name and time when, no account could be given ! That the first winter they were frozen up in lat. 66° 11' 11", long. 82° 52' 30"; and the second winter at Igloolïk, lat. 69° 20' 42", long. 81° 44' 34". North-West Straits,

69° 48′ 16″ highest latitude, and the greatest distance 83° 37′ 15″ west longitude. That they found inhabitants very civil and useful, about sixty in number, round-faced and greasy; and that they discovered about 600 miles of coast, but many days not more than forty miles per day. They brought home in the *Hecla* seven dogs and in the *Fury* fifteen, which dragged an anchor of great weight from ship to ship ! The dogs are large, with erect ears, yet appear docile, as they were unconfined in the long-boat and the ships—very clean. Mr. Fletcher and son from Rochester called.

" *Saturday, 25th.*—Very fine sun ; second day of Gravesend Fair. Mr. Fisher of the East India House (formerly of Rochester), an able antiquary and historian, called.

" *Monday, 27th.*—Boa-constrictor and crocodile at the fair.

" *Tuesday, 28th.*—A masquerade ball at the fair.

" *Wednesday, 29th.*—Heard a Hudson's Bay ship had arrived south ! and put into Falmouth damaged !

" *Friday, 31st.*—Hard rain in the night. Many young cod-fish (four inches long) caught in Lower Hope. More rain fell in these two days than all the year.

" *Monday, November 3rd.*—Rather foggy morning : afternoon dull. George and apprentice came over. Mrs. Wallace gave rent to Mr. Harris near ten at night.

" *Tuesday, 4th.*—Very fine. Sun ; wind. Had brought me the little puffin (*Alca alle*), a very scarce bird, shot near Gravesend !

" *Wednesday, 5th.*—Abused by Mr. Walton, junior, toyman. (*Mem.* Never deal with him again.) Busy to-day assisting George P. "setting " a folio bill, sale of Gore House effects, Darenth.

"*Thursday,* 6*th.*—Casting letters for George Pocock." [Type for George's Dartford press.]

"*Friday,* 7*th.*—Sent letter to Mr. and Mrs. Paul, settlers, Van Diemen's Land.

"*Saturday,* 8*th.*—Sun. Paid Mrs. Deare, for making me a new shirt, 1*s.*

"*Sunday,* 9*th.*—Sun. Dry; fine. Geo. A. Pocock, viz., George Admiral Pocock, did the first posting broadside, demy, for Thomas Braves of Gore House Farm.

"*Tuesday,* 11*th.*—Water rail, 2¼ ounces, brought, shot in Lower Hope.

"*Friday,* 14*th.*—Boring in market for a fountain spring.

"*Sunday,* 16*th.*—Read in newspaper of the death of my friend, P. Kerkman, at Ealing on the 7th. It was my intention, the first time I went to London, to call and see him; but delays are very bad! Mr. Kerkman was a compositor at Mr. Nichol's, Red Lion Passage, and married the widow who kept the respectable public-house adjoining. He then dealt in printing materials, of whom the writer (R. Pocock) first purchased his press and types on commencing printer at Gravesend; and Mr. K. wanted to have put his brother, a stout Irishman, apprentice to (me) R. P.; but he did not appear bright enough for that business, so Mr. P. K. got him a commission in the East London militia (I think this was the regiment). Mr. P. K. quitted the public-house and got into the firm of Lackington and Co., booksellers, Finsbury Square, and afterwards, I understand, commenced coach proprietor, and resided at Ealing, where he died. He has a son a barrister, who, I am told, promises fair to become an ornament to the law.

" *Tuesday,* 18*th.*—Received a packet from Mrs. Smith, Camer, containing dried specimens of plants and confirming the grass I found near Swanscombe Wood (S.E. part of field) to be the Panicum viride, as I thought; and that the sea-pea is peculiar to Walmer (near Deal) in Kent. And that the rare specimen I sold her (in chalk) is called '*Lunulites*' by Mr. Mantel, of Lewes, who has given a plate of it in his works on fossils. Prize-fight at Dartford.

" *Wednesday,* 19*th.*—The men boring for water in the Market Place have got down 140 feet through chalk and flint only; but now have come to some hard substance, which they have not been able to penetrate these two last days. Exchanged with Mr. Ryan, surgeon at Mr. Warren's, six medical books for No. 12 picture, 'Human Life.' Mr. Berry (a gentleman going out to settle at Kingston, in Jamaica, as secretary to Beckford Wildman, Esq., M.P.) drank tea with me, and promised to send humming-birds, &c.

" *Friday,* 21*st.*—Sun. The men have bored 151 feet in the Market Place, the wages for which come to 30*l.* ; viz., 6*d.* for every ten feet boring, viz., advancing from the first ten feet 6*d.* per foot extra every ten feet.

" *Saturday,* 22*nd.*—Mr. Alder, a learned and scientific gentleman, called and had some conversation, saying he had had a public disputation at Newcastle, at the request of the mayor and corporation, to confute the principles of Sir Humphrey Davy's safety-lamp. He informed me the high sheriff of Northumberland,— Selby, Esq., was writing a 'History of British birds,' &c., &c.

" *Sunday,* 23*rd.*—Went in evening to spend an hour with Mr. Alder, and with much pleasure saw his draw-

P

ings of the coal-pits and their various strata. Drank, for the first time, whisky.

"*Monday,* 24*th.*—Had three more twelve-rayed star-fish from Whitstable Bay, brought me. Mallam's sale, where I bought nails at threepence-halfpenny and fourpence-halfpenny per pound.

"*Wednesday,* 26*th.*—Read letter from Frances describing Dulwich College, &c.

"*Thursday,* 27*th.*—Dan. Bryant bought steps of Mallam for a shilling, which were mine.

"*Monday, December* 1*st.*—George Pocock came and "set" a job for the Mayor about the watermen's apprentices being so rude.

"*Friday,* 5*th.*—Walked to Grays to Mr. Blaker's. Visited the brick-fields, where many bones of the mammoth, or elephant, were found about a fortnight since, in the clay-earth, fourteen feet down. Mr. Ingram of Little Thurrock, just by, has a very large one found there; and in the spring of 1823, a socket bone of this animal was found there which measured four feet in circumference !—so I was told to-day. The men who were at work sold me two large pieces for a shilling; and in the brick-earth were nodules of a roundish form, and hollow, which the men said were called 'race,' or 'rase,' and often met with in brick-earth, and if put into the brick would make it blow or spoil the brick. They always remembered it being called 'rase;' I shall call it a tophus for the present, until I am contradicted by superior judgment. It has much the appearance of a bubbled ball, hollow within, and of a calcareous substance.

"*Sunday,* 7*th.*—Observed in my walk to Grays on Friday only two birds on the sea-wall—viz., a chaffinch

and a lark—except gulls, although the sun shone delightfully; then whither are the birds emigrated?—
this is worth an inquiry. I think the history of birds
very imperfect! I forgot to mention that upon wash-
ing one of the large bones I brought home on Friday,
it frothed like soap. In afternoon visited Mr. Alder
and looked over the numerous views he had got together of Kent placed alphabetically, and although I
was there five hours could only look over letters A,
B, C, and his portraits.

"*Monday, 8th.*—Served on a jury on a sailor killed
by a block during the storm on Thursday last, coming
out of the Firth of Forth, about twenty miles from
the Isle of May, the inquisition stated it was on board
the *Prompt,* Captain Miller, of Leith, about two ante-
meridian, which words the foreman of the jury, John
Hopcraft, senior, did not understand, and asked Mr.
Matthews, the town clerk, their meaning, which made
a smile among the other jurymen. The verdict was
'accidental.' The deceased, John Banes, had a wife
and three children living at Leith, and through the
motion of Mr. Hubbard, one of the jurymen, the seven
shillings coming to the jury was given to the widow
and children : the other expense of nineteen shillings
the captain readily paid.

"*Friday, 12th.*—Went by Newman's coach to Dartford.

"*Saturday, 13th.*—Windy. Mr. Nelson, the under
water-bailiff, called on me for information about the
open navigation of Yantlet Creek into the Medway.
He said Mr. Smith, a person of the Isle of Grain, had
indicted the City of London because they had ordered
him (some short time since) to open the communication,

P 2

which he effected by thirty men in twenty-four hours ; and that Mr. Isaac Starbuck, an aged pilot of Graves- end, remembered about sixty years since going through a bridge of eighteen feet span on his way to Snodland Paper Mill with paper stuff,—and as he (Nelson), in cutting open the bar or communication between the Isle of Grain and the hundred, had found the foundation of the former bridge, he desired me (R. Pocock) to give him what information I could about any ancient map or document relative to Kent in favour of the said city, which I did by saying that Symon's map of the county I thought the best; but it is very surprising, although so many have been published, not one yet (1823) may be called even nearly perfect, as they are very defective by not pointing out the different ferries, locks, impediments, improvements, and many other remarkable things worthy of notice.

" Mr. Nelson lives at Barge Yard, Lambeth, and has been a very active officer for many years to the City on the Courts of Conservancies.   When the great whale was taken to London (which I accompanied to sell its description, on a speculation that answered well, having measured, named, and described it), Mr. Nelson daily visited it, and I spent the evenings with him and the proprietors of it until it was ordered away by the City and Admiralty as a nuisance (each claiming it as their privilege).

" *Wednesday,* 17th.—George went to Rochester, having been disappointed by Mr. Evans, the book- binder, in his work.   At about nine at night the storm so violent as to blow several bricks off the chimney, and the *General Harris,* East India ship, ashore, on the north side near Grays.

" *Thursday,* 18*th.*—George P., came over to acquaint me that he had pacified Mr. Caldecote about his books which he wanted to have bound. Mr. Caldecote is an author and a barrister, but now old—above eighty (?).

" *Friday,* 19*th.*—Heard that one Pallet was hung in Essex, on Monday last, for the murder of Mr. Mumford, which he had done on the Monday before! Quick work !

" *Sunday,* 21*st.*—Dull. Spent the evening in looking over more of Mr. Alder's views of Kent, but could not get farther than the letter G. Many are very rare; and among this copious collection saw the conduit of Maidstone, drawn by my friend Mr. T. Fisher of the East India House, who favoured me with a visit about a month since; and others by my friend Mr. Tracy of Brompton, the bookseller, who always wore a three-cornered hat!

" *Tuesday,* 23*rd.*—Read a letter from Dungarvon, in Ireland, only written there on Saturday last, and received at this place, Gravesend, this morning! giving an account of the cheapness of living, viz., a goose for 9*d.*, 8 lbs. weight; two fat ducks for 3*d.*; beef, 2*d.* per pound ; mutton, 1¾*d.* ; sheep's head and pluck, 3*d.*; whisky and brandy, 3*d.* per quartern; porter, 3*d.* per quart ; a large cod-fish, 1*s.*; potatoes, 2*d.* per stone ; and other articles in proportion. Received a *latitat* from Rose.

" *Thursday,* 25*th.*—Went to Dartford (walked) and eat a Christmas dinner with George P., and drank tea with Mrs. Saxton, who is a very frank woman, with a large family, widow of Lieut.-Colonel Saxton, and keeps company with all the principals in Dartford.

Heard that the man had died whose legs were broken by the caravan the other day. Very mild; I may say warm. Saw furze in bloom, with many other flowers there having been no frost or snow yet to hurt any flower.

" *Sunday, 28th.*—Mr. George Pocock came over, and we drank tea with Mr. and Mrs. Alder, both of whom we found scientific persons, well acquainted with chemistry, geology, and biography, in which last Mr. Alder has made a great collection of the natives of Kent, and also Northumberland! Mr. George P., was to have been home to have heard a charity sermon in Dartford Church, by the Rev. George Musgrave Musgrave, A.M., of Brasenose Coll., Oxford, chaplain to the Right Hon. the Earl of Bessborough. Mr. George Pocock married Miss Kezia Smith of Brasenose College!

" *Monday, 29th.*—A comet said to have been seen this morning, but it is more likely to have been Jupiter rising just before the sun, as I hear Jupiter is in conjunction with the sun (?). Lightning in the evening, but distant. Jupiter is said in the *Weekly Despatch* to be in conjunction; but Mr. Peen finds by White's 'Ephemeris' it ought to be opposition !

" *Tuesday, 30th.*—Received a letter from my daughter Sally, saying she had engaged herself to a lady, Mrs. Parker, No. 12, Terrace, Clapton, and that she goes on Thursday next. Received letter from George Pocock, desiring me to lend him the great hammer, rolling tools, lettering tools, backing hammer, some basil, and anything else in the binding business. Mr. R. Peen called this evening, saying it again lightened in the S.E., and that the comet had been seen three nights, about one or two in the morning, in the E. or E.S.E., with its tail perpendicularly, but not high from the horizon. The late comets brought very warm weather, and within this last week it has been warm, or very mild! Sent a caravan box to Sarah Pocock (by Mrs. Wallace), by Newman's coach, to be left at the Flower Pot, Bishopsgate Street, until called for.

"*Wednesday, 31st.*—Heard that the comet, first seen about the 29th, had been announced in the newspapers. This morning Mrs. Saxon (wife of Lieut.-Colonel Saxon, of the East India Company's Artillery) called and breakfasted—and I went with her on board the *Berwickshire*, East India ship, with her son Charles, to get him a berth in any capacity, but without success. I gave her a letter of recommendation to Henry Blanchard, Esq., No. 1, Broad Street, near the Royal Exchange, whose brother is an East India captain."

Referring to the whale mentioned under date the 13th December, the "Encyclopædia Britannica" tells us that "an ancient perquisite belonging to the Queen Consort, mentioned by all our old writers (and only therefore worthy notice), is this : that on the taking a whale on the coasts, it being a royal fish, it shall be divided between the King and Queen, the head only of it being the King's property and the tail of it the Queen's. 'De sturgione observetur, quod Rex illum habebit integrum, de balena vero sufficit si Rex habeat caput et Regina caudam.' The reason of this whimsical division, as assigned by our ancient records, was to furnish the Queen's wardrobe with whalebone."

"The editor of the ' Encyclopædia ' is ignorant upon the subject of whales, as the whalebone is taken from the mouth not from the tail."

# CHAPTER VIII.

Harsh poverty!
That moth, which frets the sacred robe of wit,
Thousands of noble spirits blunts, that else
Had spun rich threads of fancy from the brain :
But they are souls too much sublimed to thrive.

WILLIAM CHAMBERLAYNE.

IN the before-going Journals which have been set forth
so fully, and perhaps even wearisomely, a very good
means of gauging both the general course of life, and
to some extent the character of their author is afforded.
The reader must remember that he had never received
any education except as a stripling at the Gravesend
Free School, and all he afterwards acquired had come
by his own unaided powers of observation. But these
powers had enabled him to amass no inconsiderable
knowledge upon many subjects with which the public
mind was not then so conversant as at present; indeed it
would be an act of injustice to estimate his attainments
according to the lights and advantages of this day,
when the diffusion of books and other means of
popular instruction brings knowledge almost to every
threshold. He was looked up to by many of the
poorer of his townsfolk much as Goldsmith writes of
the Schoolmaster :—

Yet he was kind, or if severe in aught,
The love he bore to learning was in fault;
The village all declared how much he knew,
'Twas certain he could write and cypher too;
Lands he could measure, terms and tides presage,
And e'en the story ran that he could gauge.

Having now completed all that has been recovered of his Journals, we come to the MS. which our unwearied author had (p. 199 supra) expressed his intention of publishing. It is entitled—

OBSERVATIONS
and
MEMORANDA
in
BOTANY.
By Robert Pocock,
Printer and Bookseller,
Gravesend,
Kent.
1821.

And in a later part of this MS. he has, amongst other information, made the following entry :—

" Rare plants found by R. Pocock, in the vicinity of Gravesend, not generally mentioned by authors, nor in his ' History of Gravesend :'—

" Scirpus sitaceus. At reservoir, Randall Wood.

" Caucalis daucoides. White Hill Field, near to Thong Lane.

" Echinophora spinosa. Marshes, bottom of Gally Hill Lane, north.

" Isatis tinctoria. In Randall Wood, five or six plants (1820).

" Lepidium ruderale. Northfleet Dockyard.

"Avenaria verna. Ruffet field (south side), Southfleet.

"Orchis hircina. About Wilmington and Roe Hill.

"Ophrys aranifera. Waste ground about Green-hithe chalk-pits.

"Centauria solstitialis. In Old Road, between Gravesend and Northfleet.

"Myosurus minimus. In ditch-side north of Shorne Battery.

"Plantago (proliferus?). Two roots apparently distinct, or perhaps come from one root joined under-ground. I have observed them four or five years past on the saltings (next the river) between Mr. Rosher's house and Red Lion Wharf.

"Milium lendigerum. In old gravel-pit near East Tilbury.

"Symphytum. About Dartford Paper Mill.

"Erysimum precox. In walk from church to Mill Hill, Shorne. This plant is not mentioned by Dr. Withering in his 3rd edition.

"Campanula hybrida. In Chalk gravel-pit.

"Pencedanum silans. Greenhithe Marshes, east side.

"Anagallis cerulea. Fields about Luddesdown.

"Sordylium. From Tilbury Fort to Chadwell.

"Euphorbium exiguum. Fields to Swanscombe.

"Typha angustifolia. Ditch at Lower Shorne.

"Jasione montana. Tilbury (East) gravel-pit.

"Papaver hybridum. White Hill, towards Thong, September 30th.

"Antirrhinum orontium. White Hill to Thong.

"Lithospermum purpuro-ceruleum. Swanscombe Wood, April.

"Anagallis tenella. Northfleet Brooks, September 12th, 1813.

" Scilla autumnalis. Chalk gravel-pits, Aug. 20th to October.

" Samolus valerandi. Tilbury Marshes to Chadwell.

" Turritis glabra. In Randall Wood. This is what I supposed was the wood Isatis tinctoria.

" Veronica montana. Gad's Hill Wood.

" Ruppia maritima. In ditches.

" Panicum viride. Field next or near Swanscombe Wood, by Spring Head Lane, wherein is the halk hole, September, 1823.

" Erysimum cheiranthoides. In Mr. Pete's garden, November 5th, 1824."

The reader will have noticed a reference in the Journal for 1823 (on p. 181) to his—

ERRATA;

or,

A Peep into some Books:

Whereby

Many errors of Authors

are pointed out,

And the volume and page noticed;

So that

The mistakes can be easily corrected

with a pen,

' As a benefit to truth and future readers.

_Motto._—Before one Author finds fault with another,

he should correct himself—

WHICH IS DONE.

By (me) R. Pocock,

Author of the "History of Gravesend,"

" Memorials of the Tufton Family,"

" Margate Water Companion,"

&c., &c., &c.

London:

Sold by Sherwood, Neuly, and Jones, Paternoster Row—

in which, treating of his own "History of Gravesend," he says,—"The author now regrets that this volume is neither printed with a good pica type, nor of a fashionable size. In it we find page 165 wants to be transposed to 164, because the occurrences do not follow in regular order of time (the narrative of the Duke of Albemarle being in 1667, and the building of Tilbury Fort in 1683). Secondly, in page 119, so much as relates to the Manor of Melestun should be cancelled; because the author, by closely following Hasted's 'History of Kent,' has fallen into that historian's error. The mistake perhaps was originally made by the transcriber of Domesday using an *l* for an *r*, and so Melestun for Merestun,—Merestun being in the Hundred of Shamel, whilst Melestune is in Toltingtrough Hundred. Mr. Hasted thought Melestun meant Parrock, but on looking over Henshall's 'History of Britain,' I find no mention of Parrock in Domesday : hence Mr. Hasted made a wrong conjecture.

"As an apology for the type made use of in the 'History of Gravesend' (since which time typefounders have greatly improved its beauty), the author assures the public that on a second edition, for which he is preparing, and should be glad to receive hints for its improvement, they shall have no cause for complaint : nor yet of the paper, which shall be a quarto demy size."

This second edition never saw the light, nor is it believed that the author ever completed his " Errata;" but it will not be inappropriate to follow up his self-accusations in reference to the Gravesend History by stating that he has really little to charge himself with, considering his opportunities of information. We are indebted to Mr. W. H. Hart, F.S.A., for pointing out that the foundation by Roger Orger (p. 126) of a daily mass in Milton Parish Church upon an endowment of two messuages, two oxgangs and a half of land, &c., was really a foundation in the parish church of Melton Mowbray; but in this Pocock did but follow Hasted, and it was only by recently turning to the inquisitions of February 20, 11 Edward II., No. 101, that the error was detected, as the name of the county is suppressed, while Milton-next-Gravesend used to be written Melton. Again, it might perhaps here be added that the reference to the first meeting-house for Protestant Dissenters, at p. 93 of his History, is inadequate, since on the 6th of July, 1702 (1 Queen Anne), a meeting-house for Baptists is certified in the " Bishop's Registry " at the instance of nine of the inhabitants, whose names are recorded.

But the discovery, which would most have pleased our historian, was denied him, viz., the will and the executorship accounts of his great fellow-townsman of 1280, Richard of Gravesend, who then ascended the episcopal throne of St. Paul's, upon which he sat for twenty-three years, until 1303 ; great, not for his occupation of that important see, but for his personal character and attributes. Especially would he have yearned in sympathy at the Prelate's taste for books. His Holy Bible, laboriously and painfully written out in thirteen volumes, and even at the then currency valued at forty-one pounds sterling, he appropriately bequeathed to his nephew Stephen ; and his other works, no less than fifty-five volumes MSS., were valued in the same early currency, according to the executors' inventory, at 116*l.* 14*s.* 6*d.*—and comprised, besides three other copies of Holy Writ, books upon theology, and canon and civil law.

Indeed a few lines may well be devoted to the interesting will of this local precursor of Pocock, as a lover of books; and no reader who takes up the Bishop's will fails to cull many evidences of his kind, domestic, and amiable character; his recognition of his obligations to his predecessor in the See of London, so emphatically expressed by the word "promoter;" his touching wish to be laid side by side with him on the floor of their common cathedral, with the stony record cut into the pavement (as in fact his remains were), until in subsequent troublous times both remains and the memorial were destroyed, either in the reign of Edward VI. or early in that of Elizabeth.

In the same testament the Bishop gave to his niece Alice, daughter of his brother, Sir Stephen Gravesend (living at Parrock, then the local squire), one hundred marks for her marriage portion; while to his brother himself he forgave whatever he owed him. And to his nephew, Richard Gravesend, forty shillings.

Nor indeed could a testamentary document of the kind scarcely be indited which expresses in simpler and more touching words the hopes of the testator in regard to the life to come; and as Pocock would have given this record (had it been known to him) prominence in his History, so its present disinterment may now be not inappropriately dedicated to him, if it be to some small extent reproduced in these pages. The Will runs in the usual official Latin of the day, of which the following is a free and fair translation :—

" In the name of the Father, and of the Son and of the Holy Ghost, Amen: A.D. 1302, the second day of September : I, Richard, the unworthy Minister of the Church of London, make and establish my will in the following way. In the first place, to Thee, O Holy Redeemer and powerful Saviour of souls, my Lord Jesus Christ ! I commend my soul. To Thee, O great High Priest and true Pontiff of souls, I commend the whole people of London City and Diocese, beseeching Thee by the medicine of Thy wounds upon the cross, both for me and for them, that full pardon of our sins being granted, Thou wilt grant us in Thy mercy to enjoy the beatitude promised to Thine elect for ever !

" I give and bequeath my body to be buried in the Church of St. Paul's, London, next the tomb piously recording the memory of my Lord Henry of Sandwich, my patron " [Bishop of London from 1262 to 1273], " so that my tombstone be side by side with his on the pavement, that is if I should happen to die near my cathedral church. If however at any distance, then I elect to be buried in the nearest conventual church.

" For the uses I have made of earthly things, I beg pardon from the Creator of all things, and that by what I have retained I may not increase my sins, but it may the rather lead to salvation."

Further on, in remembrance of the poor of his native town, he says, " To the poor of Milton and Gravesend I bequeath ten pounds," a bequest altogether distinct from the twenty-seven pounds (or more if necessary) to be distributed to the general poor at his funeral. Nor is the Bishop's appeal at the end of his will to Robert

Archbishop of Canterbury devoid of interest, when he says, " I humbly beg out of kindness, as for old companionship and our common country's sake, that he will undertake the burden of this executorship, beseeching him and the other executors, by the sprinkling of the blood of Jesus Christ, that they would be such true dispensers of my goods as they would themselves wish to have when their own turns come."

Thus Bishop Gravesend expresses himself, dying the 9th of December, 1303 ; and his body, taken to London on the 15th, was, after an impressive funeral on the day following, quietly laid under the floor of his cathedral, below a simple stone of " ten pieces."

Though it does not appear in his will, he founded and endowed the Divinity Lecture at St. Paul's, originally attached to the chancellorship of the church.

Pocock had traced out (as the fact was) that the Bishop's same nephew Stephen, of Gravesend, to whom his uncle had bequeathed his best Bible, became, in A.D. 1339, curiously enough (after three other intervening prelates), himself Bishop of London, a see he occupied till 1398. Being a man of inflexible probity he felt unable to recall his oath of allegiance to King Edward II. after his deposition, and for this he was imprisoned ; and while the Earl of Kent lost his life on the same account, Stephen was ultimately released and pardoned by Act of Parliament in 1336, his previous accusation being that after the death of the king, September 21st, 1327, he had disseminated rumours that Edward II. was still living.

Returning to Pocock's career as a topographer, it is believed to have been a few years afterwards that our indefatigable author drew up his—

PERAMBULATIONS THRO' KENT;
or,
Objects in that County
worth seeing
near
The Principal Towns
in 1827.
By R. Pocock, Gravesend.
Describing a Kentish Journey of about
330 miles,
Performed in        days,
With the probable expense
attending the same.

The
KENTISH BOOK OF ROADS;
or,
The Traveller's Companion
through
The Turnpike Roads
in the
County of Kent.
Describing
The different cities, towns, villages, gentlemen's seats,
remarkable buildings, fine views, and other objects
worthy of attention in the neighbourhood,
With the
Distance in miles from London to the several towns, &c., and from
one town to another on the several roads; the rates of postage,
market-days, &c.
By R. Pocock, Gravesend, Kent.
London :
Sold by Sherwood & Co.,
And by all Booksellers and Turnpike Keepers.
Price Sixpence.

But, alas! for his own *ways* and means! His Journal
entries of the month of May, 1823, clearly show the
bourne to which Pocock's worldly affairs were rapidly

Q

hurrying. What an insight does not the following entry afford?—

"Waited on Viggers about the taxes due, 34s., who behaved very violently, saying he would not give me any indulgence!—no, not an hour! Walked over to Northfleet with some parish receipts" [which he had printed for that parish], "but came away without the money."

In February, 1822, he had presumably asked the mayor, Mr. Millen, for a little pecuniary help, who appears to have assented if he could find a surety for repayment; and the extract from the Journal conveys his clear apprehension of the considerable difference between the number of his literary, antiquarian, and natural history acquaintances, visitors, and customers, and those of his true friends, real and judicious. The entry runs as follows:—

"*Saturday, February 9th*, 1822.—Fine day. Mr. Millen (the mayor) kindly offered to be my friend (in case I could find a friend). Some author has observed a man may think himself happy if he finds six friends in his life. I have often said I keep three books: a little one for my friends, a large one for my acquaintances, and a small one for my customers. My late wife used to say our acquaintances were so numerous that we kept a public-house without profit. The best sentiment to give in company is, 'From injudicious friends, good Lord, deliver me.'"

And two years later we find that the printing of the third edition of the " Guide for Gravesend," the first edition of which was printed by Pocock in 1817, had passed out of his hands, and had gone into those of his respected competitor, Mr. T. Caddel, his declining means now exhibiting all the symptoms of early financial dissolution and catastrophe. [This work was written by a visitor.]

The mischief culminated—this burden of impecuniosity—this terrible scourge of poverty, to which unworldly men knowing little of that which is sordid are ever so prone to fall victims—this mischief with which Pocock, like others of his class, knew no mode of grappling, was advancing with sure and steady steps, and was now about finally to engulph him. It came at last, when his furniture and household effects were taken in execution. This he would have borne, and borne perhaps with equanimity; but his museum and his deeply-prized and laboriously-formed collections—his fossils, his butterflies—were sold and dispersed (see p. 243); and he himself, alas! became houseless and a wanderer.

Fortunately, as his Journal has shown (p. 203), he had lately established his son George as a printer at the neighbouring town of Dartford, and there he himself found a resting-place for the soles of his feet, cast out of his native town, impoverished and ruined! Happy privilege, which gave to the son to be a refuge to his broken-down father!

But this refugee was not a man to surrender his attachment to the pursuits of his life, or give up the practice of them by self-prostration. On the contrary, he began to repay his new neighbours by sedulously setting to work to complete a singularly full, complete, and exhaustive history of that town and its adjacent parish of Wilmington (forming together a separate hundred, one by no means unentitled to the attention of the antiquarian and the topographer), and he followed up this labour of love with so hearty a good-will that even now it is computed that the MS. materials remaining extant, are equal to an octavo of 600 pages. The difficulty, however, with him was not the labour—not at all,—his industry, and his love of information, whether ancient or modern, impelled him forward in spite of ordinary obstacles ; but it was his poverty—here was the bane.

We offer no excuse for presenting the prospectus, title-page, and preface of this latter work, with which he may truly be said to have "been in labour," asking that it may be remembered that, owing to circumstances, they are but rough drafts, which he would have corrected and improved had events permitted.  He was a great admirer of Hasted, the historian of Kent, and had defended his good name and fame, as we have seen, in the "Gentleman's Magazine," especially in 1812, and he wished this new work in the land of his adoption, or of his proscription, to have corresponded in type and character with, and to have formed an extra volume to, Hasted's "Kent" (in eight volumes octavo).

It is considered that Pocock's flight to Dartford occurred in the spring of 1827, as the author has seen a letter from his friend and fellow-antiquary, Mr. Clarke, addressed under date the 31st of March in that year to him, "under the care of his son, George Pocock, printer, Dartford;" though it is equally clear that the poor-rate receipts for Gravesend for use subsequent to Easter were printed by the father, and bore on the foil of each, " R. Pocock, printer, Gravesend, Kent;" such receipts are, however, invariably prepared and printed several weeks in advance.

It may savour of encroachment upon the reader to set forth *in extenso*, not alone the draft prospectus but the dedication also, and the somewhat singular prefatory remarks to this " History of Dartford and Wilmington ; " but the extenuation is to be found in the circumstance that these lines will constitute all which will ever appear of this his last abortive and strangled-for-want-of-means compilation ; and as we have very sparsely dealt with his printed works, since, having been published, they are so far accessible ; so in the case of an unpublished MS., as it never can be otherwise known or come at, a little more licence seems permissible.

# CHAPTER IX.

Ah, worthless wit! to train me to this woe:
  Deceitful arts that nourish discontent;
Ill thrive the folly that bewitch'd me so!
  Vain thought, adieu! for now I will repent—
And yet my wants persuade me to proceed,
For none take pity of a scholar's need.

    .      .      .      .

Ah, friends!—no friends that then ungentle frown
When changing fortune casts us headlong down.

THOMAS NASH.

WHEN, alas! it is remembered that all the careful preparation of 600 pages octavo for this Dartford History was doomed to fall flat, prostrate, fruitless, and still-born for want of a few pounds, how forcibly we are struck by the marvellous and chilling dependence of mind upon matter. Such failures, indeed, enable one to appreciate the value in bygone days (before the vast increase of readers supplied a remedy), of that encouragement which wealth and position offered to talented poverty—a relation which admits of being as dignified as it may be degraded; for what fair-minded judgment would fail to recognize, in such kindly and timely encouragement of letters, that the needy author far more than repaid the patron by linking him as a joint tenant in the in-

heritauce of gratitude of the future. Without further delay, let us produce Pocock's own words:—

"1827.

" PROSPECTUS FOR THE HISTORY OF DARTFORD. .

"Printed for the author; a *poor* old man with a
*proud* spirit of independence which do not agree and
who can ill afford it. He is obliged by his loyalty
and duty in obeying the laws of the land, to make a
present of eleven books when finished (*value above
eleven guineas*) to the British Museum and other
public bodies.

" Ready for the Press and will be published, *for
subscribers only*, when a sufficient number of names
are obtained to cover the expense, in one volume,
price *one guinea, in boards*, illustrated with plates and
copious notes—the type to correspond with Hasted's
octavo edition of 'Kent,' to which it may be deemed an
extra or supplementary volume—

THE HISTORY OF
DARTFORD AND WILMINGTON,
IN THE COUNTY OF KENT;

extracted from parish records, registers, wills, and
documents of authenticity, comprising various departments; viz., ecclesiastical churches, chapels, priories,
buildings, monumental inscriptions, chantries, antiquities, cemeteries, medals, coins, tournaments, traffic,
commerce, manufactories, government, biography,
heraldic information, geology, sewers, agriculture,
botany, natural history, military stations, bowmen,
palace customs, manors, views, walks, recreations,
chronology, and other miscellaneous information;
with some account of the environs, *by R. Pocock,*

author of the 'History of Gravesend and Milton in Kent;' 'Memorials of the Tufton Family, Earls of Thanet,' 'Margate Water Companion,' &c.   Subscriptions received at the Banking House of Messrs. Masterman and Co., Gracechurch, London.

### " PROSPECTUS.

" Our topography commenced in the reign of Queen Elizabeth, and was at that time considered a new, principal, and leading feature in fashionable literature; it has embraced attention and employed the pens of several eminent writers from the days of the respected Lambarde, the famous Camden, the useful Thorpe, the decorative Gough, Grose, &c., down to the *laborious Hasted*, with his own contemporaries, Denne, Cousens, Parsons, Noble, &c.

" The numerous events which have happened in the county of Kent have caused many topographical publications, and although most of the considerable towns in that opulent and pre-eminent county have been written on and particularly described, yet the much-frequented and thriving *town of Dartford has had no Historian* to commemorate its various occurrences. The noble persons who have resided, passed through, and assembled there at different periods as warriors, soldiers, Royal bowmen, cricketers, &c., make the subject well worthy of inquiry.  The monastery or nunnery with its religious community, the once royal palace, its antique church, its ministers, one of its singular cemeteries, its numerous charities, its extensive manufactories, commerce, traffic, famous mills, manors, descent of manorial property, pedigrees of principal families, illustrious passengers, anecdotes, biography, coins and medals, heraldic bearings, natural history (Dartford warbler, a bird but little known), antiquities, well-frequented market (Horticulture and agriculture), scarce botany, customs, sewers, societies, chronology, walks, recreations, &c.,—all combine to form materials sufficient to make a volume of interesting matter enough to make above 600 pages; all which substance was by Mr. Hasted, for want of local knowledge, time, and assistance, contracted into only nine pages. No more perhaps was then possible considering the bulk of his great provincial work; but it would be unpardonable in a local historian did he not extend all the information in his power, by elucidating and enlarging on many points in history which remain obscured and partially treated with, whilst he found subjects of either utility or entertainment, particularly on the commonly talked-of rebellion under Wat Tyler, the origin of paper-making by Sir John Spilman (whose tomb as such is daily shown in Dartford Church, and whose story is followed through tradition from one historian to another without any one having had the boldness to break this link of error and set truth in the right path). Therefore the present author has undertaken this desideratum, hoping the volume will frequently be referred to, and that it may be favourably received by the public.

"Whilst the author flatters himself he has done his duty with respect to collecting materials and introduction of several interesting plates, the engraving of which have come very expensive, yet he would wish to make a still further addition (provided circumstances afforded the means) in order to render the work more valuable. A few more plates might be judiciously placed, and by

some thought requisite, towards which he humbly
solicits aid; many valuable and scarce records yet lie
with much dormant information, hid in our churches,
public libraries, and private families, especially with the
clergy of the adjoining parishes, whose assistance in
this undertaking he humbly requests, by referring to
the register books of their parishes, where many curious
memoranda are frequently discovered, which he begs to
solicit, and which may be forwarded to the printer prior
to the publication.

"Whoever employ themselves in works of this nature
are well aware of the perplexity and mortification which
accompanies the labour. The impatience of some;
the lukewarmness of others; the sneer of the self-con-
ceited; the austere behaviour and the silent contempt
which authors experience, is enough to dishearten
an attempt to be useful. Repeatedly has the author of
the present work sent letters without having answers
returned. His presence upon asking for information has
been thought troublesome. Others wait to have the
opinion of reviewers; others, more cunning, say we can
read it at the circulating library for a few pence; but
the author retaliates on this class of readers by
endeavouring to keep the book from their sight,
assuring them most faithfully that no more copies will
be printed than subscribed for, and that after the
period of publication no copy can be procured or seen
unless through the favour of a subscriber. Nor can a
subscriber individually have more than *one copy in one
name*, which name will be *printed on the title-page*. This
*novel mode*, although attended with additional expense
and trouble, will be adopted to secure the subscriber, and
render his copy more scarce and valuable, to which he is

entitled as the friend of the author, for without his subscription the work never would have appeared.

"In the progress of this History, whilst some small obstacles and delays have occurred on one side, it is but just to acknowledge the kind friendship and assistance the author has received from the communications of Charles Clarke, Esq., F.S.A.; John Latham, Esq., M.D.; — Rute, Esq., F.L.S., &c., surgeon of Dartford, for his list of rare plants in the neighbourhood; the Rev. Mr. Currey, of Wilmington; the lately departed and much-lamented Rev. Mark Noble, vicar of Barming, &c.; with other gentlemen and ladies,—to whom the author will always consider himself under obligation.

"To announce a work of this nature we must have recourse to advertisements, letters, packets, and many thousands of handbills printed and distributed to gain subscribers. The carriage of a single packet is not an object; but many come expensive (especially when paid by an author not abounding in riches). Therefore he humbly solicits that early communications and subscriptions may be forwarded free, or at *as easy a rate as possible*, and the mode pointed out by which the book may be conveyed when finished, for which purpose he has appointed agents at various places, and named persons to receive subscriptions on the *three principal roads* leading through Kent—viz., to Dover, Ashford, and Tunbridge Wells—whose receipts will be proper vouchers.

"If this undertaking is accomplished *with any small profit*, the author will proceed to describe the other parts of the county of Kent."

It may be here stated, by way of parenthesis, that the author was quite competent to have performed, had he received encouragement, the contingent promise thus made, since his collections for a " Topography of Maidstone " alone were advanced and considerable. Indeed these pursuits had been the labour of his life, the collection of material illustrating the past history of Kent, and its considerable towns, was ever and anon a work interthreaded in his business and recreation.

We will now give the dedication of his Dartford volume :—

"DEDICATION.

"To Thomas Caldecote, Esq., Barrister-at-Law.

" Sir,—Be pleased to accept this dedication as a tribute of respect due to yourself, for three reasons : first, that you are the only gentleman I have found on record (as a barrister) having honoured the town of Dartford with his residence ; secondly, your ready compliance to lend me those scarce and valuable books the Registrum and Customale Roffense, and also Hasted's volumes of ' Kent,' &c., from which I availed myself by making several relevant extracts, which acts of kindness convince me you are a true promoter of literature; and thirdly, you having been an author, an arduous task, well know the tedious research and perseverance which is requisite to put a book of this sort into print. Also, my sincere thanks are due to those ladies and gentlemen who have favoured me with their names, not only as subscribers but with genuine information. They truly may be called *friends* who have so readily come forward to patronize the present volume by their subscription ; for without that kind assistance, prematurely paid through the hands of Messrs. Budgen and Co., bankers, Dartford, and their agent in London, this

work could not have been completed !  The word *friend*
is often mentioned by persons in discourse, and nearly
as often misapplied ; it was not understood by Dryden,
Shakespear, Peachem, or Mathew ;  South only appears to have given it some value and its true sense ;
Johnson himself is silent,[1] although he justly hinted
at it in his preface to Lord Chesterfield, otherwise he
would have repeated it on his return from Scotland ;
and Sheridan also would have been glad to have found
it, just previous to his death, among the numerous
train who followed his remains to the grave !  For this
mockery of friendship and empty honour he is not alive
to resent by his pen ; neither is Professor Porson !
Permit me now, dear friends, whilst I have life and
gratitude left, to subscribe myself

"Your most thankful historian,

"ROBERT POCOCK."


The following is the title-page and preface :—

## THE HISTORY
### of
## THE HUNDRED AND PARISHES
### of
## DARTFORD AND WILMINGTON,
IN THE COUNTY OF KENT :
Comprising
Their Antiquity, Commerce, Manufactures, Customs, Ecclesiastical
Buildings, Charities, Societies, Monumental Inscriptions, Re-
creations, Biography, Botany, Geology, Views, Walks, Natural
History, with some account of the Environs ;
viz.
Erith, Chiselhurst, Darenth, Sutton, Horton, Farningham, Eynsford,

---

[1] See "Johnson's Dictionary," 8vo edition, 1760.

Erith, Crayford Stone, Greenhithe, Swanscombe, The Crays;
and Miscellaneous Information.
Illustrated with Plates, price One Guinea (the Volume),
in extra Boards.
By ROBERT POCOCK, Senr.
Author of the Margate Water Companion ; Memorials of the
Tufton Family, Earls of Thanet; History of Gravesend, &c.
*Motto.*—" Pro captu Lectoris habent sua fata Libelli."
" Books take their doom from each peruser's will ;
Just as they think, they pass for good or ill."

*Gibson's Camden, Preface.*

" If books are well chosen, they neither dull the appetite nor strain
the capacity,"—" but polish and perfect at the same time they
please and entertain."—*Gent.'s Mag.*, June, 1802, p. 15.
" Whoever thinks a perfect piece to see,
Thinks what ne'er is, ne'er was, and ne'er can be."
Printed by G. A. Pocock, Lowfield Street, Dartford.


## PREFACE.

" Topographical information is as important to the
district it describes, as the history of England to the
Kingdom of Great Britain. Hence arises a due con-
sideration of its value, for if a fictitious ideal novel of
three hundred pages large type, written in haste, is
worth seven shillings, what ought double the number
of pages of true historic composition to be worth, extracted with care, collected by scraps, copied out fairly,
written and rewritten repeatedly with much labour and
great loss of time by the author, who has endeavoured
to introduce all the original matter he could obtain ?
The reader, therefore, himself can now calculate about
what price the volume before him should be charged
to the public.

" From the perusal of history and biography, we are

able to judge the actions of our ancestors, whereby we can avoid their vices, reject their follies, and improve our morals; such documents exhibit excellent lessons by showing the rise and fall of princes, or the revolutions of states, all which changes have been chiefly brought about by the pride of man, who too often forgets himself in good health, and only knows when on a bed of sickness the proper duty he owes to his superior.

" Since the commencement in forming this volume some doubt has arisen whether it would be proper to notice what Mr. Hasted (the historian of Kent) has written (his work being already in the hands of the nobility and principal gentlemen of the county), to incorporate it with what we have gleaned ; or to strike out a new plan by giving the whole in the form of a biographical and chronological history. At last the incorporation preponderated, in consequence of the number of years elapsed since Mr. Hasted's death, the scarcity of his voluminous work, and the many therefore who have it not in their possession: besides, our subscription being one guinea for an octavo, we are unwilling the subscriber shall have any cause of complaint ; but that he shall have enough for his money, we have illustrated the work with several interesting plates, and also introduced (we hope not irrelevantly)some pleasing digressions, extending the volume to above 600 pages, as we promised in our prospectus.

" Among the various publications extant, few have appeared as a helping rule for topographers and authors; therefore we have inserted our synopsis, which will serve, not only as a partial index, but a

guide for the departments which a local history should
contain.

"To understand this history clearly, first think what
England is in the present reign of King George the
Fourth, and what it was at the most early period
on record; and note the progressive changes and improvements it has undergone.  In 1829 we have every
kind of fruit, vegetable, art and science, known
throughout the world, and brought (it may be said) to
this land of milk and honey.  Our ancient forests,
woods, and waste lands have been mostly grubbed and
turned into cultivation for corn, grain, and useful
herbage, of which there are now produced more than
ever known at any period before.  Only revert to the
time Queen Elizabeth came to the throne, in 1558, this
great pride of English history (far more praise has been
given to this tyrannical lady than perhaps she deserved).
We had then no cherries, but the little common black
indigenous berry of our country.  No variety of vegetables, but what were brought from the Netherlands!
We had then no potatoes to feed our people, nor
mangel wurzel to feed our cattle.  No turnips, for they
were first introduced into England by Lord Townsend,
secretary to King Charles I.  Mangel wurzel was
brought over by Doctor Lettsom.  Although potatoes
were brought to Ireland in 1565, by John Hawkins,
from Santa Fé in New Spain, they did not become the
general food of the Irish until after the Revolution.
We had no East India trade!  No West India
trade!  Lean meat and fish of the coarsest sort was
the daily food!  Porpoises we find brought to table;
and bull beef (tough enough we have no doubt) was
frequently a prominent dish (every parish kept a bull,

which was let out, the profits going to the parochial revenue, as seen in many of our churchwardens' books), but, to make the beef more tender, prior to the death of the animal permission was given to bait it with dogs, a sport which afforded the vulgar a treat, but which is now looked on as a cruel pastime, and seldom resorted to by the more refined. Queen Elizabeth seldom had a meal without red herrings and salt fish.

" If we add more to the deficiencies in the reign of this female monarch, we shall say,

" No gas to light our palaces, streets, or houses.

" No telegraph (which was invented by Claude Chappe, a Frenchman, who died in 1805).

" No telescopes (they being invented, in 1590, by Jansen, a Dutchman).

" No observations for navigators (Jupiter's moons being not discovered till 1610).

" No spring pocket watches (they being invented by Dr. Hook in 1658).

" No tea from China, nor fine China pottery ware.

" No coaches to ride in, they only coming into fashion in 1588.

" No coffee, it not arriving in England till 1652.

" No mustard.

" No porter ; no carp fish.

> ' For hops, pickerel, carp, and beer
> Came to England all in one year.'

" No umbrella to screen the face from the rain or sun ; a large cloak with a hood was the only covering to protect the head.

" No daily post to communicate at a distance.

" No surgeon in the land with skill enough to amputate a limb.

R

"No Alpine strawberries, for they only came in 1760.

"No magic lanthorn to amuse.

"No comfortable Bath stove to warm by sea coal.

"No microscopes to expand the mind by viewing the millions of animated nature heretofore unknown.

"No British writing paper, till John Spilman in 1588 made it in Dartford.

"No feather bed to sleep on, the chambers then having clean straw laid down in lieu. (Copy from Chalk Church book.)

"No steam vessel to convey quick intelligence.

"No mahogany, rosewood, or satinwood chairs or tables, nothing but chestnut, oak, or walnut-tree chairs or stools.

"No Royal Society to reward inventions.

"No Geological Society to investigate the strata of the earth.

"No fossilist, conchologist, or natural historian.

"No Horticultural Society to adorn the garden and please the eye.

"No Hard's Royal Farinaceous Flour, as made at Dartford, and extolled throughout the kingdom for making the best puddings, of which the Queen, if now living, would often have a taste.

"No rich graziers like the present, nor cattle shows, nor oil-cake as made at Dartford to feed them.

"No carpet to ornament the floors, straw being then used and green rushes.

"If then we had no such luxuries of foreign trade, of what goods did our merchandise consist? Who were then our merchants? I believe at that time very few English; but Jews abounded in every part of the world, and appear to have taken the lead, as they do to this day in the principal parts of Asia and Africa.

"And as to our buildings : to glimpse at ancient times, the Romans came after the Phœnicians and built edifices, but with what materials ?  We have none of their fine Corinthian or ornamented columns remaining, as are seen in Rome and Italy.  No, the buildings are mostly of rough stones of our own country, with a few Roman flat tiles worked in with them, made or collected on the spot, or brought from some neighbouring lord of the soil, to whom a fee or grant for such permission must have been previously obtained.  Hence a partial commerce in building materials commenced, while Eastern produce was in the hands of infidels and Jews, who made annual excursions, resting in certain places for disposal of their commodities (among which we find spices as one of the most ancient) at a certain period of day, from whence originated the festivals, fairs, and marts, of which a further account will be given.

"When we behold an old castle, or building, and observe that the materials with which it is constructed are not the produce of its soil, a natural question arises, from whence were the bulky substances obtained ?  by what means ?  by whom ?  and how paid for ?  Here the study of lithology and geology will arise, and the author congratulates himself that the pleasure and knowledge he gained from the study of fossils, by Dacosta, procuring also a specimen of each sort described, with some choice minerals and a copious museum which he collected (all lost ! this will be explained in the life of the author, about to be written), tended to fix on his memory the different indigenous substances of different countries !

R 2

" On entering Westminster Abbey at the great door, and looking up on the right hand to a monument, we hardly know which most to admire, the courage of the hero, the grandeur of the pyramid, or the judgment of the artist, who has gone in unison with the design, for it is the monument of that naval conqueror who took Gibraltar! The sculptor has not only displayed his taste, but has brought over, and actually employed his chisel on, part of that famous Rock itself!

" In the Conqueror's time, and shortly after, we find Caen stone, from Normandy, introduced into our castles and buildings, many instances of which are seen; for example, the base of a window in Stone Castle, also at Rochester Castle, the White Tower of London, &c. This trade continued with France until the Gothic architecture was introduced, when we find Kentish rag stone, with flints interspersed; then came a period, about 1400, when flint stones, flat-faced and squared, were used. This pretty species of ornament reached to King Henry the 8th. And in all those centuries we find the English procuring many of the above materials from a distance, and at great expense, without once using bricks like the present, there being none in old Stone Castle, although they might have been made near the spot, and would have worked in more squarely and easily. Thus the art of brickmaking in England appears of modern invention. Small clinker bricks were imported from Holland and the Netherlands; and English bricks, made of no particular size. Afterwards came in use Act of Parliament bricks (so called), made in England of a certain dimension, the duty from which and the quantity made has been within the present century immense, and seems to be rapidly increasing, especially in the years 1824 to 1828.

" During the time Calais was in our hands, wool was the staple commodity, and those who dealt in it were persons of great credit, for it paid a considerable revenue to the Crown at Sandwich, which was the chief port for its exportation. Other textile articles have come in gradually as the fashion has infected the nation. At one time many mortgaged their lands to go to the holy war. Another time the building of churches, chantries, and nunneries engrossed their thoughts. In Queen Elizabeth's reign great differences arose between Papist and Protestant. In King Charles 1st's time an obstinacy reigned on the part of royalty and its adherents. In Charles 2nd's time levity and immorality prevailed (yet we pray and rejoice by ringing bells for the glorious Restoration; surely it is high time to drop the festival of this day and also November the 5th, which only keep up a party spirit). In King George 3rd's reign a thirst for art and science flourished, particularly geography, topography, balloon flying, and novel reading. In King George 4th's time, brickmaking, building houses, and speculative companies, accompanied with failures of bankers, and bankruptcies, especially among the booksellers and printers; at the same time Bible societies, missionary meetings, anniversaries, preaching sermons, with National Schools, abounded, whilst the public were accommodated by gaslights and steam-packets.

" The author most deeply regrets the loss of numerous ancient deeds, old armour, and manuscripts, from the church of Dartford, sold by the parish officers (a few

years since) for a paltry sum. A sum may fairly be
paltry, but ought the conduct of any parish officer to be
such? No, they who are the guardians of the parish
should endeavour to maintain our trade and support
the poor within it, but not encourage foreigners, when
the work can be done equally cheap and masterly by
workmen within the parish. The above manuscripts
would have elucidated and added much to the history,
not only of the parishes but of the country, because
formerly there was the habit of depositing valuable
records in churches and religious houses, as a greater
security from whence it was presumed no sacrilegious
person would attempt to rob or disturb them.

*" O Tempora ! O Mores !*

" In this compilation, for compilation it may mostly
be called, the author has culled the sweets, and made
extracts in words, from those well skilled in the history
of the country, in preference to anything he could himself write or suggest, for if he had ventured to amend,
he should, in many instances, have failed altogether.
' He will not pretend this collection is free from mistakes ; no wise man will expect that, for he that copies
after others (as collectors of histories must do) cannot
always be sure he writes truth. Who is so careful (says
Camden) that, struggling with time in the foggy dark
sea of antiquity, he may not run upon rocks?'

" The author thought to have found a treasure of
ecclesiastical information on looking into Bishop
Gibson's ' Camden's Britannia,' 2 vols. folio, but to
his surprise and disappointment the Rev. Prelate was
quite silent under the head of Dartford Nunnery. And
even the laborious Hasted has been very scanty, only
giving the name of one nun with a few prioresses !

These desiderata have been most kindly supplied from Coles and from other MSS., through the means of Mr. Dunkin, of Bromley, to whom the public, and the author especially, are under great obligation. Also to such other gentlemen who have endeavoured to assist the author

" There was a period when prayers were publicly offered up for the dead ; and although the custom is nearly obsolcte, yet the author cannot forget the names of Thorpe, Camden, Lambard, Kilburne, Denne, Noble, Hasted, and many others, hoping they exist with God, enjoying more bliss above than when on the terraqueous globe. Thanks are also due to the living for assistance in this work; particularly to my old friend Charles Clarke, Esq., F.S.A., my young friend William Crafter, Esq., junior, in repeated instances, William Upcot, Esq., of London Institution, for beginning my subscription book, &c., B. Tanner, Esq., of Maidstone, and others, for their kind endeavours, especially T. Fisher, Esq., whose name commands respect."

# CHAPTER X.

From sorrow here
I'm led by Death away—why should I start and fear ?
If I have loved the forest and the field,
Can I not love them deeper, better there ?
If all that Power hath made, to me doth yield
Something of good and beauty—something fair—
Freed from the grossness of mortality,
May I not love them all, and better all enjoy ?

ROBERT NICOLL.

So much for the Prospectus, Dedication, and Preface of this great work, of Pocock's defeated hopes ! He had too early rejoiced over the circumstance that the artists lived at Dartford who had furnished the drawings and plates, that there also the work had been *written* and the type *composed* by himself; the pages to be printed, *imposed*, and worked off by his son G. A. Pocock, and also bound. A *combination*, he says, scarcely to be paralleled ; but in point of fact cruel fate drew a hard and fast line between the preparation of the drawings and of the MS. text, and all that was to follow of the fair performance.

It was not until 1844 (to forecast the future) that a history and antiquities of Dartford was published, and then by Mr. John Dunkin, to whom the above graceful reference (p. 247) was due, and who, in his Preface, referring to Pocock and these his labours in the same field, writes :—

"The late Mr. Robert Pocock some years since circulated proposals for a History of Dartford which his death, and then the dispersion, if not destruction, of his collections prevented ever being fulfilled."

In the preceding preface grateful allusion is made by Pocock also to Mr. Charles Clarke, F.S.A., who in the History of Gravesend is mentioned also as a literary person settled at that town ; but in neither statement did it appear, as the fact was, that Pocock had equally and laboriously devoted himself to the acquisition of antiquarian details for his friend in connexion with Rouen and other towns in Normandy—a friendly assistance which was well repaid by Mr. Clarke in aiding Pocock's researches into the earlier historical transactions connected with the county of Kent. Another kind friend (a friend departed during the work) finds mention and acknowledgment, to whom Pocock had opened some of his trials, viz. :—The Rev. Mark Noble, Incumbent of Barming, Kent, F.S.A., who wrote to Pocock, in September, 1826, in reference to the projected History of Dartford and Wilmington, as follows :—

"DEAR SIR,—I shall answer your letter as methodically as I can. I am extremely hurt that you have been in any distress. The best consolation I know is the Book, which is given us in mercy to comfort us here and lead us to where only true joys are to be found. I applaud your intention of writing an history of Dartford and Wilmington. I desire you to make me a subscriber for a copy."

This writer is the accomplished author of " The House of Medici," " The Genealogy of the House of Stuart," and many similar works.

His wife, Mrs. Sarah Noble, was ever sensible of our author's ready assistance in her botanical tastes, and an appreciation of it is shown by many acknowledgments, of which the following is an instance :—

"*April 28th,* 1828.

" Sir,—I feel myself very much obliged by the great trouble you have taken to procure me the lizard orchis, which I prize very highly ; and I assure you they look quite well after their remove. I carefully preserved the chalk rubbish you sent with them, and planted them on the same bed on which you saw the military orchis when you were here last summer. I was very glad of the military one you sent, which I shall send in the autumn to a daughter I have in Staffordshire, who is really and scientifically a botanist. The other plants I have taken care of, and they all seem likely to grow, and I hope you will see them flourishing when your promised visit takes place in the summer. At present, I am sorry to say, my daughters have not found any of the plants enumerated in your list, but I hope the spring and genial weather will introduce some of them to us ; but I suspect that plants which have not already a place in your collections must be very scarce indeed. Mrs. Cresswell requests I will return her compliments and thanks for your valuable present of shells, which she admires exceedingly, and has in part arranged them in drawers ; the others are carefully put up, as she cannot extend her liberality so far as to part with them to her collecting friend. Our youngest daughter, and two of Mrs. Cresswell's children, are much indisposed with the hooping, which disturbs the fond and anxious mothers night and day. You are the only person I have ever known that succeeded in transplanting the orchis tribe. The bee, the fly, and birds' nest were frequently found in the woods around us; but owing to cultivation on the one hand, and ignorant and pretended botanists on the other, they are become very scarce. I find great difficulty in keeping the fly alive; I had two in the garden last summer, but both died in the winter, and one I placed under a cucumber frame with my auriculas is alive and hearty.

      " I am, Sir,

         " Your very much obliged,

            " SARAH NOBLE."

These letters have been set out the more readily since the former of them shows that Pocock had to some extent " opened his griefs " to the venerable and accomplished clergyman (his kind correspondent); but although a member of the Established Church, the times in which Pocock's lot was mainly cast were not those in which the Church of England was characterized by any general religious fervour or activity, and we shall search in vain for any indication in his Annals that he personally exhibited any exception to the fashionable lethargy of the day in this respect. On the other hand, the religious reflections to which he gave utterance in his " Dartford " Preface, at p. 239, are of unimpeachable propriety and force, and of appropriate application.

In his poverty and dejection there is evidence that our author formed the design of writing his autobiography, the record of his life, its pleasures and its trials (indeed he interpolates as much in the above Preface, see p. 243). Of this there have been collected snatches and extracts such as the following, but they are few and meagre; still their reference to himself is sufficiently shown by the prefix of " Pocock's Life," in his own hand :—

" POCOCK'S LIFE.

" How happy is he—born or taught—
That serveth not another's will;
Whose armour is his honest thought,
And simple truth his utmost skill."

These lines are very characteristic of the independence, not to say impatience of character, which Pocock exhibited throughout his career, and which is often indicative of that struggle for leisure and means of study against which he had ever to contend. Impecuniosity carried with it then greater and more formidable consequences than now exist, and the actual confinement for debt was not a contingency which poor Pocock could exclude from his thoughts. In another extract, headed by him with the words " Pocock's Life," we find the following :—

" POCOCK'S LIFE.
" A prison is a place of care,
Wherein no man can thrive;
A touchstone sure to try a friend,
A grave for men alive.

" Mem.—I think this verse was written by Mr. Cotton, when confined in gaol."

At one time he indited his own epitaph, in a hopeful strain, trusting that his memory might live in his native town as the author of its annals. Thus he wrote,—

" An Epitaph.—The register of this parish records the birth and death of Robert Pocock (son of John and Martha). He made his exit on     18  , having existed the space of        years ; but in that time he produced a ' History of Gravesend and Milton,' with other works, which will perpetuate his memory."

At some other period, when haunted by his embarrassments and apprehensions of arrest, he wrote,—

"The Gravesend historian finished his writing on     18  , when     years old, being arrested by Death."

Under his own hand, and speaking of himself, we have the following painful retrospect of these his later days ; he says,—

" After being driven from house and home, destitute of money, furniture, &c., and experiencing more distress and mortification than falls to the lot of many,"—

His son George lingered at Dartford near his father's tomb till about 1835, when whatever few relics remained were presumably sold by auction, and he himself left for South America. He had seen service in his youth under Sir Gregor McGregor, and he died in the service of Queen Isabella, at Santander, in 1836, six years after his father.

The scant memory which yet lingers at Dartford—the retreat of this reduced and broken-hearted man—

points to a man of an independent spirit, of a mien and deportment above the accessories by which he was there surrounded. Already conspicuous and solitary, in the rapidly shifting fashions of the day, by the persistent retention of his pig-tail, he was there baited and brought to bay by fortune, and languished under ever-receding hopes. His efforts to float his " History of Dartford " failed for want of subscribers, though the scanty list was extended by the pathetic introduction of the names of all his children—an extension of its length of little advantage to its strength. The poor old man having thus battled with adversity with a perseverance beyond praise, and having pushed his last literary load up to the summit of attainment—all in vain—a sense of pity seems to cry out for some release from the unequal struggle. The lines of Thomson come to our thoughts involuntarily :—

> Come, ye who still the cumbrous load of life
>  Push hard uphill; but as the farthest steep
> You trust to gain, and put an end to strife,
>  Down thunders back the stone with mighty sweep,
>  And hurls your labours to the valleys deep,
>  For ever vain! come, and, withouten fee,
> I, in oblivion will your sorrow steep,
>  Your cares, your toils, will steep you in a sea
> Of full delight; oh, come, ye weary wights, to me!

His son George, of whom he had made a practical printer, and who was ready and willing to assist, possessed no funds by which this goodwill could be realized. His filial duty had already provided his homeless parent the covering of a roof; and possibly still further troubles would have supervened, had not death, in kindly pity, noiselessly and quietly eased the harsh strain, and closed the old man's career, with all his cares and disappointments. For on the morning of the 26th of October, 1830, there they find him as he lay in his bed, stricken, so the doctors said, by heart disease.

His body was quietly laid in the neighbouring churchyard of Wilmington. Little notice was taken of his death, and no record, either of wood or stone, ever marked the place where they laid him.

And here also we will leave him, peacefully laying down his freight—three score years and ten of final disappointments, struggles, and cares—in the little picturesque churchyard of his old friend and fellowantiquary, the Rev. Samuel Denne, in the midst of that rural scenery which (student of nature as he was) he traversed so oft, and which he loved so well.

> Farewell, ye blooming fields! ye cheerful plains !
>   Enough for me the churchyard's lonely mound,
> Where melancholy with still silence reigns,
>   And the rank grass waves o'er the cheerless ground.
>                               MICHAEL BRUCE.

FINIS.

# APPENDIX.

THE following is a list of most of the works actually printed or published by Robert Pocock:—

"Pocock's Child's First Book, or Reading made Easy. Bound in embossed paper, price sixpence.

Pocock's Child's Second Book, being a further improvement in learning.

Pocock's Spelling Book, or the Children's Reading and Spelling united. Strongly bound in leather or canvas, being the two preceding articles bound together, price one shilling.

A Chronology of the most Remarkable Events that have occurred in the parishes of Gravesend, Milton, and Denton. To which is added a list of the Mayors for the last forty years; also an obituary taken from the monumental inscriptions in the cemeteries of the parishes of Gravesend and Milton. By R. Pocock, 8vo, pp. 38. Gravesend, 1790.

Giles' English Governing or Parsing; recommended to schoolmasters, and private teachers of Grammar, as the most easy method of attaining a thorough knowledge of that science. Nothing of this sort has ever appeared in print. Bound in leather, 12mo size for the pocket, and printed on good paper and type, price two shillings.

The History of the Incorporated Town and Parishes of Gravesend and Milton, in the county of Kent, selected with accuracy from topographical writers, and enriched from MSS. hitherto unnoticed; recording every event that has occurred in the aforesaid town and parishes, from the Norman Conquest to the present time. (By Robert Pocock.) 4to. Gravesend, 1797.

Kentish Fragments, gleaned from the Hustings on Penenden Heath; a Poem, containing Sketches of the most eminent Characters, and of the Events and Disasters, at the late General Election of 1802, for the county of Kent, with a state of the poll in 1796. 8vo. Gravesend, 1802. Sixpence.

The Picture of Human Life: or variety of food for the mind; consisting of valuable matter calculated for the pleasure and instruction of readers of every class, among which, besides those articles selected from the best authors, are interspersed many original pieces never before published. In twelve numbers, price sixpence each.

Clarke's Observations on the Tunnel or Road intended to be made under the River Thames at Gravesend. 4to stitched, price four shillings. Much learning is displayed in this pamphlet. 4to, three shillings and sixpence. Gravesend, 1799."

[In reference to which Sir Edward Knatchbull, Bart., writes to Pocock as follows :—

"January 27th, 1799.

" Sir,—Yesterday I received your letter, dated the 1st, and also Mr. Clarke's book with Observations on the intended Tunnel under the Thames, for which I am

s

much obliged to you. I wish it may answer; I have very much my doubts about it.

     " I am, sir,

        " Your most obedient servant,

           " Edwd. Knatchbull."]

" Memoirs of the Tufton Family, Earls of Thanet; containing not only an historical account of that family, but many digressions, replete with anecdotes &c. 8vo, in boards, price seven shillings, 18 .

The Everlasting Song-Book, with original Rules for Behaviour in Convivial Societies. Bound in red, price two shillings.

Gravesend Water Companion, describing all the towns, churches, villages, parishes and gentlemen's seats, as seen from the river Thames, between London Bridge and Gravesend town. In two parts, 12mo, pp. 60. Gravesend, printed by R. Pocock, 1798. Reprinted in 1802. Also, Margate Water Companion, see page 28, supra.

Sea Captain's Assistant, or Fresh Intelligence for Salt Water Sailors; containing, among a variety of maritime articles, a naval chronology, the list of Trinity House pilots, with those of Deal, Dover, &c. Price one shilling.

God's Wonders in the Great Deep, giving an account of the most wonderful and amazing deliverances of sailors at sea. Price one shilling.

The Antiquities of Rochester Cathedral, with the monumental inscriptions; decorated with a plate of the Cathedral. Stitched, price one shilling.

The Toast Master, and Directions for Conducting Yourself like a Gentleman. Stitched, price sixpence.

" Memoirs of the Families of Sir E. Knatchbull, Bart., and Filmer Honeywood, Esq., 8vo, price sixpence. Gravesend, 1802.

The Charter of Gravesend, with all the laws relating to the watermen using the ferry between that town and London. 4to, stitched in marble, three shillings. Gravesend, R. Pocock.

Rules for Playing the new and fashionable Game at Cards called Boston, introduced into this kingdom by the Russian officers who visited Chatham. Price sixpence.

Laws of the manly Game of Cricket. Price threepence.

The Royal Soldier : a sermon.

The Life and Death of John Carpenter. Printed by R. Pocock, Gravesend, and sold by all other booksellers, 1805. 12mo, Gravesend, 1805.

A Guide for Gravesend, by a visitor. Printed for the author by Robert Pocock, High Street, 1817."

Numerous parish and business papers, of which on the 8 August, 1787, are his earliest known printed particulars and conditions of sale (auctioneer, Anthony Peck) of Roger Man's properties in High Street and Church Street ; sale to be held at the Catharine Wheel, in High Street.

# ROBERT POCOCK'S FAMILY.

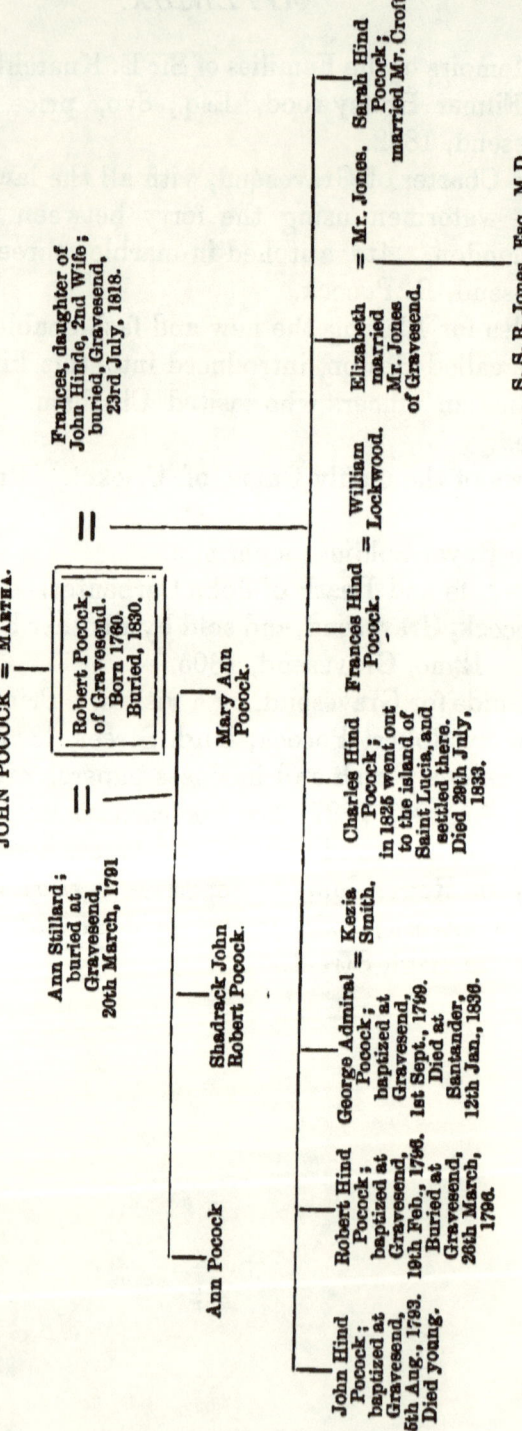

JOHN POCOCK = MARTHA.

Ann Stillard;
buried at
Gravesend,
20th March, 1791

= Robert Pocock,
of Gravesend.
Born 1760.
Buried, 1830.

= Frances, daughter of
John Hinde, 2nd Wife;
buried, Gravesend,
23rd July, 1818.

Ann Pocock

Shadrack John
Robert Pocock.

Mary Ann
Pocock.

John Hind
Pocock;
baptized at
Gravesend,
25th Aug., 1783.
Died young.

Robert Hind
Pocock;
baptized at
Gravesend,
19th Feb., 1786.
Buried at
Gravesend,
28th March,
1796.

George Admiral = Kezia
Pocock;                Smith.
baptized at
Gravesend,
1st Sept., 1790.
Died at
Santander,
12th Jan., 1836.

Charles Hind
Pocock;
in 1825 went out
to the island of
Saint Lucia, and
settled there.
Died 29th July,
1833.

Frances Hind = William
Pocock.            Lockwood.

Elizabeth
married
Mr. Jones
of Gravesend.

= Mr. Jones.  Sarah Hind
                   Pocock;
                   married Mr. Croft.

S. S. R. Jones, Esq., M.D.

# INDEX.

LONDON:
PRINTED BY GILBERT AND RIVINGTON, LIMITED,
ST. JOHN'S SQUARE.